NO NIGHT AS DARK

NO NIGHT AS DARK

Underground. Undersea. Unrelenting.

A David Langwonaire Thriller

JOHN MYLROIE

No Night as Dark: Underground. Undersea. Unrelenting. (David Langwonaire Thriller Series)
Published by CIKM Publishing
Starkville, Mississippi

Library of Congress Control Number: 2023901422

MYLROIE, JOHN, Author
NO NIGHT AS DARK
JOHN MYLROIE

Paperback ISBN: 978-1-959594-03-1
e-book ISBN: 978-1-959594-02-4

FICTION / Thriller / Crime

Book Design by Michelle M. White
Cover Image composed of photos from: Teerayut/stock.adobe.com, razihusin/istockphoto.com, and Kateryna Kukota/istockphoto.com

CIKM

Dedication:
To Elva and John Mylroie, who bequeathed me with sound genes,
and nurtured my soul and intellect for joyful success
on my own terms.

CHAPTER 1

A FORTUNATE ACCIDENT

"DRIVE FASTER, WUWAN, we are late, very late" Joanie hissed, trying to be the friendly American but angry because Wuwan had arrived behind schedule and now they were missing her deadline. Joanie's driver was going quickly, if not fast, along the streets of Jakarta, which, as always, were filled with cars, trucks, busses, pedestrians, motor bikes, rickshaws, and other modes of human transportation. It was noisy, smelly, and confusing, while at the same time being fascinating, fluid, and entertaining. She marveled at it all, seeing glances into the car and the excited expressions of those onlookers. A boldly red-haired westerner with sharp features that made her look like a bird of prey, accentuated whenever she left a vehicle and stood up, her six foot frame dominating the Indonesians around her.

A big beat-up cargo truck suddenly pulled out from a side street right in front of the Suzuki Jimny she and Wuwan were in. Wuwan tried to stop but all he did was slide the passenger door of the little SUV into the front wheel of the big truck. Joanie screamed as her window shattered into flying fragments of glass and she hit the side of the door with a sharp impact. No side air bags, at least none that worked in Jakarta's heat and humidity. She was stunned, her head had hit the door post; she felt conscious but distant, as if watching from afar. Her right arm shrilled its pain; she couldn't move, and the door was flat up against the huge truck tire. She could smell the tire rubber, old oil, and new gasoline.

Wuwan was out of the car, just standing, not knowing what to do. Several sidewalk vendors came up and physically lifted the car and pulled it away from the truck. Joanie's door would not open. A boy reached in the driver's side and hit the levers that dropped one and then the other front seat back and flat. Other men reached in and carefully lifted Joanie out of the driver's side, where a woman ran up with a large green shawl and wrapped it around Joanie to insulate her from the men who held her form. Joanie could hear music, then realized it was the sound of police vehicles swarming to the scene, their alarms blaring. She passed out, wondering why she was wrapped up like sushi in a pancake.

Joanie heard voices. Her head was foggy, and her right arm felt heavy, or maybe pinned; she couldn't move the arm but it hurt, a dull throbbing. Her efforts turned the throb into spikes of pain, and she lay back, limp and moaning.

"Joanie, are you all right?"

It was Matt's voice, the head of security at the Embassy. What was he doing here? Where was here?

"What happened? How is Wuwan?" Joanie's words were ragged, uneven. Matt Coglin was a Foreign Service Specialist specializing in community outreach, which was cover for his behind-the-scenes efforts at maintaining Embassy security. His work was complementary to the marine guard unit and the Embassy's spies, both acknowledged and unacknowledged.

"Joanie, what happened? We need to know the details," Matt's voice held concern. It seemed to be more concern than one in Joanie's position deserved. She was just an intern, specializing in educational issues, difficult work in a Muslim country where the roles of women in society were different than in the United States. Six months, summer term and the following fall semester, then she was back at college. Today she was to visit a private high school for females only, her assigned task as she could walk the halls without an escort, sort of opposite to what was the common situation in some Muslim countries where women required an escort by a male relative to be out in public.

"The big truck pulled out in front of us. Wuwan tried to stop, but the car skidded, my side hit the truck. I'm sorry I missed the school performance. How is Wuwan? It wasn't his fault." Joanie's words tumbled out, her facts overlain by her worry.

"Were there men with guns?" Matt's voice carried intensity, urgency.

"I didn't see any, several men worked hard to get me out of the Suzuki, a woman gave me a shawl to cover myself." Then Joanie opened her eyes, she didn't realize until now she had them shut. Shut because she didn't want to look at her right arm, didn't want to see the damage she could feel.

"Good, good," Matt muttered to himself.

Joanie looked around. There were two U.S. marines in full combat gear standing by the door. She was in a hospital room. She understood the reason, but why the guards? "You think it was a kidnapping attempt?" Joanie's voice rose as the implications dropped into her cloudy mind.

"You will do fine here. Your arm is broken in two places, but not compound. A mild concussion. You will be up and about in a few days. They know how to treat trauma here." Matt had not answered her question, and he walked out the door, his grizzled visage turned away, his short stature moving briskly. He looked Indonesian when he wanted to.

※　※　※

"What have we got?" Ambassador Linton asked. For once, a career man and not a political appointee. He had hoped for Thailand, but understood that for a Muslim country like Indonesia, a male at the helm was better politics on this side of the world.

"Joanie's lucky, so we are lucky," Matt replied. "It appears she was hurt in a true traffic accident. The drivers of those big trucks think they own the road, and that everyone wants to get out of their way.

Wuwan was in a hurry, they were late. It was 'bam' and Joanie doesn't make it to her destination."

"So, she was to be taken at the school, like the other three?" The ambassador had come up through the ranks, had done most embassy jobs, and was now the right person in the right spot.

"I believe so, and I would like your permission to spirit Joanie Dellows out of the hospital tonight and keep her here in the Embassy incommunicado," Matt said, his voice controlled. Joanie Dellows was a sideshow to the main problem.

"So the kidnappers of the other three won't know what happened?" Linton could see the advantage of some slight confusion in what had to be a major, well-organized plot. "So, who has been taken?"

"Phil Cannoczic, a Consular Fellow; Walt Pinny, of the Foreign Agricultural Service; and Jim Pastick, the Foreign Service Generalist working on oil and gas economics," Matt replied. "All taken after they entered the school they were to visit today. Done quickly as they walked what we think was a vacant hallway. A subtle kidnapping. It increased the chances of getting away."

"You said Joanie was lucky, and therefore, so were we. What did you mean?"

"A female in the hands of Islamic terrorists is always bad news. Having only males taken reduces angst up the line," Matt was being realistic. Gender did matter. "We need to keep this quiet, keep a lid on. The terrorists will want big publicity, so we say nothing and let them make the first move."

"I agree. I'll contact some people I know at the CIA and brief them personally," Linton replied. "Then I will do State. Where do you think our people are now?"

"Best case, still on Java. Worst case, they are already on a small inter-island freighter moving to someplace where the terrorists have more control." Matt was glum; these captures rarely had a happy ending. He wasn't guessing about the freighter.

"This will end badly, heads chopped off and all that," Linton was also glum. He had lost friends in other postings.

"Maybe not. Some information came in late today. We may have an actual lead," Matt tried not to sound hopeful; there was much analysis yet to be done, but he had hope of a rescue. They would just need the right person. Wuwan and his driving skills may have saved those three after all.

CHAPTER 2

ACCOSTED

THE LINE SHUFFLED SLOWLY. David was reminded of those old black and white newsreels of men in bread lines during the Great Depression, lines that wound around corners, and the side-to-side swaying of the men as they moved forward step by step. The future here, in the Atlanta Immigration and Customs line, was far brighter than for those men. The air had that unique aroma associated with people who had completed long flights from many countries, a mix of natural and imposed smells. All he had to do was get to a kiosk, flop down his passport, look at the camera, and get on through to his connecting flight back to Montgomery and Alabama Southeast University. He had classes to teach tomorrow, lectures all set up, and he looked forward to it. Unlike some of his colleagues, he enjoyed teaching. For him, there was a bit of missionary zeal to it. As he told a colleague once, "If I taught at Harvard, it wouldn't matter, those students are going to succeed no matter what I do. Here at ASU, I think I can make a difference, get a few students to a place they otherwise wouldn't reach." His colleague had said "good luck," and gone about her business. He had a tremendous diversity of students in terms of ability, motivation, and personality. He had students who could have gone to Harvard, others for whom the three best years of their lives had been eighth grade, and most somewhere in between. It made for a difficult teaching environment, keeping the good students' interest and not losing those so far behind, in the classroom and in life.

David spent a lot of time traveling, which meant a lot of time in lines, waiting to board a plane, waiting for luggage, or waiting at Immigration, as he was now. At such times he often went into revelry, thinking about tasks ahead, or days gone past. But he never lost situational awareness; he always paid attention to his surroundings. So, when two men in black suits came down the left side of the hall and let themselves into his line, he was fully alert. He wondered who they were after, as their clothing and attitude spoke of routine and casual use of power. It was a surprise that both men stopped in front of him.

"Dr. Langownair?" the lead man, thin, under six feet, asked. David's name is spelled Langwonaire, so it's supposed to be 'Lang won air ee', which no one ever got correct the first time. He understood the vowel problem at the end of the name, but not the consistent reversal of the 'o' and the 'w', both in writing and in speech. He ignored the mispronunciation.

"Who are you?" David answered.

The taller man stood behind the shorter man and said nothing. Clean shaven, flat eyes. The initial speaker said, "That is not important now. You need to come with us."

"No," David replied, his voice conversational as if he had been asked if he wanted cream and sugar. He had seen them coming. He didn't like their air of authority, didn't accept that he was to simply submit. He explained his thoughts in a single word.

That answer woke up the taller man. "We can force you," he said.

"You can try," David responded. "No identification, I must assume you are criminals attempting to rob me."

"That is ridiculous," the shorter man sputtered with exasperation.

As all of this had been going on, David had kept moving with the line, but people around him were now watching, a simple form of entertainment in the boring shuffle of a queue. "Not ridiculous to me, to be accosted in a public place by unidentified strangers." David said.

"I can haul his ass out of here," the taller man said to his colleague, a message meant for David.

"Suppose I point at you and shout 'gun, gun' and start to run, what do you think happens here?" David proposed. "You want me to come with you? Fine, I'll meet you at the other side of Immigration."

The shorter man shrugged his shoulders and said, simply, "OK." He led his taller companion over to the line for pilots, diplomats, and officials, and they both went through, without showing any ID or documents. David shuffled on in his line, got to a kiosk, then on to the official in the booth and he was quickly through. His two potential interrogators were waiting. As he walked past them the tall one grabbed his arm.

"I need to collect my bag and put it through to my connection," David complained.

"Not a problem. Your bag has already been taken care of," the shorter man said. "Now, please come with us." Still holding David's arm, the tall man followed the short man past the security checkpoint and into a *Do Not Enter* posted hallway.

"May I hit the restroom first?" David asked.

"No," the tall man said, as abrupt as David had been. They went up a flight of stairs into another hall, opened a door on the left side to a room, pushed him in, and closed the door. David tried the door, simple hollow-core tan wood. Not meant to stop a determined effort to escape. It was, of course, locked. The room was about five meters long and about four meters wide; David now thought in metric as his field work was usually overseas and it was metric almost all the time there. He also considered it easier to use. The room had beige walls, a white hung ceiling, and a tile floor. It was barren except for a table, one by two meters, and two simple metal chairs. The door was in one corner with four LED lights in the ceiling. Nothing too fancy. A camera was up at the wall and ceiling junction midway along the shorter wall with the doorstop. There was a light switch by the door and an outlet on each wall. The light switch worked. His escort had removed his backpack and cell phone when shoving him into the room, but he still had his neck pouch and his pocket contents. The neck pouch was useful, few people saw it, almost impossible to be lost to a pickpocket.

What to do? He asked himself. And the immediate response was … nothing. He would have ended up here no matter how he had treated the two men. He knew he was clean, he had no record, not even a moving violation for twenty years. He carried nothing illegal, he had permits for his field work. This wasn't about what he had done; it was about what they wanted done, 'they' being as yet undefined, but there weren't many options. He was a caged animal for now, so he did what a caged animal does: he inspected his surroundings. He examined the walls, which were sheetrock, so not a true confinement space, more for interviews or interrogation. There was a slight water stain in one corner, at the corner of the wall separating the room from the hallway, the side away from the door. The table was near that end as well, placed long axis parallel to the wall with the door, a chair on either side. A good spot for viewing by the camera, as the interviewer and the interviewee would both be seen in profile.

David didn't do well with inactivity, and he evaluated his situation. He assumed a worst-case scenario. It was easier to pull back from that mental position than to hurriedly escalate if things went south. He pulled the table over to the short wall by the door, stood on it, and looked at the camera. It seemed standard. He gave it a wink and then jumped down and crawled under the table. He took his pen out of his pocket, unscrewed it, and used the exposed lip to unfasten the screw holding the outlet cover plate. It came off. He pricked his left pinky finger with his mechanical pencil and squeezed out a drop of blood. He stuck that finger past the outlet socket and put the drop of blood on the back of the socket fixture. Then he wiped his finger with a tissue from his pocket, tore off the bloody part, and let that piece of paper float to the floor behind the socket. He then replaced the cover plate, came out from under the table, and pulled it back to its original position. He left the necessary, indisputable proof that he had been in this room.

David sat in the chair that faced across the table to the wall and the other chair and he waited. He understood that he was supposed to cool his heels for a while, but that someone would eventually come in to explain what this was all about. Or not. A softening-up process of sorts. He let his thoughts float.

He had believed he would be a biologist. Growing up with no siblings had made loneliness his friend, frogs and birds his companions. It seemed appropriate he would look into their lives and lifestyles for a career. In college he had discovered the Outing Club, had gone in a couple of caves, and had been hooked. Caves revealed nothing unless you went into them and sought out their byways and their ends. When the caves became hard, with cold water, tight crawls, and deep drops, the caver population was winnowed. Gone were the Saturday adventurers; still remaining were the aficionados, the true believers. David found he fit into this group as none before. Who you were mattered less than what you did as a small team, pushing the limits. Going around a corner in a newly discovered passage and realizing that you would see what no human being had ever seen before was a thrill that was not repeated by whitewater rafting or mountain climbing, where the end goal could be seen from afar. In a cave, you had to go there to find out. No excuses, no side bets, no substitutes. It fit David, that mentality, an earned arrogance, a justified abruptness. It had carried him forward, and still did.

His draft status sent him into the Navy soon after he had married Elaine. When he came out, she moved on and so did he, to geology and the study of caves. He wondered about his marriage, how it had flared like a Roman candle and then sputtered out. The Navy was partly at fault, that forced separation, hungers unsatisfied. He and Elaine did not initially realize how unusual their relationship was. They were sexually matched to an extraordinary degree, but otherwise shared little. Some of his older caving buddies would talk about how their marriages were gray, that they did sex once in a while, almost as a duty, because married couples were supposed to. David was filled with confusion, he and Elaine couldn't wait to get into bed, or the back seat, or the back lawn. Then they would do their own thing, go to movies with friends but not with each other. Visit family separately, dine out but not together.

Then come home alone and hop into the sack together and love it. The strangeness of their relationship became more apparent to them. The Navy took them apart, and each found different releases. David had liked Elaine the way one does a cooperative co-worker. Then he took a different job, college professor, she had long since moved to the west coast to pursue something, perhaps someone. He didn't know and he didn't care. His energies went into his career, and he was careful with his intimacies, taking his joy when far from home, maintaining friendships but never committing. Finding women of a like mind. Always glad to see him, never sorrowful when he left, knowing there would be a next time. A non-commitment commitment.

He had been a professor for decades, moving up the ranks, easy to do at a small school in the Alabama state system. He avoided administrative posts, reveled in his cave research, and joyfully honored his commitment to his students. He began work in The Bahamas; the caves there were fascinating and no one knew how they formed, the models developed on continents didn't work. David figured it out and won some fame within the small community of cave scientists. He used to say it was all about the fish-to-pond ratio. If it was a small pond, you were a hell of a big fish. David's ponds were islands all over the world, and he knew their caves as no one else did.

CHAPTER 3

REVELATIONS

HE DIDN'T WAIT LONG, maybe fifteen minutes more, when the door opened, and a tall woman, perhaps forty, in a tan pantsuit, dark hair, little make up, carrying nothing in her hands, strode in, closing the door behind her. She walked directly up to him, stopping mere inches away. He stayed seated.

"That is where I sit," she said sternly.

"Apparently not," he replied.

She stood her ground. He, too, remained seated. "Did you hear me?" she demanded.

"You have multiple choices," David responded. "You can fight me for this chair, you can sit in the other chair, you can sit on the table, you can sit on the floor. Or you can leave." He said this looking straight ahead.

She stood next to him, having not moved during their brief exchange. Now her foot began tapping, just a little, quietly. A tell, David thought, simple black flats, easy to kick with, great to run in. She then abruptly walked around the table and sat in the other chair. The fact that she had no file, no documents, impressed David. The camera would be the record keeper, and she either had his data in her head, or she felt it didn't matter.

"What were you doing under the table?" she inquired.

David's first impulse was to say he had been masturbating, but that wouldn't be useful. Although to say he wouldn't have been interested in how she responded would have been at least partially untrue. "I used the table to examine the camera," he said. "Then I examined the underside of the table to see what might have been placed there."

"Do you think this is a James Bond-type of situation?" she asked, an aggravated tone to her voice.

"More like flight of the dumble bees," David answered.

"You will cooperate, or there will be consequences," she demanded.

"With whom, on what, why?" he asked, all legitimate questions.

She was unfazed or uninterested. "I can have the IRS audit you and take your life apart."

"When making a threat," David replied, "the interrogator needs to achieve two thresholds. First, the threat must be relevant to the target. I have my taxes done professionally, by a CPA, who assumes all the risk. I take every benefit I can, but I do not cheat on my taxes. Therefore, your threat fails the first threshold. May I visit the restroom?"

"No, you may not," she stated.

David got up, walked to the end of the table, unzipped his fly, and urinated into the corner with the water stain. He finished, zipped up, and sat back down. "That is the low point in the room, it will stay there," he explained.

His interviewer had not moved; she glanced over to the small yellow pool, then back at him. "Suppose I told you failure to cooperate will mean you will not leave this room alive," she proposed, with a mean little smile.

"The second threshold you must achieve," David continued, "is that the target has to believe the threat will be carried out. So, while I take a threat on my life seriously, I do not believe it will occur. By the way, in an interrogation, it is best not to provide information to the target."

"What information?" she asked.

"That you cheat on your taxes," David replied. "You threatened me with something from your frame of reference. It failed because I am not in that frame. You would be fearful of an IRS audit, so you assumed I would be too." David glanced up at the camera, "now they know it, too."

She couldn't help herself; she took a quick glance up at the camera.

"You also have now put yourself in a dangerous position," David said, as he stood up again, and spun his chair around so that it hit the wall behind the table with a bang, the back of the chair facing his interviewer. "I am now between you and the only egress from this room. If I wanted you dead, you would be dead right now." Then he took the chair back around the table and sat down.

"What would that achieve?" she remained cool, confident.

"If I truly believed I was to very soon die in this room, my goal would be to extract a cost from the offending party," he said seriously.

She threw her head back, laughing. David launched himself over the table, put her head in an armlock against his chest, and leaned forward, flattening her face against the tabletop. He whispered in her ear, "All I have to do is rotate my body like a crocodile, and your neck snaps. So, let's cut the crap and get down to business. I know why I am here, and I know your problem." He released her head and slid back across the table into his chair.

Her aplomb was gone. Her hair was a mess, her blouse crooked. "Would you have really killed me?" she asked.

"If I really believed I was to die in here, today, maybe," he began. "But then a star goes up on the wall, people talk about it for a few days, and speak of your carelessness and the bad outcome that carelessness produced. It might be better for me to pop one of your eyeballs out and gouge your face so you can never look comfortably in a mirror again. Then the talk goes on for years. They would ask, 'how is she doing now, how does she cope?' You would always be a living reminder of my death."

She stared at him for tens of seconds. He said no more. Then she swallowed and said, "You know why you are here?"

"Of course, but what I suspect is going on requires a high level of clearance, I imagine," he said. "Have you been read in, or were you brought in to get the ball rolling like the two clowns down in Immigration, and you actually know very little?"

At that point, the door opened, and a man with thinning blond hair, wearing grey slacks, a flannel shirt, sneakers, and no tie, walked in.

"Molly, let's retire to the office," he said, "I have worked with academics too long, and I miscalculated. My apologies."

"Its OK Glenn, I guess I was a bit rusty myself," she answered as she stood up.

Glenn led the way out of the room, Molly motioned David should follow, and she brought up the rear. This trio went out and down the hall, up another flight of stairs past security guards who took David's picture and gave him a 'visitor pass' as Glenn and Molly waited silently.

As they went down the hall, Molly was trailing the two men. Glenn said, "You were rough with Molly. Was that necessary? Would you like me to return the favor?"

"You can try," David said, "I am a bit tired of the ineptitude displayed so far, and I needed to make a point. Satellite office, you folks have gotten soft and forgotten some of your craft."

"Actually, we came in today," Glenn offered.

"Then it is worse than I thought," David responded. "I'll put it down to jet lag."

That comment made Molly give Glenn a searching look. Then Glenn coded at a door, opened it, and waved David and Molly in. Typical office, carpeted, small couch, small conference table, desk, several comfortable looking chairs, pale blue walls. Glenn looked to Molly, indicating she should start. No one sat.

"You said you could tell us why you are here," she began. "You also indicated that we were not professional. Can you explain?"

"To accost me in an open line full of internationals you haven't vetted was incredibly stupid," David scolded. "It told me, and any cogent observers, that you were CIA."

"How did you come to that conclusion?" Molly asked.

"You are not supposed to carry out certain activities in the U.S.," David answered. "Taking me before I officially entered the country allows you to maintain that fiction. Later, when I talked about putting a star on the wall, you accepted it."

Molly looked to Glenn, who shrugged his shoulders. "You also said you knew what this is all about. Do you care to explain?"

"Why would the CIA, or any federal agency, want to talk to David Langwonaire, in a public setting, instead of in my office in Alabama?" David began. "You have a problem, it involves a cave, most likely in an island setting. You are in a hurry, a rush, which in part explains the clumsy action done this morning. So, what would induce that behavior, and cause you to seek me out? The cave contains something. Maybe WMD? Maybe a hostage or hostages? I think it is the latter."

"Why is that?" Glenn spoke for the first time on this topic.

"Outside of a few locations, a WMD in a cave is harmless. It has to be taken somewhere to be a threat," David postulated. "In that case, you sit and watch, and by seeing who comes and goes, you ferret out the network of individuals involved. But hostages, they are in immediate danger. Extraction becomes the central issue. To do that, you need to know about the cave. Someone has done their homework, and tracked me down, they realize that island caves are different than the usual caves found on continents. That difference could be critical to mission success. However, it is a trap."

"Why do you say that?" Molly asked.

"Because you already know the hostages are in a cave, and you know where!" David exclaimed. "They want you to know. I guess that it is not military hostages, as DIA would be all over it, not you folks. Not tourists, either. You couldn't keep it secret. I expect federal workers, probably diplomatic personnel, not top echelon, but people in the trenches."

"Why them?" Glenn asked.

"They want to draw you in, they want you to think you can get the hostages out," David said. "The people taken hostage were carefully assessed, not only to be a soft target, but to be people you would want back while keeping the whole operation secret."

"Well," Molly said, "if you think your story is correct, where are they being held?"

"Initially, I thought of the Persian Gulf, maybe Socotra," David began. "Then I thought, too public, too busy, routine. This attempt is special, a trap, with a longer view. So perhaps try to get the world's most populous Muslim nation involved." He paused.

"Which is?" That from Molly. She already knew, she was testing David.

"Indonesia," David answered. "They have kept the lid on pretty well since the post 9/11 Bali stuff. They also have very strong feelings about their post-colonial identity."

"How so?" Glenn inquired.

"They spent centuries under Dutch colonial rule, then got a few years of Japanese occupation as part of World War II and the East Asian Co-Prosperity Sphere. When the Aceh earthquake occurred in 2004, they initially wouldn't let U.S. helicopters land with relief supplies, they had to hover and roll the supplies out onto the ground."

"Because?" Molly asked.

"They didn't want any foreign military, of any type, setting foot, or landing gear for that matter, on Indonesian soil," David answered. "Later, things were negotiated to allow landings, but it is that initial gut reaction that you need to be aware of."

"Why is this 'gut reaction' important?" Glenn questioned.

"So, if the hostage takers can get the U.S. military to do a hostage extraction, and the perpetrators can make it blow up in the faces of the U.S., it would be a diplomatic and foreign policy nightmare. Desert One on steroids."

"Desert One?" Molly inquired.

"The failed hostage rescue from Iran during the Carter administration," Glenn offered. He went on to ask David, "where in Indonesia?"

"If they want to create an incident," David responded, "they need to set it up where a military action would be easy for the U.S. So, I think eastern Indonesia, perhaps within helicopter range of Mindanao Island in the Philippines.

"Not Palawan?" Glenn asked.

"That gets you close to Malaysia, not Indonesia," David replied. "That's my pitch. The problem is, if any of the hostage takers has done their homework, and has eyes on me, then that stupid approach at Immigration will have let the cat out of the bag. When do I get to go home?"

"Well, we need more of your insight and expertise, we haven't even begun to talk about the cave site yet," Glenn explained. "We will get you re-booked back to Montgomery when this is over. We do have your luggage."

"I have classes to teach tomorrow." David said.

"I will call your department and say that you were a witness to an on-board altercation, and we have asked you to stay in Atlanta while we take statements and investigate," Glenn said. "I am going to have lunch brought up from Subway. Want anything?"

"Chicken Teriyaki, no pickles or peppers, plain chips, a Coke," David replied. "And bring my backpack up here, please." It looked like he had piled supposition on supposition, and it was either correct, or they liked how he thought on his feet. His backpack appeared in minutes, with the short guy in the black suit as sherpa. Glenn and Molly excused themselves and went out in the hall.

"Do you believe this guy, Glenn?" Molly asked. "He was dead on about everything."

"What about you? He threatened you with being dead," Glenn responded. "Are you OK?"

"I got schooled on interrogation, I can tell you that," Molly replied. "I am OK, but he did scare me."

"When he had you in the headlock?" Glenn asked.

"No, earlier," she began, "when he said that if he wanted me dead, I would be dead already. The look in his eyes was just so matter of fact. He sees, he decides, he acts. Don't piss him off. What did you say to him in the hall?"

"I told him he was rough on you and asked him if he wanted me to return the favor. He replied, 'you can try' and it did make me think."

"What do you think he was really doing under that table?" Glenn inquired.

"We can ask him that later. What do we do now?" Molly asked.

"We read him in, he knows most of it already. We can't just let him walk out." Glenn answered.

"He understands operational security," Molly replied. "He is right. We really botched it this morning. Do you think we blew it already?"

"I hope not, but it does show that we need to act quickly," Glenn said. "We pay a lot of very smart people to analyze intelligence data, and then we grab this guy off the street and he figures it all out, from essentially one data point, in real time. I'd like to get him on contract."

CHAPTER 4

BAD IDEAS

LUNCH CAME TO MOLLY AND GLENN in the hall. They took the bags from the security guard and stepped back into the office, setting the food down on the conference table. This time, they all sat.

"So what were you really doing under the table?" Molly asked between bites of her tuna sub.

David looked at her, and at Glenn. "Am I in?"

"Yes, you will be fully read in. You know most of it already." Glenn responded.

"I put blood on a piece of tissue and dropped it down behind the power outlet on the wall," David said.

"To prove you had been in that room?" Glenn asked.

"A little bit of insurance. I was concerned that it had been a mess so far, and that I might need to document my where and when status," David explained.

"I see," Glenn replied. "Well, as you have probably surmised, your hunches, guesses, assumptions — all were pretty much on target. We have information that the hostages are on an island off the western end of New Guinea, Pulau Ternate. For now, we will skip why we think the information is truly reliable, and that our knowledge is at this time not known by the hostage takers."

"OK, let's bring up that island on Google Earth unless you want to use your own imagery," David suggested. "You have a pinpoint location?"

Glenn was now at the desk, as images began to appear on the flat screen above the conference table. Molly moved her seat over next to David's to look up at the screen. They both kept munching on their subs.

"The cave in question is south of a small village called Wadjol," Glenn explained. "We have imagery that shows sea cliffs and beaches. The cave is in the cliff behind one of those beaches." The screen was using Google Earth and the scan grew and grew until David could see the site clearly. "The local name for the cave is 'Gua Liang Sireh' which supposedly translates to 'Pepper Lizard Cave'. We know hardly anything about it, except that it is supposed to have many chambers and passages."

"Have you looked at the Dutch caving literature?' David asked. "There was a guy named Hummelinck who wrote about caves in the Netherlands Antilles and in Suriname. He was Dutch. Perhaps he, or a colleague, did work in the Dutch East Indies before it became Indonesia."

"We did a search on the cave name, nothing came up," Molly interjected.

"The name now is an Indonesian name. It may have had a Dutch name when originally documented," David explained, recognizing it could have had a pre-Dutch name as well. "There might be a map. The cave is in an easily accessible position. The cliff entrances are probably visible from the water. It could have been documented by a naturalist, a minister, a miner."

Molly left the room while David looked at the images.

After a few minutes, David asked, "How old is this image?"

"2014," Glenn replied.

"Too old, get something newer."

Molly came back into the room. "I have people working on the Dutch name possibility."

David wondered why they were showing him old imagery. "Where do you think you would come in with your extraction team?" David saw the hesitation on both Molly and Glenn's faces. "I can probably figure it out, if you have 'need to know' issues. But, either I am read in or not. What do I find if I look it up in a current Google image myself? Where is your LZ, your landing zone?"

The image blanked out, the Google Earth program was shut down. A minute later, a new image shifted into position. "This is our stuff," Glenn explained. "We plan to use this soccer field here," he said, highlighting a cleared rectangle east of the cave area.

David looked at the image. "Back out a bit; more, a little more. OK, come back in, fill the screen." David studied the image again. "Well, it is a trap all right. Lots of casualties, lots of prisoners."

"How so?" Molly asked.

"First of all, a soccer field has been built kilometers from anywhere," David noted. "Who uses it? Better still, how long has it been there? Whoever built this field thinks they know soccer, but they don't. Can you put a scale bar on the image?" A scale bar came up, in feet. "Metric as well, please; OK, good."

Then David stood up and walked around the table so he could point things out on the image. "Soccer dimensions are in yards, not meters, but the eighteen-yard-deep penalty area boundary is eighteen *meters* out from the goal. Second, the curve on top of the box is supposed to be an arc, not a semicircle."

"Why an arc?" Glenn asked, "I was always a football fan," he added, as if in explanation.

"It is football everywhere except in the U.S.," David commented. "The point of the arc is to meet the rule that every direct kick must have all defenders at least ten yards away. A penalty kick is special in that all players, offensive and defensive, except the goalie and the one taking the kick, must be outside the penalty box, and also ten yards away. The penalty stripe is ten yards from the goal, but the penalty box is eighteen yards deep. So, to make all other players ten yards away from the ball, the arc was added."

"So the field was laid out wrong. That doesn't make it a bad LZ," Molly argued.

"It does if the sole purpose of the field is to have you use it as the LZ so you can be ambushed," David countered. "This is a current image?" Glenn nodded. "Can we go back six months?" No field at all. "Can you put up current infrared?" That image came up. "See, no plant stress in front of each goal, which means the field has hardly, if ever, been played on." Then David pointed to two parallel rows of circular spots going the length of the field. "That is where they put the IEDs. The only question is whether they plan to blow them up·at landing, or afterwards, so they could have a ton of prisoners."

Glenn was the first to respond. "I see what you are saying. And I agree. I have information you lack, and it isn't supposed to be shared at all, but you have seen stuff we haven't, and given us leads we didn't think of, so I am going to give you some specifics. Realize that most people at Langley don't know what I am going to tell you, and no one else here in Atlanta does either. Molly, you OK with this?"

"Yes, go ahead, we need all the help we can get," she answered.

"I take it, then, that the two gentlemen who met me at Immigration have no idea why they were collecting me," David speculated.

"Correct, only that they should avoid any public display," Molly said. "Your threat to shout 'gun' and run made them follow your instructions. You are also correct that we did it because of CIA rules, and that was a poor decision. My decision."

David appreciated that she owned up to what could have been a colossal error.

"Here is the full story, as best as we know it," Glenn began. "Six days ago, three consular officials were kidnapped as they drove to three separate minor events involving educational institutions. We believe a fourth person, a female, was to be taken as well, but she was involved in a minor traffic accident and ended up in the hospital with a broken arm and a concussion. The three kidnapped males have disappeared."

"So how do you know where they are?" David interrupted.

"We had been watching a fellow we thought might be a courier or underling in what appeared to be a local terrorist organization. They were extremely well-funded, and we couldn't figure out what they were up to."

"Now you know?" David asked.

"Yes," Glenn replied, "now we know. The day of the kidnappings, we had this individual under surveillance. Our watcher had just received a call saying we had a problem, as the kidnappings had taken place minutes before, with one failure, when the guy under watch suddenly left his building, hopped on his motorbike, and took off. Completely unusual behavior for that fellow, who always did his proper quiet and careful exit protocols. Acting on a hunch that the rapid departure was a result of the fourth kidnapping going bad, our agent entered the building, accessed the fellow's room, and found on the table a jump drive lying next to a cut-open cucumber with a jump-drive-sized interior hole. Our agent popped the jump drive into his scan device, copied all the files, replaced the jump drive, and left the building unobserved, we think."

"So that is how you know where they are, and you believe they don't know you know," David offered.

"Again, correct, but it gets more interesting," Glenn said. "There were just two files, one a set of instructions, and one a letter. The letter was a set of orders to the hostage takers that they were to execute the hostages, one-by-one on four separate days, with the female to be the last, starting in a little over three weeks from the day we got the file."

"I see," David responded, "so why the rush?"

"The set of instructions told this operative to set up a minor courier to get caught with the letter a few days before the first execution," Glenn explained.

"That is brilliant!" David exclaimed. "For weeks, they will release threatening videos, with pleading hostages, then you get a tip and bust the courier and see that the executions will start soon, assuming we will rush pell-mell into their trap. The courier also provides the cave location. So that is why you thought an ambush could be avoided — you planned to get ahead of their schedule."

"That is how we see it," Molly said. "In any event, we need to know about the cave, and what we can expect when we get there. That is why we, uh, collected you."

"You need a better extraction plan," David announced. "You currently plan to come in at night with Navy Seals in a series of helicopters, flying in from Philippine territorial waters where you can stage without any diplomatic problems."

Molly and Glenn looked at each other. "You have a better plan?"

"This kidnapping operation took place in Jakarta?" David asked.

"Yes," Glenn answered.

"Then the hostages were moved over 2,400 kilometers to Pulau Ternate. That is a long way. They had to do it by boat, probably a small inter-island freighter. If it does 10 knots, which would be good, our hostages are arriving today." David looked at the two agents.

"That is our estimation. We feel they recently transferred to a small boat and will make final landfall at the cave area from that," Glenn explained. "We are trying to check with satellite data, but there are dozens and dozens of possible ships and boats."

"I think they have to have some help from inside the government, to allow a few inspections to be missed or done without rigor," David suggested. "Do we provide them military aid in the form of equipment?"

Molly said, "I think so. I can check."

"OK, do so, and see if they made a request for night vision equipment, and where it went," David followed up. Molly left the room. David looked at Glenn, "can I hit the men's room? The floor here is carpeted."

"I need to go too," Glenn said, which may or not have been true, but they went down the hall and took care of business, not talking at all.

Molly had come back. "You were correct again, David. Five months ago, the Indonesian Marines made a request for 100 night vision sets. They were delivered a month ago."

"You cannot do any follow up at their end. It will alert them," David said. "I am willing to bet some of those sets are in Pepper Lizard Cave right now, not for use in the cave, but at your planned night helicopter landings."

"You suggested you had a better plan," Glenn commented.

"This group expects Navy Seals by helicopter at night from the east of the cave," David began. "Instead, we send in a fast-attack submarine with fewer personnel, lock out in the morning, in daylight, scuba to the coast, go up the cliff, take the bush route to the south end of the cave, enter, get the hostages, and leave by the same route."

"Where do we get the submarine?" Molly asked.

"Pull rank, get a fast attack boat to Guam, load up there and head off. We could be extracting them in a week," David stated.

There was a knock on the door, Glenn opened it a crack, received a folder, and shut it again. He sat down at his desk and looked through the folder. He looked up at David. "You are beginning to scare me a little, David. Thijs Daan, a Shell Oil petroleum geologist, had an interest in caves, and in 1929 he entered our cave and did a simple survey, producing a map. He called it Goedenavond, which translates to 'Good Evening Cave'. He passed a piece of paper over to David.

"This is actually a really good map, excellent for the time it was done!" David exclaimed. "It has cross sections, and a fair amount of passage detail. With this map, I can get your guys into the cave unseen, through the cave, and get the hostages out."

"How do you get them out? Once you have them, there will be pursuit," Molly said.

"The usual. Blow something up to distract them," David said.

"Did you just say you would lead this group?" Glenn asked.

"If you want it to succeed, yes," David replied. "If you want dead Seals and dead hostages, then no."

CHAPTER 5

JOINING THE COMPANY

DAVID SPENT SOME TIME SIGNING government documents. His pay would be substantial, but of no use if he died over there. He had essentially no family. His ex was long gone to the West Coast; they had no kids. His parents had passed away, and he had been an only child. He had colleagues at ASU, he socialized occasionally, often far from campus, but his real life was his field work in caves on islands around the world with fellow 'true believers' from a spectrum of places and social positions. His 'Friends of the Field' as he liked to call them. He also had professional colleagues who did similar or allied research, most of those were good buddies as they were true believers as well. If you worked in cave science, you always had to deal with a bit of social stigma, the 'spelunker' label. It created somewhat of a bunker mentality. The public thought people who went in caves were weird, but if someone got trapped, then it was all celebrity. When asked about the difference between spelunkers and cavers, David always responded, "Cavers rescue spelunkers" and left it at that.

Glenn came back into the office. It wasn't Glenn's office; he was squatting so he had a place to work. "How is the paperwork going?" he asked.

"The paperwork is fine, similar to the state bullshit we do for Alabama bureaucrats," David replied. "But we do have a problem, which is, how to make me disappear, as it were, without tipping off the perpetrators? The easiest way to determine if there is any interest in me is to have an asset just watch and see who visits me when I am on campus. There's a fair number of foreign students on campus, one could be an observer."

"Well, we could fake your death, or say you ran off with an undergrad, or you embezzled from a grant," Glenn suggested. David's statement reeked of self-importance to Glenn, but then, what if the man was right?

"Glenn, I want to go back to my job when this is over," David began, "I am a tenured full professor at a place that accepts my research as legitimate. I can't go into a type of federal witness protection. You need to be creative."

"There is little we can do to make you disappear without arousing suspicion," Glenn advised.

"How about a cave rescue on Farallon da Madinilla in the CNMI?" David suggested.

"CNMI?" Glenn asked.

"Commonwealth of the Northern Mariana Islands," David replied, "quasi-U.S. territory, left over U.N. trustee islands from World War II, still associated with the U.S., but self-governing. They have U.S. Post offices, U.S. Fish and Wildlife works there; Saipan has a small U.S. National Park. And, of course, a large U.S. military presence, especially on Tinian."

"So how does this Fernando Island fit in?" David asked.

"It's Farallon da Madinilla, the northern most of the limestone Mariana Islands. Everything else north of it is volcanic, most of which, like Anatahan and Pagan, are still active," David responded. "The key is that the island was used as a bombing range and weapons-testing target until biologists made them stop because a lot of sea birds nest there. It is uninhabited, and off-limits to everyone as there is so much unexploded ordnance lying around. A small place, but suppose we had some Chamorro fishermen get ship-wrecked there, and they can't be found? Maybe they hid out in a cave and need to be rescued? So the Navy brings me in. It's public but still a bit hush-hush because at times the island has been a bit of an embarrassment to the Navy, like Vieques off the coast of Puerto Rico was a few years ago because of a similar target-practice history."

At this point, Molly, who had been setting up the extraction team, came back in. "It is going to be difficult fielding the group we planned for," she said. "We have so many assets pre-positioned in Europe, Syria, and South Korea that pickings are slim back here in the States."

"How many did you want for your original plan?" David asked.

"We had planned on four helicopters, thirty-six Seals, plus pilots, and flight managers," Molly answered.

"For my plan, we need only seven," David stated. "Your plan was clearly a bust- and-grab operation, which even if they didn't know you were coming would have been high-risk. Seven gives me my keeper, then a pair for each of the three hostages. It takes time to move through a cave, especially with inexperienced Seals and three possible compromised hostages."

"We can do seven easily," Molly answered.

"Can I help vet them?" David inquired.

"No, you can't see that much detail," Glenn said. "Even I won't see the files, only Molly."

"Well, I can tell her what I want and then see what she comes up with, right?" David countered.

"That will work," Molly answered. "Tell me what your criteria are." She sounded a bit frustrated, having to deal with the demands of a small-time academic.

"Obviously, anyone on file that has caving experience would be top priority. See if any were members of the National Speleological Society or university outing clubs," David offered. "On the flip side, any hint of claustrophobia is bad. Size will be an issue. We may need a few of them to be smaller than average. I understand that is not how Seals are recruited, but there will be physical constrictions in the cave that big, muscle-bound guys will have trouble with. They can rear guard as the rest go forward, and perhaps haul my ass out of there as we bug out."

"What equipment will you need?" Glenn asked.

"Get my luggage up here and I'll break out what I need," David replied. "I don't know what standard gear the Seals come with, but they should have knee pads and elbow pads. Not what athletes wear, but what cavers wear, lightweight, simple in design, easy to use. It is important that the Seals understand there will be no use of any night vision equipment, no helmets, and certainly no balls of string."

"David, we have a crash pad here in the terminal, and we will all stay there tonight," Molly said. "If I can get a flight set up, we will leave as soon as possible tomorrow. The CNO already knows we are taking assets."

"What about our submarine, is that approved already?" David questioned. "I only asked for it five hours ago." David's voice was inquisitive, not demanding, not whiny, not arrogant — matter of fact.

"When Molly and I were assigned this task, we were told to move fast and get anything we needed, that we had authorization all the way to the top," Glenn replied. "We will have a Virginia Class fast-attack nuclear submarine at our disposal in Guam within thirty-six hours."

"The joys of VLF, I guess," David said. He saw the blank looks on both their faces. "VLF stands for very low frequency; it is a way to get a signal to a sub at depth in salt water. Low bandwidth, but it can tell a sub with a single word to come to periscope depth, put up the regular radio aerial, and receive a data-rich message."

"We are doing pizza here tonight," Glenn said. "I am keeping you under wraps."

"Wraps are good too," David replied, licking his lips.

CHAPTER 6

SURPRISES

"I THINK WE SHOULD MODIFY THE DIVERSION PLAN," David advised, taking a sip of root beer as they ate in the office Glenn had confiscated at Molly's direction to be their Atlanta headquarters. "A rescue mission in the Marianas is not sinister enough to require my assistance. Instead, how about considering making up a right-wing neo-Nazi group going to Farallon da Madinilla to harvest explosives for future terrorist activities?"

Glenn put down the mushroom and sausage pizza slice he was holding. "Make it more of a clear and present danger situation?"

"Keep the 'rescue' cover story for my department, they won't like the idea of thwarting a white nationalist movement; it is, after all, Montgomery." David replied. "Anyone investigating my absence will see that we are trying to cover up my true mission and will see that the true mission is in the Marianas, and not Indonesia. I'll need to be seen boarding a patrol vessel or destroyer. Then I sneak off and board the submarine, which doesn't appear until the vessel I am supposed to be on has left port."

"This action is a lot of work to counteract a surveillance that we don't know even exists," Molly countered.

"This kidnapping and lure project has been at least six months in the process," David answered. "That's when the soccer field was built, that's when the night vision equipment was ordered. The terrorists don't see me as a threat, they see me as an indicator of what you folks know. If I am under watch, then right now they are nervous that we know more than they think we do. If it can be shown I have been picked up to do a different task, they will relax. It can also work in our favor if we can spot who has been watching, here at the airport, whoever you send to ASU, and when I deplane in Guam and board the vessel to Farallon da Madinilla in Orote. I assume the MATS flight will go into Anderson?"

"We were thinking of using a Gulfstream 6500 jet into the naval air station, but Anderson Airforce Base would be more routine," Molly responded.

"I have published quite a bit on the caves of the Mariana Islands. The terrorists, if they think watching me is important, will know that," David added. "My being called in makes sense as we are not looking for stranded sailors who want to be found, but white nationalists who don't want to be found. Cave expertise would be critical."

"So, who do we send to ASU?" Glenn asked.

"Send someone in a naval officer's uniform," David replied. "There is significant respect for the military in the South. Someone in a black suit would be viewed as 'Deep State' and not trusted. He should ask to see the University President. That will start things moving down the chain of command."

"He?" asked Molly.

"It is Alabama, we play to their preconceptions," David answered, understanding her viewpoint. "The President will tell the Dean, who will tell the Department Head, who will get my classes covered. While the officer will ask for secrecy, it will leak out of a bunch of campus offices. If there is anyone watching, they will know the back story. On Guam, you will need to see that the true story gets leaked in a believable manner. Then we hope that they were either not watching at all or are watching and bought the story."

"The officer does what with the University President?" Glenn inquired.

"He starts off with the typical stuff seen in the movies, 'it is a matter of national security', the usual mumbo jumbo. The Prez will eat it up. Present a letter from the CNO, read it aloud, explain it, ask for full secrecy, and leave. I assume you will have either an NCIS officer, or one of your operatives, to do the job. The tall guy from this morning would do well. He has gravitas and a no-nonsense manner." David laid it out as if he were teaching his students: here are the facts, here are how you interpret them, consider special-case conditions, such as the agent's gender.

Once again David was alone in the room while Molly and Glenn left to set up the various elements of the scheme that they, mostly David, had pieced together. It was easy to dismiss those two as cardboard cutouts; they revealed little about themselves. That was the way the spy business worked. Their goal was to be flat, unremarkable, to leave no hints, no threads, no loose ends. To be unremembered. He felt they were even imitating his style of language, as if they had an innate need to blend in, to be inside and not outside. He didn't have even their last names, didn't know if Molly and Glenn were their real first names. It didn't matter, there was a job to do, and he would do it with those he had available. His choice in life was similar, to be unremarkable except in a few things that were important to him, like caves and teaching.

David had an image of the full Western Pacific up on the screen and was facing away from the door looking at the image when the door suddenly popped opened.

"Who are you?" a voice commanded.

"Well, who are you?" David replied as he turned, his ID badge was on his sports coat, which lay over the back of his chair, and was not visible.

"I am the TI, and I don't know you," the man said. He was maybe four inches under six feet, a bit rotund, balding. "I'll ask again — who are you and what are you doing here?" the man demanded.

"I am here by invitation. My name is Karl Mallin, and I am a mining engineer," David lied. The imperious air of the man, his demands, his posturing, had set off alarm bells in David's head. He decided to be very careful, Glenn and Molly said this operation was tightly held, few at Langley knew about it. What was a stranger in Atlanta doing here, asking these questions? He knew the door code.

"What business does a mining engineer have with the CIA?" the man demanded back.

"And you are who?" David asked again. "Have you been read in? And what is a TI?"

The man paused for a moment, realizing his ID badge was front and center and it had the name 'Harold Willard' on it. "TI means 'Team Inspector', I check on activities across the CIA for procedures. I wasn't told about you."

"And I wasn't told to expect you." David countered. "I have work to do."

"What work is that?" Willard asked.

"Apparently we are missing some people in Indonesia and I am to see which mines on Irian Jaya have been recently closed down. They could be used as possible hiding places," David said with a smile.

"I see," Willard responded. "Good to know you are helping get our four people back." He abruptly left the room.

David wondered what that was all about. He didn't want any more interruptions. A good thing he had zoomed the image out and it wasn't focused on Pulau Ternate when Willard had suddenly appeared. He placed a chair against the door handle and went back to looking at close-ups of Pulau Ternate; he didn't want to risk any more interruptions.

CHAPTER 7

MOLE ASSES

ABOUT AN HOUR LATER THE DOOR OPENED, or rather it tried to be opened, but hit the chair. David strode over to the door and asked, "Who is it?"

"It is Glenn. What's up?"

David pulled the chair back and opened the door fully. "I had a visitor."

Glenn looked startled. "Who was it?"

"His ID tag said 'Harold Willard' and he was quite abrupt." David replied. "He asked a lot of questions. I think he is a problem."

Just then Molly came in through the door, saw the look on Glenn's face, and said "What is going on?"

"Willard was just here, interrogating David," Glenn answered.

Molly and Glenn turned simultaneously to David. "What did he want?" Molly initiated.

"What did you tell him?" Glenn followed, viewing it as source to sink.

"My ID badge was covered up, so I told him I was Karl Mallin, a mining engineer, and I was looking at old mines on Irian Jaya as hiding places for missing people," David responded.

"You lied to him?" Molly was astonished. "Why?"

"He didn't seem right, I got a bad vibe from him, so I decided to play a role, thinking I could always say later I was only being careful," David answered. "He said he was a 'Team Inspector' checking on procedures. I didn't believe any of it."

"Who do you think he is?' asked Glenn.

"He hunts for moles would be my guess, but I think he is the mole," David ventured.

"Why do you say that?" Molly asked.

"He said he was glad I was on the project, and he hoped I could help get our four people back," David stated.

"So what?" Glenn seemed distracted, and rightfully so.

"He knows four were to be taken, but doesn't yet know only three actually were," David replied. "To me, that indicates advance knowledge of the plot, and it also indicates good security on your end. Once he learns only three were taken, let's hope he forgets his offhanded comment to me."

"Jesus H. Christ," Glenn muttered. "Willard is out of the loop for this mission, he shouldn't know actual planned versus executed numbers. There is no reason he should be here in Atlanta! We may have a watcher on the inside."

"What was he doing here?" Molly asked. "How did he get the security code for this room? I bet he knew we weren't in the room, I bet he was really surprised to find David aka Karl in here. He was poking around."

"Nice job misleading him, David," Glenn said. "Willard has exceptional authority and access through his TI position. But he still has to demonstrate a need to know in order to get specifics. He understands we have been assigned to a missing persons problem, but that is all. He can question anyone, anytime. They need not answer if he has not been read in. The security guards on this floor didn't tell him there was a third person. Jason and Paul need to be advised to say nothing about their duties this morning, or Paul's trip to Alabama tomorrow. We'll tighten things up even more."

"Would it help if Willard got wind of neo-Nazis in the Marianas?" David suggested.

"Yes, that would be good," Molly responded. "If nothing else, it distracts him from what we are doing here. If he really is a mole, which I very much doubt, then it would reinforce our attempt to hide David's true mission."

"He's a mole," David said in a flat voice, surprised, maybe affronted that his word was doubted. "It was written all over him. Short, a bit fat, balding, he went into the CIA with dreams of grandeur, and it hasn't worked out. He has a Napoleon complex. This is his secret fantasy. He is showing everybody up. Treat him as a mole, and we will be safe. He knows more than he should, let's keep his knowledge level where it is."

Up one more flight of stairs was a series of rooms with bunks, showers, and toilets.David's single suitcase was there. He had had enough luggage lost or delayed to know it was better to travel with a backpack that had everything he needed for a couple of days. A backpack also didn't need to be gate-checked, a real advantage over a roller bag when making a close connection. He opened his suitcase and took out his field gear he thought he would need for this expedition. Molly had obtained a standard military duffle for him, so he began to re-pack. Elbow and knee pads, gloves, field pants and shirts, underwear including his silk pair, a tropical field work favorite in case crotch rot set in. He didn't plan on rigging any drops or climbs; he would let the Seals use their equipment that they worked with all the time. Some simple civies for on the submarine went in the duffle, his field boots, and his wetsuit booties. He kept his waterproof LED lights, his Suunto compass and inclinometer, and Disto measuring laser. He also brought toiletries, an encrypted laptop, a camera and associated chargers, his field hat, some nylon webbing, and a Swiss army knife. A leatherman tool from his checked luggage went into his backpack — he wouldn't be dealing with TSA security. He set his alarm for 0500, rolled onto his bunk, and went to sleep. Glenn came in sometime that night and crashed; David noticed but made no sign. Plenty of time for conversation on the long flight to Guam. Glenn had indicated he was going along but would stay on the sub. Molly would run things back at Langley.

He was up at 0500; Glenn had said 0530 would be fine but David wanted extra time to get himself together. Shave, shit, and shower, a routine he learned in boot camp a long time ago. He hadn't wanted to do time in the Navy, but it beat Vietnam, so he had made the best of the situation. He put on field clothes and made sure he had his jacket and vest; he had heard MATS flights could be cold. Backpack on, duffle under his arm, he followed Glenn out of the room and down the stairs to avoid elevators and being seen. Into a black SUV driven by the shorter of the two men from yesterday's incident at Immigration. The vehicle amused David; it might as well have said 'CIA Spy Vehicle' in big white letters along the side. The driver was Jason, he assumed, from the names that floated out during discussions about who went to Alabama the night before. Inside was a bag with a few doughnuts and coffee for Glenn and hot chocolate for David. The SUV took a round-about route within the airport in the early morning gloom of false dawn, ending up at a hanger area with numerous military aircraft, one of which was a C-5A. They drove up to the plane's back ramp, which was down. Glenn and David exited the car with their gear and climbed up the ramp into the cavernous hull of the aircraft. Jason never said a word. The SUV drove off.

They walked the length of the interior to where a vertical sheet of thick fabric separated an area with twelve typical airline seats in two rows of six from the rest of the plane. The seats looked lost in the vast width of the place. The door ahead went to the crew spaces, David assumed. Glenn secured his duffel in a wall locker; David did the same. The two rows of seats had ample space between them, and the seats were widely spaced side-to-side as well. Plenty of room for big men to sprawl on what would be a flight of about sixteen hours. Two typical airline lavatories stood along the port wall, locked in place.

"This is our priority area. No one but crew will come in here," Glenn announced. "Everyone else, plus cargo, rides in the back. We boarded first to keep separate from the routine passengers. The gear you requested for the team is in the locker next to the lavatories."

The sound of feet on metal banged away, coming closer. The curtain parted and seven men in camouflage uniforms with duffels and bags of gear came in the compartment — the Seals. They looked at Glenn, then at David.

Glenn stepped forward and introduced himself. "Lieutenant, I am Glenn, mission leader. You are to be the operational commander. David," Glenn said, pointing to David, "will be your situational advisor. Have you been briefed?"

"Lieutenant Shopov, Mr. Glenn, sir. We have not been briefed except to be told we were going underground and anyone not comfortable with that should inform Command. We are to receive our briefing and instructions during the flight."

"Very good, Lieutenant. We will do introductions now and brief once airborne," Glenn said. "First names only." That instruction was a bit late for the lieutenant.

The lieutenant was Josh, there was a Rob, Wu, Tim, Pete, Sam, and Jesus. Sounds from the back indicated that the plane was being loaded. David would be with these men for the next sixteen hours, then not see them again until they were all onboard the submarine. On Guam, they would go their separate ways; the Seals would not know anything about the diversion plans involving mythical neo-Nazis. Seal Tim was a master diver and would be in charge of the underwater passage route from the sub to the coast of Pulau Ternate. Navy divers on the sub would handle the actual sub lock-out to ocean transition and return. David had not had a tank on for decades but assumed, much like riding a bicycle, that it was all in his muscle memory. A crew member came out the forward door, told the people in the compartment to buckle up, and then she went on to the rear of the plane to tell the passengers there, in their seats along the sides of the compartment, to do the same. Cargo was piled high and tied down along the axis of the plane, she had to walk around it in a circle to reach everyone. She returned without further comment, entered the forward door, and closed it with care. The engines lit up, the plane moved, and after a very short taxi, did its roll and then was in the air.

Molly was in the air too, flying back to Dulles and then back to Langley. Dr. David Langwonaire had been a surprise, they had sought to pick his brains and the toss him back into the waters of society, too insignificant to matter. Well, he mattered now, and Molly felt the heat of the man's understated intensity still. So different than Glenn, who had mimicked him in voice and action, classic technique to keep a subject at ease, except Glenn did that to everyone. She had done it, too, but somehow she felt it was different. Langwonaire had pissed in front of her without a care, then he had threatened her, laid his hands on her, literally held her life in his possession. Then he had released her life, as they had intended to release him. The lesson wasn't lost on her. She prided herself on her professionalism, it was her identity. She had no personal life, she had unused vacation days by the trunk-load. She wasn't lonely as much as unfulfilled, her career was a distraction from all the confusion that was life. Her career was her anchor — did it secure her or drag her down?

CHAPTER 8

THE FIRST INVESTIGATION

JOANIE WAS FEELING BETTER, but that was just her meds working. Her head had cleared, at least to the extent that the pain treatment for her broken arm allowed. She had been working on writing up the details of the events that led to her traffic accident with the truck, but it was slow going, her memories were still sorting themselves out, she pecked out words on the notebook computer slowly with her left hand. Then Matt came into the room, which was not her apartment in the city but a place within the Embassy, usually used for important visitors, and it had a whiff of opulence. She was here for her security, she had been told, but she suspected they wanted to keep her close for other reasons.

"Good morning, Joanie," Matt said, his voice carrying true warmth. Joanie respected Matt, he had a flair for his work, and he always made those around him feel comfortable. He said it was his way of disappearing, by creating a glow that would hide him from prying eyes. "How are we doing today?"

"Still getting my thoughts together, I apologize for being such a drag on operations."

"Not a drag at all, a key witness we hope can help us figure out what happened, and why," Matt kept his voice mellow, his eyes on Joanie, but softly, as if he was embarrassed to stare. "What can you tell me about Phil, Walt, and Jim?" Matt used only the first names, to make it seem less official, less urgent.

"Well, Phil was excited, he likes interacting with what he calls the next generation. Jim saw it as a chore, but he always does it with good cheer." Joanie paused, looked out the window next to her bed.

"And Walt?" Matt had noted the omission, it spoke volumes.

"Walt didn't like the work, he wanted to be in his lab growing seeds or whatever he does, he complained all the time." Joanie looked back at Matt; her eyes were full of tears. "He hit on me, all the time. At first, I tried to be polite, but he kept pushing. Finally, I told him to stop or I would report him. He told me to do it, then he could get out of this place. He hated it here. Then he hated me." She began to cry, more of a weeping, trying to hold it in.

"I see," Matt replied, and he did, it began to fall into place. Someone had to leak information about the timing and routes the four embassy employees would take, the plans at the destination. "Did you make a complaint?"

"I did, through the priority hotline. I was supposed to get an acknowledgement, but it never came. I assumed that it had been discarded, that there was no corroboration or proof. So I just tried to gut it out." Joanie took a deep breath. "They can have Walt and do what they want, but Phil and Jim are such good people, always nice to me, never an advance or suggestion."

"OK, that was very helpful," Matt said, and he turned to go.

"It was Walt, wasn't it? Joanie accused. "He didn't like Phil or Jim, he envied them, their easy way with people, how they were rewarded for their performance."

"They did perform well, Walt did not, there was no favoritism," Matt countered.

"It doesn't matter what you think, it matters what Walt thought." Joanie was now fully awake, fully alert, the cobwebs gone. "He set this up, he thinks he will get some prize, some bonus. He is a dead man and doesn't even know it."

"We don't know that, Joanie. This is a private conversation between you and me." Matt looked hard at her, such that she drew back deeper into her bed. "Keep it that way. We will do a formal debrief after this all sorts out. You have been cleared for duty, Wuwan too, although I don't think he will be driving for us again."

"It wasn't his fault, you or I could have done the same thing," Joanie protested.

"Well, maybe so, but we did not and he did. We will keep him on staff with a task that keeps him in the Embassy," Matt replied.

"Keeps him safe, you mean, like me."

"There is that benefit. You are medically done here except for check-ups. You can go back to work tomorrow." This time, Matt did leave.

"So, what do you have?" Linton asked as Matt settled himself in across from the Ambassador's teak desk, as dark as he. The Ambassador had a first name, he never used it, it was 'Ambassador' or 'Linton' or for important times, 'Ambassador Linton'. Matt suspected his high school nickname had been 'Lint' or 'Dustball' or something like that.

"Based on communications with Langley, very secret, an almost off-the-record contact, we are told that a mole may exist here and that we should be cautious." Matt was careful with his words.

"Great, just great, a mole hunt, my favorite activity. Well, it isn't me, and I doubt it is you, so that leaves everyone else," Linton was chuckling, but at the irony, not the situation. "The first likely candidate is Joanie Dellows. Comes in as an intern, no one knows her; she is the only one of the four not taken. Stages a traffic accident as cover. Now she is in here, 24/7, and can continue to monitor our actions."

"Not possible, I have investigated that angle, it was truly a traffic accident. People were waiting for her at the private high school. She was to be taken." Matt understood that Linton knew better, was this a test or something else?

"I agree, however I received this morning a 'for your eyes only' communication from the TI officer at Langley, which suggested exactly the scenario I presented to you."

"You got a direct communication from Harold Willard? That is not protocol. Neither is sharing it with me." Matt was concerned, the boat was getting leaky.

"You didn't see the communication, you only heard it verbally from me, it was only my eyes" Linton laughed. "I don't know the man. What can you tell me?"

"A typical internal investigations guy, a rat like all the rest across law enforcement in the USA," Matt answered, his disdain obvious.

"We need internal controls. You do that for me," Linton protested.

"The position is only as useful as those who hold it," Matt was forceful in his answer. "Willard likes his power, and he applies it where it gives him the most satisfaction. I bet he wants to come here and run the show himself as regards the hostages."

"Just so. I informed him no, we have all the skills and personnel necessary already here, so don't worry. It's a State Department decision, not a CIA one, so I have control." Linton's reassurance was good, but Matt thought a confirmation with Molly back at Langley might be useful.

"So who is your candidate for the inside job?" Linton pressed on.

"Walter Pinny. He checks all the boxes, spurned by Joanie Dellows, poor job performance, always complaining'" Matt offered. "I'd like to see his communication records."

"Have at it, keep me informed, stay off the usual Langley circuits." Linton waved Matt away, his arm moving like a branch originating from the teak desk.

CHAPTER 9

LIFT-OFF AND LESSONS

GLENN STARTED THE BRIEFING, explaining that three hostages had been taken, and that a large Seal team was to fly in and try to extract them from a cave in eastern Indonesia in about three weeks. That was what the kidnappers expected, but that is not what the U.S. was going to do. Instead, the schedule had been advanced, to use a small team that went in via submarine and executed the extraction. A sheet had been hung on the forward bulkhead, and Glenn used a computer projector to show the general location of the island, then close-up images to show the precise location of the cave, with an overlay of the cave map done by Daan in 1929. Glenn asked for questions.

"Will we use open circuit or rebreather to make the sub-to-coast transition?" asked Tim, the dive master.

"I leave that choice to you and your navy colleagues on the sub," Glenn responded. He flipped back a slide to show the general position of Pulau Ternate. "The edge of the island platform is less than 300 meters from land, the shallow offshore is quiescent. The sub can get close and still be in deep water. As a result, the swim is short. The team will go in at sun-up."

"A daylight extraction?" questioned the lieutenant.

Glenn turned to David. "Would you like to explain?"

"Uh, sure," David responded, caught by surprise, a rare event for him. "The terrorists are expecting us to come in at night, by helicopter, from the northeast, in three weeks. We will do what is called 'escape in time and space'. We will come in two weeks early, in a different vehicle, from the opposite direction, in daylight. Intelligence indicates that the terrorists are urban based, so an open field setting will be foreign to them. They may rely on some local but poorly trained support." David touched the projector and zoomed in on the island picture. "Satellite imagery shows the cliff line of a rocky point south of the beach fronting the cave. That cliff has a few small caves, one of which," David pointed to a spot on the south-facing side of the point, "has an opening onto the top surface of the point. We will use that as our landing site. From there, I will lead you to the southern-most possible entrance to the cave, and we will go in."

"You will be with us? You are an old man!" the lieutenant exclaimed, obviously agitated.

Glenn stepped forward but David signaled him back. "The key to a successful mission is to be able to find, enter, and traverse the cave without detection. The cave involved is called a flank margin cave, and it is very different on the inside than most caves any of this team has ever been in. How many of you have done wild caving?" No hands went up. "How many have taken a tour in a show cave?" Rob and Pete put up a hand each. "OK, route finding in a cave is different than that in a building. Regular caves, such as found in most of the USA, are either active or abandoned underground stream passages. They have a flowing water origin and a water destination when they form. Flank margin caves do not. They are very mazy, passages end unexpectedly, and passage size varies from tiny to very large. Rob, what cave did you visit?"

"Blanchard Springs, in Arkansas," Rob answered.

"And you, Pete?"

"Carlsbad Caverns in New Mexico," was Pete's reply.

"What you saw in Carlsbad is what you can expect on Pulau Ternate, only very much compressed in the vertical dimension," David explained. He put up the Daan map of the cave on the screen. "The Daan map shows that the cave has numerous entrances in the cliff that overlooks the beach south of the village of Wadjol. Those entrances were produced as the cliff line eroded landward and chopped into the cave. There are some entrances from the top. These," David said, pointing to a couple of small circular structures, "are water input sites. The larger ones," David pointed to a few more circles of larger diameter, "are collapse features that lead into the cave's upper level. We will try to enter by way of the southern-most entrance, which the Daan map shows as having daylight as seen from the inside, but partially blocked by rubble. We will have to do a little digging, but satellite imagery shows that the site is in the bush back from the cliff face, so we can work unobserved."

"The map is almost 100 years old. What if we can't dig in at that point?" A good question from Wu.

"Plan B is to go to the next entrance in line, but the risk that it is actively guarded will be higher," David responded. "We take what we can get." He continued, "The profile of the cave shows that it has two main levels, a very low and sprawling upper level, most of which is a meter or less in height, and a much larger set of passages and rooms, but more laterally constrained, in the lower level, where we feel the hostages are being kept." David indicated several chambers on the map at the north end of the cave. "The two levels connect in multiple spots. I suspect that the upper level is not utilized and that we can traverse unseen to a region above the larger chambers and determine where the hostages are."

"How likely is it that we will have to haul them up and out?" The question came from Jesus. A small man, lifting big people would be an issue for him.

"It is quite possible, you will need to carry line and pulleys with you, plus the necessary webbing and rigging gear," David replied. "It may take a 2:1 or 3:1 rig to lift them efficiently and quietly. To get back to the lieutenant's original question, I am going because I know how to find, traverse, and exit a complex cave such as we see here," David pointed at the cave map. "I can carry my own weight and my personal gear. You guys will have to sherpa the team gear. I also want about five kg of explosive and several timing detonators. We may need to make a distraction or seal a passage from pursuit." David had made his case; he would see how the men responded. They commonly used local human resources in their clandestine field work. How did they view him — local, exotic, or just old?

"We were told not to bring any night vision equipment, which sounds crazy for working in the dark. Why is that?" asked Sam. It was like they took turns so everyone got to participate.

"All right guys, hear me out on how we will configure for traversing the cave," David announced. "We won't use night vision equipment for a number of reasons. First of all, we have to see the cave as our opponents see it, to understand how they would guard and patrol the cave. Second, the equipment allows no peripheral vision, which would be a real problem. Third, it is bulky, and we will be in confined spaces. Fourth, it is electronics, and they don't do well in the cave environment. We will use simple hand-held LED lights on lowest power."

"Why not headlamps?" asked Rob, as if on cue.

"The beam of the headlamp follows your head movement," David explained. "Our heads will be on a swivel, the cave is complex, and we have to check which route actually continues north, keep a look-out for guards and for obstacles. We can't be sending light beams all over the cave. When you talk to someone with your headlamp on, you shoot the beam right into their eyes and kill their night vision. You control your hands much better, and there is no lag time between when you want to turn off the light, no reaching and fumbling for the headlamp switch. Light discipline will be the most significant task you will face."

David saw the men look at each other and nod; it wasn't rocket science, what he had said, it was just new information. The Seals processed and accepted it in real time. The battlefield doesn't allow detailed consideration or a vote — it is react or die. David could see he was earning trust, not by ordering, but by teaching.

"The cave has many entrances," David continued, "and we will be in the cave in daytime, so an odd light pattern inside the cave won't be unusual for those who are in it now. Speaking of discipline, we have to be quiet. Sound can travel very efficiently in a cave. Odors too. No aftershave, no deodorant, no scented soap. Best if no one showers for twenty-four hours prior to the mission. Westerners smell different to Asians, mostly because of our meat and dairy diet. If we are sweating enough to stink a bit, we smell more like a dead or dying small animal, which will help us."

David, from long experience, could remember how he could tell a lot about another group in a cave before he saw them: that one individual in the group was a smoker, that they all had gear that smelled new, that their voices carried anxiety, how their lights never moved. That fixed light beam meant they weren't looking at the cave, but only at the way out. Spelunkers.

David pulled a flashlight out of his pocket. "Each of you will have two of these. They are flat, so they won't roll when set down. They have two switches. The left switch is low power — this is what we will use. The right switch is high power, and if pushed a second time, medium power. I thought about disabling the right switch, but maybe a small piece of duct tape over it will prevent accidental engagement. Each light has a neck cord." From his backpack, David pulled out kneepads and elbow pads. "These pads are what cavers use and are what you will use. They are lightweight, rugged, and simple. We will be doing a lot of crawling. This equipment will keep things easy and allow rapid and silent motion. No helmets — they increase your cross section and make a distinctive sound when they hit the ceiling. You will need to be careful, avoid sudden moves, and know that if you hit your head, it doesn't make much sound as long as you don't curse. A watch cap works well if you want some padding." Finally, David pulled out a cave pack. "Each of you will have a cave pack like this one. It goes over the shoulder and has a waist strap. You wear it along your side so you can easily negotiate low passages. In it goes your second light, your water bottle, a power bar or two. Nothing in your pockets. Anything in a pocket always seems to work its way out during a crawl or climb."

Wu asked, "What about weapons?" The turn-taking continued. It wasn't to establish status or pecking order, it wasn't to kill time. The men seemed relaxed, looking at one another with a smile, making a soft joke as the plane hopped and skipped through minor turbulence.

It was a gradual, step-by-step interrogation of David, to see what he knew and if it was enough; to see if he had command focus, had a strategy that overlay the tactics. The Seals knew the military was hurry up and wait. The key was how to wait, how to prepare, how to keep an edge.

"I defer to you on that issue," David replied. "Inside the cave, I recommend only a side arm. Multiple reloads if it makes you feel better, but we are not looking for a fire fight. If we get in trouble, we exit immediately at the nearest entrance. Pursuers will be able to move faster over the cave than we will be able to inside it, and we will get out-flanked if we stay in the cave. We get outside, and we run for it. We can have assault rifles stashed where we enter the cave at the south end."

"What will you use?" asked Tim with a hard look, sizing up David to see if he was a participant or just extra baggage. Would David fight if necessary? Tim was all about teamwork, about shared responsibility; he came from a family of eleven. He was also a diver, and you never dove alone.

David reached into his backpack and took out a pistol, courtesy of Glenn. "A .45-caliber service automatic. A real man-stopper, it functions under almost any conditions, and I know it well. I will carry two full clips as reloads."

"You expect we will have to shoot our way out?" Tim followed up.

"I want to be able to shoot my way out if I have to," David said. "It is like bringing a raincoat on a hike. Having it prevents rain, not having it invites rain." As if the Fates cared what you did, he thought without saying.

"Footwear?" asked Sam, one of the larger men. Shoes and how they fit were more important if you were big and heavy.

"What works for you in the field," David responded, emphasizing the individual. One-size-fits-all is unacceptable when the team has been selected not as a formless group, but a machine with specific parts for specific tasks that fostered overall unity. "I use tight-fitting wetsuit booties with a thick felt sole for this sort of work. Lightweight, can handle the jagged surface rocks we will encounter on the hike over to the cave entrance. Good friction for climbing. I'll have lightweight long pants and long-sleeved field shirts, a field hat I'll leave at the entrance. I will have gloves, but I usually don't use them. I do better if I literally have a feel for the cave. If we do this right, they won't know we have even been there. We leave nothing behind that identifies us in any way. My shell casings, if I have to fire, could be from a local who has a left-over WW II service automatic."

The discussion went on. Some of the men wanted to know more about the cave and how it formed, others wanted to know how they would make the transition from the water to the coastal cave and up into the bush for the hike on to the selected cave entrance. David finished the initial briefing by saying, "Once we are on the submarine, we will need to work with the Navy divers there, and ship's command, to see how we actually do the lock-out and get our gear in waterproof carry bags. I assume they have scooters with an octopus rig, and we will be able to glide in to shore." To that statement, there was widespread agreement.

CHAPTER 10

QUIET DESPERATION

PHIL CANNOCZIC SAT IN THE NEAR DARK. Light leaked in from the blocked oval passage that led from this room to the main cave. At least he thought it was a cave; the walls of this chamber had a natural curvature, and there were a few stalactites dimly seen on the ceiling. A small hole to nowhere was up there, too. The floor was gritty, dirty sand, there was a plastic tarp that they slept on along one wall; the other far wall had a twenty-liter plastic paint can with a snap-on lid. That was their latrine, and it added a mild stink to the room. Phil assumed the lid was not for their own nose benefit, but for those who came in twice a day to deliver a simple rice and beans meal, and a jug of water. They ate from the communal plate with their fingers. As with Muslim tradition, they ate with their right hand only, and used the left for any action that might cause contamination. They shared the same water jug, passing it around as if it were filled with moonshine.

They had come here by way of a boat, a small freighter based on how it rocked in the sea and the sounds it made. They were kept in a storage room with the same two pieces of furniture: the paint can, and the tarp. Jim and Walt had deferred to Phil, he was senior in rank, such as it was in an embassy, and he had tried to keep them calm. No one talked to them; they were given no instructions except pushed to where they were to be, their hoods taken off at that moment as the door shut them in. No one told them not to talk, so they did so in low voices. Hell, Walt snored louder than they talked. The room light never went off, but it wasn't bright. They weren't being maltreated; they were being ignored.

Six days on the boat, based on twelve meals served, then a man came in, put the hoods back on, and they were walked out of the room, up a steep set of stairs, then carefully placed hands helped them down a rope ladder and into a smaller boat. Phil could feel no beating heat, no light penetrated the hood, so he assumed it was night — perfectly reasonable for a prisoner transfer. He deliberately didn't think hostage; hostages commonly didn't survive. A prisoner? Maybe a prisoner exchange or buy out. He didn't see himself as kidnapped, but as captured. Such thinking kept some of the fears away, back in a corner, where all they could do was gnaw at him.

In the cave, Phil relished the memory of the transfer, the sound of birds, voices in a language he didn't understand. The gentle movement of the small boat, the sound of waves breaking gently on a beach. Then a soft bang as the boat hit something solid, and hands hauled him up to stand on a flat, hard surface. There was a dock or wharf at whatever place they had come to. They were walked a short distance until the solid surface became sand, well packed. Then the air changed, sounds had echoes, and they must have walked into the cave. Not a mine, not a tunnel, but a natural feature. Hopefully not a tomb, thought Phil. Many voices, the floor occasionally uneven so that they stumbled now and then. Pushed in their backs to bend over, their heads brushing rock above, then the hoods taken off, and they were here as a wooden slab covered their entry point. In minutes their eyes had adjusted to see their dark-gray interior space. Were they already buried?

Walt was quiet for long stretches of time, then he would talk rapidly, almost gibbering, about how this wasn't right, how it had been a mistake, that soon it would be all OK. Then he would go silent again. Jim was calm, but his fear was manifest. He jumped at every sound that leaked in from outside their prison chamber. Phil understood Jim's fear. Jim was gay, and at risk if their captors were fundamentalists. Phil was more realistic about their fate. It would be common to all. Probably execution by beheading, recorded and broadcast to the world as a signal of their captor's loyalty to their cause. Phil tried to keep religion out of it; religion was just the vehicle by which their captors' hate could be carried.

While Jim spoke of a hoped-for rescue, Phil understood that extraction of them alive was a distant possibility. Walt seemed to be in some fantasy world where their captors released him and him only. Phil wondered at that, realizing that someone at the Embassy had released their travel schedule. Or a person or persons on the outside had done a lot of homework to find out which schools were hosting what Americans on what date. Had Walt sold them out? If so, it had been incredibly stupid for Walt to think he would be rewarded for his treachery. If it was going to be a sequential beheading, Walt was likely to be the first. The most expendable, the one with unique knowledge of their situation.

Phil wondered about Joanie. Had she been taken, too, and kept separately from her three colleagues? That made sense, to isolate the female from the males. While Phil thought in terms of being a prisoner, he knew he was not. Prisoners get interrogated, and no one had spoken to him, or to his co-prisoners. They weren't taken for their knowledge of the Embassy or of American policy; they were functionaries. Their captors apparently knew this fact and didn't bother to try and extract secrets the prisoners didn't have. Their value was in their lives, and the maximum reward would be distilled from those lives before they were ended. The true value was in the ending itself, a snuff flick produced as foreign policy by a stateless regime.

Phil had little to do but think, so he thought. Actually, he remembered. He went over his childhood, his days growing up in a loving family with siblings and friends, parents who cared and gave solid life lessons. How would Mandy react, to see his head fall from his shoulders in a spurt of blood? Would she even watch, to see his very end, his last moment of life in her life? Or would she never watch it, wanting to see him alive in her memory and not headless and dead on a flat screen? She was to have come out in September, when her summer field work was over. They were going to start a life, they had talked of marriage, of children, of their career together. Phil still had hope, he was still alive. He thought of men on death row. Was it better or worse to know the end date, how much time you had left? Was it better to not know until the last few minutes, when they came for you with their long, sharp blade? Here, Phil was uncertain of how many days had passed. Counting time was difficult in the dark chamber. He could count meals as he had on the boat — it appeared to be two a day no matter the setting. If so, it had been only three days in this dark place.

Phil waited; he comforted Jim, who had a partner back in the States. Walt seemed to not want comforting, although he clearly needed it most. Phil felt Walt carried guilt on top of his fear. Self-inflicted guilt, Walt had to own it. He would die for it. Phil continued to believe in hope even as passing time whittled it away. Soon, he would be only a splinter.

CHAPTER 11

FLYING, STILL FLYING

THE FLIGHT DRAGGED ON. David had the team try on what they would wear in the cave, then wiggle around under and through the seats. Then they did it again with the lights off, testing the three light settings and practicing light discipline. The team seemed to fully understand how poor light use would compromise the mission. Josh, Wu, and Jesus were the smallest, and would be in the lead with David; Sam, Tim, and Pete were larger, quite robust, and would not fit in a very low squeeze. Rob was the only average-sized person other than David. Hopefully, the cave wouldn't have any really tight spots on the route they would use. Sam would carry the explosive and the detonators; the rigging gear would be disbursed among the remaining six. They took a break and Glenn opened a cooler from a locker and passed out warm chicken noodle soup and ham sandwiches, crackers, and chips. From another cooler came fresh fruit and cold drinks. The team ate, made some small talk, then took a planned rest, all the Seals nodding off within minutes; they knew to get sleep when they could.

"So, what do you think?" Glenn asked David as they sat side by side on the coolers, away from the napping Seals.

"The mission won't fail because of them," David answered. "They are fit, no surprise, but mentally flexible and willing to evaluate my planning and offer constructive comments. I worry about a bunch of stuff, most of it out of our control."

"Such as?" Glenn offered.

"Was a watcher involved and will what we have planned put them off the scent?" David replied. "Is the submarine commander going to work with us or put his boat before the mission? Can we get to the cave unobserved and traverse it and find the hostages?"

"You control the mission in the cave," Glenn observed.

"True, but I don't control the cave." David retorted. "There are a couple of chambers at the extreme north end of the cave that appear to be likely places to hold three hostages. But what if they are in a cage in the center of a large room with people milling about? Then it gets dicey."

"OK, what is Plan B then?" Glenn was walking David through it.

"Then we have a fire fight," David answered. "We recover our assault rifles, shoot up the place, explode a bomb or two, and run for the sub. Or maybe steal a boat and go that way. Do we have recent imagery of what is docked at the cave area?"

"I get two updates a day," Glenn explained. "To get more would require repositioning a satellite, and that might alert the terrorists."

"How would they know?" David asked.

"Lots of countries track satellite positions. It is relatively simple to do, and one of those countries could be in sympathy with the terrorists," Glenn added.

"Not repositioning could be a bigger problem than doing so," David countered. "They know we are looking for the hostages. If we don't reposition then they may assume we know where the hostages are already, and things are blown. Can you reposition to get good views of Pulau Ternate but make it look like your interest is more central in Indonesia?"

"I see your point, and I think we can do what you suggest," Glenn said, stepping through the door into the crew space ahead. He came back about twenty minutes later. "Done," was all he said. They each settled into a chair and took a nap.

David slept well. He had slept in hotels, dorms, tents, and under open sky all over the world. The bay of a C-5A was just another place to flop. He had basically been kidnapped into this plot, and had gone willingly, subsuming the plot as his own, taking control, as was his wont. He had the confidence produced by long experience in unusual situations. Caving had something to do with it. Like ice diving, caving was an 'overhead' situation — you couldn't bail out by calling in the helicopter or by climbing straight up. You had to work your way back and out. If you couldn't self-rescue, you were likely to die where you were. The CIA had tried to co-op him and had been co-opted instead. They had a mission, but their design was flawed. He was confident his design was not flawed. To be certain his mission was properly carried out, he would do it himself. Arrogant? Perhaps, but also effective. David very much believed in doing your job. His concern was that he would become known because of this mission, that he would lose his self-protecting anonymity. He wasn't modest; he, instead, knew the value of being unknown.

The flight went on, long and uneventful. They ate again, reviewed plans and procedures, got to know one another. The enlisted men took David in stride. They respected motivation and expertise, and David had demonstrated both. Lieutenant Josh remained a bit skeptical — not a bad thing if it didn't distract him during the mission. David *was* an old man, he was also fit and knew all the moves and tricks of field work, both above and below ground. He knew he could do the mission if he only had to take care of himself. The mission would be a bit like a beginner's cave trip, David thought he could expect some simple mistakes by the others on the team. Josh would take special care, as he had operational command and clearly believed he knew better than anyone else. David would need to keep him under control.

David and Glenn were on the coolers again, about an hour out from Guam. The coolers were now empty — Seals didn't leave grub behind, either. David shared his concerns about Josh with Glenn. "I don't want to get into an argument about what to do inside the cave. I was introduced as 'situational advisor', whatever that means. What is my authority?"

"Inside the cave, you have the ultimate authority," Glenn began, trying to address David's concerns. David was far older than Glenn, yet at times like this Glenn felt as if a father figure, which was ridiculous but somehow true. "If you get into a fire fight, I expect you to defer to the lieutenant as conditions allow. I will make it clear to him that you have full authority in the cave and should be listened to outside of it. Josh is OK. He did a little testing of limits with you and may continue to do so. He must be sure you can do what you say, and that you will make good decisions. He wants to stay alive, keep his team intact, and complete the mission."

At this point Tim, who had woken up, came over. "How do we get the hostages from the shore back to the sub?" he asked. "We can't assume any have scuba experience."

"Actually, one of them is a certified scuba diver, I think through PADI," Glenn stated. "I can't give you his name, at least not now. One of the reasons he wanted a posting in Indonesia. The diving is fantastic. The other two, no diving experience at all."

"Tim, you are our corpsman as well, correct?" David asked. Tim nodded in assent. "We can do what they did for those boys, that soccer team trapped in the Thai cave several years ago. We drug them into compliance and haul them back underwater like a sack of coconuts. Glenn, we will need to see that the necessary pharmaceuticals are on board the sub."

"That might work," Tim agreed. "Glenn, can you get me the full diagnostics and procedures so I can be prepared?" Glenn nodded as more work was added to his sheet.

The same crew member as before came out a half hour later and told everyone to secure their gear and belt-up. The coolers and packs went back into the lockers, and the men settled in for the final approach. Anderson's runways were long and wide; the C-5A had no problem with an easy landing and taxied to a routine disembarkation point. There was passport control on Guam, as the island was part of the Federated States of Micronesia, which allowed free travel amongst all the island groups. So, to prevent backdoor access to the mainland USA, a passport was needed even though it was U.S. territory just like Puerto Rico. The other passengers and cargo were removed, then an Immigration official came to the team and made a quick note of their documents, said nothing but "Good day," and left. Anderson Air Force Base was at the northern end of Guam, a flat plateau where a cliff dropped 600 feet to a narrow coastal plain and then on into the deep western Pacific.

The Seals exited next with all their gear, into the hot, muggy tropical weather of the southern end of the Marianas Archipelago. They boarded a truck to look like a normal military contingent and were whisked away. Then Glenn and David followed, stepped into a nondescript car with their gear in the trunk, and headed south to Orote and the Navy base. David wondered if they didn't have black SUVs on the island, or had they upped their security consciousness to a safe level?

CHAPTER 12

ISLAND TIME

THEY HAD CROSSED THE INTERNATIONAL DATELINE, so it was the next day. The car drove past security at the main gate of the naval base and stopped under the headquarters building awning. David stepped out, leaving his gear in the trunk, and went into the structure. Here, it was hoped David would be observed; Glenn stayed in the car. If Willard was truly a mole, then Glenn would be associated with the Indonesian mission and David's ruse to be seen as chasing after white supremacists would be blown if he was observed with Glenn. After he came through the main door and went to the duty officer, David was conducted down a hall and into a small conference room. He was offered coffee but asked for a Coke instead. Within a couple of minutes, Glenn came in with a navy officer who introduced himself as Captain Rikkleman. He was missing his lower left arm, which was probably why he had a shore posting, thought David. After pleasantries were exchanged, they got down to business.

The Captain opened the discussion. "We believe we have everything set up. After lunch, you will go out to the pier and board the *Harrington*, a corvette. As soon as you enter the internal spaces, we will shave off your goatee and mustache, put you in a medical officer's uniform, give you cheek inserts, and have you immediately leave the vessel in the company of two other medical officers. You will go to the clinic and change back into your original clothes, which will arrive in a duffel containing your backpack. You will hang out in the quarantine section of sickbay for the time being. The *Harrington* will set sail by 1600

61

hours after boarding a party of marines. The *Harrington* will head north to work off Farallon da Madinilla and your neo-Nazi mission will be under way." Rikkleman delivered the briefing rapid fire, then paused and observed, as if he were ranging a target.

"When will the submarine arrive?" Glenn inquired.

"The *South Dakota* will dock tonight at 2200 hours and the two of you will board immediately in the dark amidst all the hustle and bustle of provisioning and equipment swaps," Rikkleman said. "The *South Dakota* will stay at the pier until after twelve noon before leisurely casting off. We do several of these re-provisioning exercises every year, this will look routine to any outside observer, including satellites and any idiot up on Nimitz Hill with a pair of binoculars. Both of you will be in enlisted men's tropical white long uniforms."

"Who is in command of the *South Dakota*?" David asked. "What will he be like to work with?"

"Captain Lionel Gardesol, a real ring-knocker but efficient and effective," Rikkleman stated. David found it to be an interesting choice of words from a man with no left hand. "He doesn't suffer fools gladly and he is not happy about being pulled in from patrol to do a rescue operation. He understands Glenn is in charge of the mission, but Gardesol commands the boat. He won't mind the Seals coming on board, but civilians will annoy him. Be squared away and respectful and things should go smoothly."

"Ring-knocker?" Glenn asked.

"Academy graduate," David explained. "Academy graduates will pat their hand on the tabletop at a meeting when an ROTC officer is presenting, to make the ring click, and remind everyone that the real navy is run by such graduates."

Rikkleman gave David a surprised look. "You are a veteran?"

"Enlisted from way back. It's we who really run the navy," David said with a smile, to which Rikkleman nodded.

"Chief Fronsan will be here in a few minutes to take you over to the *Harrington*," Rikkleman said, looking at David. "Good luck on your mission, whatever it is." He left the room.

David looked at Glenn and said, "Lots of cloak and dagger, but it is necessary and should work, if it isn't an exercise in futility."

They reviewed their mission yet again. Lunch arrived on a cart — fried chicken and French fries; fortunately, not a fried salad. They napped and chatted the afternoon away.

Chief Fronsan came in, introduced himself, and announced "Time to go." David slung on his backpack and followed the CPO out the door. He would meet up later with Glenn in sickbay. They walked across the yard, engaging in small talk. "Been to Guam before?" asked the Chief.

"Many times, doing work on the freshwater lens," David responded. "I even know what G-U-A-M stands for."

"What's that?" the Chief asked.

"Give Up and Masturbate," David replied, which got a chuckle out of the Chief. A few more war stories were exchanged about liberty on Guam and all the strip clubs down by the beach with their eager male Japanese tourists as they came up on the *Harrington*. They boarded with a salute from the officer of the deck and went below. David was immediately required to disrobe, which he did after dropping his backpack. The ship's barber shaved his face; he put on officer khakis and a baseball cap with 'scrambled eggs' on it, the golden oak leaf pattern that indicated he was of Commander rank or higher. The barber gave him two cheek inserts, which he placed in his mouth. The barber had also trimmed his hair in the back and sides. On went a pair of sunglasses. The barber showed David a mirror and David realized he did look different. His new visage didn't bring anyone to mind, but he wasn't David Langwonaire, the college professor, anymore. Two other officers with medical insignia walked up, and they all went up an internal ladder to the bridge, exited and went down the exterior ladder, saluted the officer of the deck and walked down the gangway, strolling easily across the yard towards the medical building in the distance. David was escorted past the check-in desk and down several halls to a sealed door that read "Quarantine". Once inside, he was shown a private exam room and told to make himself comfortable, and his escort left. A chair to the side, which he took, away from the medical bench in the room's center. There were some medical posters on the wall, one so old it still warned sailors about VD. A few minutes later, a yeoman second class entered with a duffel, took out his clothes and backpack, and waited while David changed back. Then he gathered up the officer clothes and cover, laid out a tropical white long uniform, left the duffel where it sat, and exited. David took a leak, then lay down for a nap.

Glenn woke him up at about 2000 hours. "Rise and shine, cave boy," he said with a grin. "We are getting room service then we get to go be sausages in the can at a thousand feet down." Glenn seemed to be enjoying himself; his affect was different. David understood the feeling. Once they were on the sub, everything was out of their hands until David and the Seals did their lock-out and swim. A cart came in, pushed by the same yeoman as before. Two steak dinners in separate trays with baked potato and a salad with fruit juice and apple pie sat on the cart. A totally American meal. Food on a sub was supposed to be good, but David enjoyed this one especially.

"I take it we are all set and things are going smoothly," David said.

"As best as can be expected," Glenn replied. "I have had a report that the interview with the President, Dean and Department Head at ASU went fine. Apparently, they were all impressed that anyone gave a damn about your research. Your job is safe, and you will probably return to a bit more receptive environment."

Meal finished, they cleaned up, and put on their uniforms. It took David back decades to wear the enlisted uniform again.

"Put your backpack in the duffel, it will get delivered to the *South Dakota*," Glenn stated. Then he handed David a clipboard. "Time to do an inspection."

David was glad to see he was a Petty Officer First Class, E-6, a rank he had never achieved in his previous tour. By now it was 2230, and Glenn led the way out of the clinic. It was dark, lighting was adequate, but David stayed alert anyway. No time to stumble. The *South Dakota* was way down the pier, with lots of activity going on. Glenn strode on through the confusion, up the gangway, and saluted the officer of the deck, who took them into the conning tower and down into the tight and cramped spaces below. Just like caving, David thought.

A Chief Petty Officer came up. "Mr. Glenn and Mr. David, welcome aboard," he said. "I am Chief Ronnals. We are a bit tight for space and I am not sure where to put you." Last names weren't important now.

"Can we get a rack in sickbay?" David asked.

The Chief gave David an appraising look. "You don't mind being in there?"

"Because of our mission, we need to be in a private place where we don't mess up routine operations," David replied. Glenn gave David an inquiring look. David continued, "Sickbay is on the roll, pitch, and yaw axis, so we won't feel hardly any motion." Not that they would anyway in a submarine at depth. But if they had to wallow on the surface, then it mattered.

To this comment, the Chief voiced agreement and led them down from the control room and aft to the mid-boat compartment that was sickbay. At the far end were two sets of bunks, port and starboard. They took the starboard side.

"The Captain will meet with you in his stateroom before we clear the harbor," the Chief said. "Do you need a meal?"

"Not now, thanks Chief," Glenn said. "We will wait here until we are summoned. Please give our regards to the Captain." The Chief left, and Glenn continued, "I'll take top bunk. I still have my prostate." A classic younger guy's dig at an old man.

David rolled into the bottom bunk and took a nap as the *South Dakota* began to prepare for its 1,600-mile journey to Pulau Ternate. The international dateline made jet lag something on steroids — like a Seal, you slept when you could.

CHAPTER 13

THE WATCHER

THE GENERAL SAT IN HIS OFFICE deep in Building 13. He liked the Western superstition attached to the building's identity. His adjutant came in with a file in his hand. "You have the update on Project Zeus?" the General asked. He never gave his name, and no one in Building 13 knew it anyway. He was just 'the General'.

"Yes sir," was the quick reply. His adjutant was smart and subservient, just as the General liked. He placed the file on the General's desk.

"Give me a quick summary, and then an evaluation," was the General's order.

"The subject, Dr. David Langwonaire, was observed in the Atlanta airport being approached by two men who were interpreted to be law enforcement agents. He was taken into custody. He had not been seen since until he appeared in Guam today. His place of employment, Alabama Southeast University, was initially told that the subject was a witness to a crime onboard the airplane he was on, and would miss his job duties the next day, but that was untrue. A naval officer visited the University the next day and explained that the subject was part of a mission to rescue lost fishermen on Farallon da Madinilla in the Marianas Archipelago. That story was also false. Our operative in Guam discovered that the island in question is being used by a neo-Nazi group to recover weapons and explosives, as it is a former Navy firing range. The island is limestone and has many caves, and the subject is to assist in finding both the people involved, and their cache of weapons and explosives. The subject was observed to board the USS *Harrington* at Orote, which then set sail north to Farallon da Madinilla."

"Your interpretation?" the General commanded.

"The subject appears to have been utilized because of his previous work documenting caves in the Marianas, both in Guam and in the CNMI," the adjutant began. "Because of the sensitive nature of white supremacist groups, especially with the current administration and given the University's placement in the deep south of the USA, a cover story of a rescue is much more palatable an explanation for the subject's duties to the U.S. Navy. Creation of such a story indicates that the subject's mission may be long. The conclusion is that the subject is no longer in a position to render assistance that could compromise Project Zeus."

"I concur," the General replied. "Inform me when the subject's mission is complete. Dismissed."

In this manner were David's concerns about the initial approach done by the CIA confirmed. The ruse to explain away that initial contact, and his subsequent absence at ASU, had worked.

※　※　※

Phil paced, it was deliberate, to keep his muscles fluid, as well as to take his mind away somewhere else. Jim did too, a half circle away from him. They both had their private space that way. Walt lay on the tarp, his back upright against the cave wall, playing with stones and pebbles he had gathered, trying to play checkers with himself. Phil was worried, the sounds from outside had changed. More voices, louder voices, languages different, one seemed to be Russian, or Slavic anyway. It was all transient, fleeting, as if people were moving in and out of a chamber, and Phil caught only fragments of conversations. Change wasn't good; change meant things were going to happen. The three of them would stay alive as long as nothing changed.

Walt had picked up on it too. He kept saying "My time will come now," then realizing the other two had heard him, he would slink down and not look up. This event happened several times. Phil was worried Walt might try and make a break for it. Jim had told Walt all about his martial arts training, and how Walt would die at his hands if Walt tried anything. Phil had merely nodded, he didn't think Jim knew any martial arts, but the lie could help keep them alive. So he paced, rested, ate, shit, and paced again. Then he slept, wondering if tomorrow would be the day, the end. He dreamed of Mandy and how she hated the song of her name. He would shoot Barry Manilow if it would make her happy. He hadn't sent her away; instead he went away, and he was sorry, so very sorry.

※ ※ ※

A second-class yeoman knocked on the side of David's bunk, and he woke immediately; Glenn did as well. "If you please, the Captain would like to see you in his stateroom. Follow me." Both men hesitated a moment to straighten out their appearance, now back in their civvies, then followed the yeoman down narrow passageways to the Captain's cabin. The yeoman knocked twice, then left the area.

"Enter," came a gruff voice from inside.

David let Glenn open the door and precede him in. The office was tiny, the Captain was seated at a small desk; he did not stand. David almost made as if to remove his cover — old, old muscle memory. He stood alongside Glenn in the cramped conditions and waited, staring straight ahead.

"I have read the briefing document from the CNO," the Captain began. "I don't like running around playing nursemaid when I have other duties to execute."

Neither Glenn nor David said anything.

"What do you require of me and my submarine?" the Captain almost growled. David thought he was stereotypical in manner, but U.S. submarine captains were a very select group, a hold-over from the days of Admiral Hyman Rickover and his iron-hand method of governing the nuclear navy. It had worked then and still produced solid results today.

"We will need to coordinate with your dive master to plan for the transfer of the extraction team to the shore of Pulau Ternate and subsequent recovery," Glenn stated. "Eight going out, hopefully eleven coming back."

"You will coordinate with Lieutenant Patterson, my weapons officer," the Captain ordered. "Don't come to me, work entirely through him. Dismissed."

David choked down an 'aye aye, sir' and followed Glenn out of the cabin. The yeoman was again in the passageway.

"I'll take you to see Lieutenant Patterson. Follow me," and he strode off without a backward glance. The lieutenant was in the wardroom with a full cup of coffee; he likely had just arrived. He stood up as Glenn and David came in. The yeoman once more made himself scarce.

"Welcome aboard the *South Dakota*," he said, extending his hand to each of the men. "I assume your meeting with the Captain was quick and efficient?"

"Quite so," answered Glenn. David had decided, for once, to keep his mouth shut. "We understand we are to work with you entirely."

"The Captain is miffed he had to break off a classic stern hunt with a Chinese nuclear submersible. He likes to keep score," Patterson volunteered. "Sit down and let's discuss your mission and how we can help you carry it out. I have a cousin in the Embassy in Cairo, so I am invested in your task." The Captain kept his officers informed, Glenn ignored the security breach, here in the enclosed environment of a submarine.

A steward came up and asked what Glenn and David would like, coffee straight for Glenn, black tea with cream and sugar for David. The refreshments came with cookies. From there, Glenn went over the operational plan, leaving out the background of how they knew where the hostages were and other non-essential details. Down here, under the sea, no one could pass on information, either by design or accident, but post-operation events had to be managed, especially if the operation failed.

"We have done several extraction missions, and we have our procedures simplified and effective," Patterson noted. "We have four scooters — each will make two trips to get all eight of you to shore.

The scooters carry two scuba tanks with octopus regulators, pressurized to 3600 pounds. Your team will transit with no burdens, no buoyancy vest, no fins, just a mask and snorkel and the octopus. The scooter driver will handle your gear, which will be in cylinders under the scooter body. We will lock-out at 80 feet and go up to 30 feet for the traverse. We will use an open-circuit system as it is simple and rarely fails. The dive profile requires minimal decompression, so we will ignore that problem. We will have already scouted the route in, so we can drop you quickly and safely. Weather reports say the seas will be calm, especially in the morning. If there is no guard or watchers, you should easily get into the cave, set up your gear, and start the mission. Questions?"

"It will be me, Josh, Wu, and Tim on the first run. Rob, Pete, Sam, and Jesus on the second run," David stated. "Glenn will monitor activities as best he can from inside the sub; we will effectively be out of contact until we return to the landing site. Total radio silence — we won't even have any radios with us. Two of the hostages will possibly be partially sedated. The third is PADI certified. We may come back by boat, in which case we roll into the water at one time and abandon the boat, hang out on the bottom on an octopus until we all cycle into the lock."

"The Captain won't like that approach," Patterson suggested.

"Then don't tell him," Glenn advised. "I have operational command. The Captain commands the boat. I have no intent to prejudice the crew's safety."

"I have a few questions," David said. "I put us in sickbay to keep us out of the way. Where do you want us to mess? Otherwise, we will stay in our spaces unless we are meeting with our Seal team. Where would be a good place to meet?"

"The crew's mess, avoiding scheduled mealtimes, meet in the back," Patterson said. "You can mess there if you wish."

"How will that go down with the Captain?" Glenn asked.

"He would prefer it that way, less disruption of his routine." Patterson replied. He went on, "I know the Captain is a hard case, but he is very competent, has the loyalty of the crew, and gets the job done with no fuss and no muss." David enjoyed the Navy lingo, unchanged for five decades.

"We intend to do the same," said David, and the meeting ended on a positive note. The yeoman did not return, but David took the lead to get them back to sickbay, where they reviewed the two meetings and then crashed in their bunks. It was approaching ship's noon when they woke, so David and Glenn went to the crew's mess, where the crew ate in staggered shifts to keep crowd size small, and all the ship's positions properly manned. They sat in the back and soon their Seal team came in and sat in their vicinity. Glenn asked Josh if things were going well and got a thumbs-up. They had already been briefed by Lieutenant Patterson on the dive plan and were satisfied. Tim wanted to go in with the navy recon team and he got permission to do so.

After lunch, Glenn and David went over the timeline. "It is 1,600 miles to Pulau Ternate, assume forty knots cruising speed, we should be there in less than two days, almost dawn local time so we can move in right away," Glenn commented, and David agreed.

"If we do get a successful recovery," David ventured, "we should isolate the three hostages and debrief them separately, right away."

"You think any of them were involved in their own kidnapping?" Glenn asked.

"Unlikely, but possible," David answered. "Each one will have their own view of their experience. Each one will have seen something a little different. A group debrief will draw them all to a common conclusion, when we want as diverse a set of observations as we can get."

CHAPTER 14

WATER AND ROCK

THE REST OF THE TRIP BECAME ROUTINE. David had Glenn reschedule sleep and mealtimes for the Seals to get them all on the same time frame that would exist on Pulau Ternate when they arrived there. Word had gotten around that they were to be left alone, so no one engaged them in conversation. Everyone gave them polite nods at mess and made way for them in the passageways. No fuss, no muss.

Pulau Ternate was at 1° north latitude, just about the same as for Singapore far to the west. It was mid September, so they would have about twelve hours of daylight with dawn at close to 0600 hours local time. David was up at 0400 hours, went down to the enlisted mess which had been alerted about an early meal for nine, and joined the Seal team in a hearty breakfast. Lieutenant Patterson came and sat with them. David gorged on ham and eggs, a pancake, a fruit cup, and tea. He didn't expect to eat again until the mission was over, although he would have a power bar and some candy with him for a boost if needed. He had brought two empty twenty-four ounce plastic soda bottles. One he filled with water, one with grape bug juice, the military jargon for kool-aid.

"Too cheap for a real water bottle?" Jesus asked him.

"Cheap is a fact," David replied. "Also, less weight and less bulk than a purchased water bottle, and it can be discarded anytime, anywhere with no regrets. And no ID." David finished up and left, doing a final toilet run and brushing his teeth before gathering his gear and heading aft to the lock-out trunk. Tim had just left the trunk, dripping wet, to report on the recon trip with two navy divers.

"All clear," he said with a smile. "We can go right up into the bioerosion notch. It is low tide, and the sea is calm, just enough ripples to disperse and hide our bubbles. The notch is broken where the cave entrance is located right at high-tide level, so we just slide out of the water and into the cave — no one above can see us. We will stage our water gear there."

David put his cave pack and machete into the cylindrical waterproof container, along with the pack from Tim, who put in his assault rifle; he was eager to go back out and get the mission rolling. The navy divers were already outside, using a hookah to the sub to keep from drawing their tanks down. Tim and David climbed up into the trunk with the water-proof storage cylinder. The hatch was swung up, sealing them from below. They put on their masks and snorkels, placed a hookah regulator in their mouths, and after a few breaths to confirm air flow, hit the 'go' switch. The trunk filled slowly with sea water; once full, the top hatch flashed a green light, and they opened the hatch and floated out into warm seawater. A navy diver took each man, switched out the trunk hookah regulator for the one on the scooter, while a third diver attached the storage cylinder under the scooter and they started for shore. Josh and Wu would follow on the next trunk cycle.

Daylight shone through the clear water, but the rippled surface kept them from seeing anything clearly above the surface, only a dark wedge that was the cliff line. The seabed was covered in hard and soft corals, sponges, and various fan worms. Fish darted about, disturbed yet curious. As they approached the cliff, the water got shallower; then they were under the notch and surfaced. The divers escorted them to the staging cave entrance and unclipped each of them from their scooter. David and Tim scrambled up into the cave and took the cylinder as the navy diver handed it up. A quick look showed the cave to be about fifteen meters wide and deep and eight meters high; but at the back of the cave, to the east, a slope led upward to daylight and the top entrance. Old stalactites hung from the inside ceiling, desiccated and crumbly from the open air and salty sea spray. Stalagmites on the cave floor were large; waves had stripped out all the small ones. Tim and David opened the cylinder, took out their cave packs, Tim's assault rifle, and the machete. They hid the cylinder in a pile of rounded, storm-wave tossed rocks along the west side of the cave and got ready to proceed. Josh and Wu appeared within minutes, and went through the same procedure, except two assault rifles came out of their cylinder. Tim was examining David's machete.

"Quite a long blade. Doesn't that make it tough in the jungle?" Tim asked.

"Actually, it is what the Bahamians call a cutlass," David explained. "The key is to use it to push the plants aside and wiggle through. Cutting makes noise, and wears you out, so I only do it where necessary. It also leaves a trail that's hard to follow instead of the superhighway some people chop."

Wu and Josh went up the slope to scout and check for adversaries. David picked up a flimsy plastic shopping bag from the wave-tossed litter on the floor of the cave and stuffed it in a pocket. He also picked up a polypropylene cord about three meters long and wrapped it around his waist.

Tim looked at David and asked, "What is that stuff for?"

"Local product I can leave behind and not give a signature from the ol' USA," David replied. "Part of the game is to keep them guessing as to who did what."

Sam and Pete appeared next, followed soon by Jesus and Rob. Everyone gathered their gear, including lights, kneepads, elbow pads and gloves for the three hostages, hid the remaining cylinders, and went up the slope to the cliff top. David was in the lead. It was a bright day, the cliff top and the bench heading back from it to the bush was irregular and jagged. To the south a beach ran to the next headland, where the lagoon platform edge came right up to the cliff. There was some kind of construction on top; it looked like a small wooden crane. David had to slip past a few jagged pinnacles several meters high to get a view north. There he found Josh and Wu keeping an eye to the beach below.

"David," Josh said, "there is a trail that ascends from the beach, crosses over this headland, and goes back down to the beach on the south side. It looks like it has been used recently, pockets of sand show fresh footprints."

"There looks like a crane on the headland to the south. I wonder if they are bringing in supplies there, as a deep draft boat could get right to the cliff, and the cargo hoisted up, then portaged north along this trail to Daan's cave?" David offered.

"Why not just use small boats along the coast?" Josh asked.

"Not all days are as calm as this one. Perhaps they have cargo that needs special handling," David offered, unsure of what was actually going on, a rare event for him and his pinpoint accurate imagination.

David then left the two lookouts and traversed the rock bench eastward to get a look at the bush. It was initially sparse as the wind and salt spray made for harsh conditions, but it soon thickened. Too low to walk under, too high to step over; it was typical island bush vegetation that could be a pain to negotiate. He waved the other five over.

"Put on your elbow and knee pads. We can scoot under some thick parts and wiggle through the rest upright," David advised. "Rob, take point and start leading the team north, keep a vegetation screen between us and the cliff top. Go a hundred meters then wait for us." David scuttled back to Josh and Wu.

"We have company," Josh said.

David scanned ahead, a party of three men, in simple tan uniforms but with what looked like AK-47 weapons, had come out of the low-lying bush to the north at the end of the beach and were strolling along the sand towards them. From their size, he assumed they were locals. David looked closely at the bush to the north.

"Is it a patrol?" Wu asked.

"More of an escort, I think," David replied. "There is a fourth person still in the bush, tracking the three soldiers." A moment later, the fourth person, in a black uniform, came out of the bush and with a brisk stride inserted himself as the third of four people in the line.

"What do you think?" Josh asked.

"I think we melt into the bush and do our mission. These guys are the ones using the trail. They don't know about us and aren't looking for anyone," David stated. "They are destination-oriented. We will avoid them. We will need to be careful coming back. Depending on how much excitement we generate in the cave, they might be alerted." He led both men into the bush where they picked up Rob's trail and soon met up with the Seals, lying in the humid and buggy shade.

CHAPTER 15

PEPPER LIZARD CAVE

DAVID MOVED TO THE LEAD, then turned around to address the men. "We can move briskly from here," David said, "but as we get closer, we will slow down to cut our noise signature." David headed north, he figured he had about 300 meters to go until he reached the collapsed cave entrance. The going was tough, as expected, but they made good progress. They slowed to make less noise, and David scanned around. He saw a gap in the vegetation to his right, east, and signaled a stop. He motioned Wu to him.

"The break in vegetation over there," David whispered, pointing, "could be the collapsed entrance we are looking for. Time to show me your skills by taking a look. There could be a guard there."

Wu slithered off, silent and difficult to see; then he was gone, invisible. David and the team waited. They had been on land for only an hour. David knew that now the mission would really begin. Wu wiggled back to David.

"Circular collapse in the bedrock, about six or seven meters across, broken rock in the bottom about three meters down, but a wisp of breeze coming up," Wu whispered. Now off the sub, he used metric. "No sign of anyone. I circled the hole. The vegetation looks untouched."

David signaled for the team to close around him. There were little blood spots here and there on the men, cuts and punctures from the dry, xeric vegetation. Their shirts were sodden with sweat. David knew he looked far better, but then he had more than four decades experience of moving though this type of bush. "Looks like we are on target," he announced in his softest voice. "Time to sequester the assault rifles. I recommend half up here, and half down in the collapse. We move forward and see if we can enter here. No sound, no light, nothing so much as a fart. Any questions?" There were none. "Wu, lead us in."

David was the first to climb down into the hole. He went to the south side and began to peer into the spaces between some large collapse blocks. He signaled Rob, Sam, and Pete to come over. "We dig here," David whispered. "Pass the blocks back to the others without making a sound. Have them place the rocks down among the blocks in the center in case someone comes by and wonders why there is a new pile of rock down here." Josh stayed up on top, keeping watch.

They moved mostly small and medium-sized rocks for about ten minutes. David then did a gentle slide down the hole between two big boulders, and under the ledge of the collapse wall and into the cave below. He turned around in a low and wide passage and stuck his head up into the collapse.

"Put my machete with the weapons and follow me down. The last man is to obscure the hole we dug with some old and dry vegetation," David instructed. He then slid back into the cave as one-by-one the team followed. He leaned back against a crusty and dry stalagmite, and watched the men come in. It was pleasant in the cave, tropically warm, mean annual temperature for 1° north latitude. Any movement would bring a sweat. Dehydration could be an issue, but the many cave entrances meant the cave was drier than otherwise would be the case. The ceiling was less than a meter high; he could slump against the wall, but he couldn't fully sit up. The stalactites, stalagmites and flowstone were dry and crumbly, typical of a cave that has become unsealed and well ventilated. The floor was loose sand, chunks of broken rock, flowstone, and old, dead, and dry vegetation. No guano, as the ceiling was too low for a bat roost. Minor air movement up and over the cliff from the open water to the west that pushed air into the cave, a faint breeze escaped up the route they had come in. Light filtered down through the collapse, and as David's eyes adjusted, he could make out some detail. To the south, the cave went only a few meters before ending in a series of blank, curved walls or rimouts, as his caving buddies called the features. Every once in a while, a small window in a rimout would lead to continuing cave. To the east, inland, a series of rimouts marked the back wall of the cave, running off to the north and northeast. To the west, a hint of daylight could be seen, probably one of the many cliff-side entrances. So far, the cave matched the representation Daan had made with his 1929 map. David signaled his team to lie in a circle facing inward, where a whisper could be heard. They looked like a giant, eight-armed starfish.

"OK, we are in, now it gets serious," David began, emphasizing that the difficulty of the bush was a minor thing compared to what was ahead. "We will hug the east wall as that route will keep us from being highlighted by the sunlight coming in the cliff-side entrances. Be careful looking left towards those cliff-side entrances. Not only will it cost you your night vision, but the glare will reduce your ability to see nearby detail. We have over a hundred meters to go before this level begins to overlap the lower level. We stay in single file." David reached up into the breakdown and pulled down a short, thin stick of vegetation about a meter long. He crawled north, with the stick in his left hand, letting the stick droop in front of him. In his right hand he had his flashlight on, with two fingers over the lens, letting only a slit of light escape, like headlights on a blacked-out car during wartime. The light was minimal but enough to see. He used his knees and elbows to crawl.

After about thirty meters of crawling, there was light straight ahead, and the east wall of the cave trended west a bit, forcing David to crawl closer to the light than he wanted. David assumed the light was from one of the open collapse entrances shown on Daan's map. It was a likely place for a guard or sentry. The hole was circular, about eight meters across, and rotting vegetation and broken rock lay in a pile on the floor. There was no rope or ladder present, and the walls were over-hung. That combination suggested to David that the opening wasn't used for routine access to the cave. It was quiet in the cave, no flowing water, no dripping stalactites, no bats. An occasional wisp of a breeze, but quiet — deathly quiet. They could not make any noise, or a guard or watcher would hear.

Ahead, the passage narrowed a bit. Josh came up along side him on his left.

"Can't we pick up the pace?" Josh asked.

"Slow but sure, Lieutenant," David replied. "Do not get ahead of me."

David continued on. The passage darkened as they put the second entrance behind them. He felt a little bump from the stick, immediately dropped it, and grabbed Josh by the collar before he could move any farther ahead. Josh turned his head, an angry expression on his face. David did not let go. He pointed to a spot in front of Josh. A line of monofilament stretched across the passage, about a hand's breadth above the floor. He signaled Wu up on his right.

"Follow the filament," David warned, "see what is at the other end, but don't touch anything." Wu crawled away to the right, and abruptly stopped. He came back.

"It's a claymore. Should I lock it in safety?" Wu asked. "Then we can cut the line."

"No, stay where you are," David commanded. It wasn't an IED, an improvised explosive device, but a manufactured one. That fact alone suggested access to Indonesian military supplies, and followed the pattern established by the night vision equipment purchase. There was some official involvement at some level inside the government or military. "Josh, follow the line to the left; again, don't touch anything." A chastened Josh went left, paused, then came back.

"The other end is a claymore, too," Josh said, his eyes a bit wide.

David looked over at Wu. "Still want to lock your end down and cut the line?" Wu gave a vigorous shake of his head, indicating no. David looked at both men in turn. "Go lock each one down, we go over the line and leave it intact in case they do a daily inspection." He passed the word back down the strung-out team and they continued on.

CHAPTER 16

ROUTE FINDING THE HARD WAY

THE CAVE BEGAN TO GET MAZY, with bedrock pillars and stalactite-stalagmite columns breaking up what had been a wide, if low, passage. Josh drifted a bit to the left, a hand pushed out with fingers extended in front of his head, looking for tripwires. David drifted to the right. Ahead he saw more light, another entrance. From the Daan map, David knew this was a smaller circular hole produced by rainwater flowing in and downward through the cave. He moved even more right to keep the entrance and its light to his left. He could see the entrance better now, and he stopped suddenly. There was a homemade wooden ladder in the small entrance. Was there a guard on duty? And where the hell had Josh gone? Had he gone left to keep the light from the ladder entrance to his right? David moved quickly to his right and got in amongst some bedrock columns and went through a very low passage, trying to circle beyond the ladder entrance. Where would the guard be placed? The guard would keep a bedrock pillar between him and the entrance, so he would be in the dark, but the entrance would light up the scene in front of him, at least during the daytime.

David was north and past the ladder entrance now and keeping bedrock pillar and stalagmites between him and where the guard might be, he went west and looked back at the area. Got him! David thought. A guard with an AK-47 in his lap was leaned back against a broad bedrock pillar, looking west where the passage was a bit bigger. Not a surprise, David realized. The tripwire had been an obvious alert of more obstacles ahead. There was something to guard, and intruders were thought possible by whoever was running this show.

The guard was watching the easiest route through this section of the cave, which was where Josh had gone. The guard suddenly leaned forward, bringing his weapon up to his shoulder, and wiggled on his butt up to a gap between two stalagmites. As the guard brought his head down to sight his weapon, David whipped off the cord around his waist, and moved quickly but silently up behind the guard, who was totally focused on what had to be Josh ahead and in his sights. David looped the cord over the guard's head, kicking the AK-47 away with his right foot while he placed his left foot square in the back of the guard's neck as he leaned back and pulled the cord as hard as he could. The guard struggled for only a few seconds before the garrote cut off the blood flow from his carotid arteries, sending him into immediate unconsciousness and after further seconds, into death. There had been no sounds but a grunt from David and rustling of the dying man, like clothes falling into a hamper. David kept pulling and pulling. Eventually Wu came up beside him.

"He's gone, David, you can relax," Wu said gently, a hand soft on David's shoulder, not to startle but to calm.

David released the cord, grooves pushed deep into his hands. Wu unwrapped the cord from the dead man's neck. The fellow looked old, his hair gray, his wrinkles now smoothed out by his final exertions. He had been given a task where all he had to do was to sit and wait, not knowing death waited as well. Wu passed the cord back to David, who mechanically wrapped it around his waist again. Josh was looking into the gap that the guard had attempted to shoot through. He had the AK-47 in his right hand. The noise it made falling through the gap must have alerted Josh to the situation. Josh looked at the guard, looked at David, and realized how close he had come to being shot and blowing the whole mission.

Tim was now on the scene. He confirmed that the guard was dead.

David snapped back into the here and now. "Everyone take a break. I have to look around." There were scattered plastic water bottles, some food wrappers, and other detritus that collects when humans hang out at a spot for long periods of time. Behind the ladder to the east was a pit in the floor, about three meters across and five meters deep. The bottom had what looked like human feces in it. The smell confirmed his assessment, with the odor of urine present as well. Two short stalagmites on the edge of the pit were smooth, almost polished. David went back to the body.

"Tim, drag him over here beyond the ladder." David ordered. Tim did so, laying the body beside the pit as David directed. "Tim, break the man's neck. Break it so it is obvious." Tim looked at David as if he had suggested Tim have sex with the corpse. David realized he had to explain.

"Look, if this man's replacement comes here, the alarm will go up, and the mission is compromised," David began. "This pit is used by the guards as a latrine. They drop their drawers, and hang out over the pit, holding on to those two stalagmites, and do their business." David pointed to the small stalagmites, burnished as if often rubbed. "If we break the neck, drop the drawers, and push the body into the pit, it will look like he slipped and fell in, breaking his neck. Sam, can you snap off one of the stalagmites?"

Sam used his shoulder, leaning in, and broke off the left stalagmite. Tim put a headlock on the corpse and twisted mightily. The gray head now flopped loosely, the skin's pallor matching the wiry hair. David undid the pants; there were no under pants, and the trousers were soiled. David rolled the body into the pit, where it landed and sprawled awkwardly across the bottom, the neck and head at an impossible angle. David then tossed the stalagmite down so it landed near the left hand. A staged accident. The AK-47 was left near the top of the pit, leaning against a bedrock pillar.

"OK folks, we literally dodged a bullet here," David said with a stern expression. Looking straight at Josh, David said, "I saved your ass twice today already. Don't count on a third strike." His gaze shifted to the rest of the team. "All of you, follow my orders. I don't give advice, I give instructions and I expect you to follow them. You can beat me up when this is all over, but we have three men who will die if we don't get this task completed." David, without looking back, continued crawling north.

There was still more light ahead, and sounds, faint voices, and routine noises made by people moving about. The map showed a collapse that had connected the two levels, totally breeching the upper level. David signaled the others to stop, then motioned Wu forward. Peering between two stalagmites, they could look down into the lower level without being observed. It was a large chamber, with daylight streaming in from a broad, arched entrance to the west. At ceiling height on the far side of the chamber, the low upper level could be seen continuing north. The floor of the upper level had collapsed to the east, and a pile of very large blocks and slabs leaned up against that wall of the lower chamber. No upper-level passage survived in the east wall, no way to cross north without going down. An occasional person strode across the lower chamber and out the gaping entrance, people both coming and going. A high-traffic area.

Wu looked over to David and whispered, "How do we get to the continuation on the far side?"

"Let's go back to the team and think this one through," David recommended. "I need to look around a bit."

The team gathered in their starfish pattern again. "OK Josh, you will get your wish. We should pick up the pace because the dead guard could be discovered anytime," David said. "But we can't go anywhere until we figure out a way to continue north. So, you all lie here except Josh." David looked at the officer. "You are with me."

David crept east toward the rimouts that made a cuspate east wall to the cave. Josh followed behind.

"Why me and not Wu? Isn't he smaller?" asked Josh.

"I need to keep my eyes on you. The others will do exactly as I say. You think about it too much," David replied. "Initiative is good, but so is situational awareness. You need more balance between the two."

Josh hesitated, then reluctantly nodded. He followed David into a small hole at the back of a rimout. The passage was small but not tight, and it turned north, then began to slope downward. The floor dropped away as a series of down steps in a narrow fissure which entered a low room, the fissure pinching down to a tight crack that ended. A low arch to the left, a half meter high, sloped down, heading west. David stuck his head into the arch, and saw that it ended against a large, tilted slab of rock, collapse material from the large chamber that united the two levels. To his left, south, numerous blocks barred the way, but faint light filtering in must be from the large entrance to the west, he thought. He looked north and saw he could turn and go parallel to the slab and wall of the cave at ground level. He did so; after about ten meters, the space angled upward slightly, the slab ended, and a more chaotic pile of large angular rocks now separated David from the big chamber. He could hear voices faintly. Keeping to the main wall on his right, he continued to slide upward. He then ducked under a huge block that sloped from high on the cave wall on his right to a pile of rubble to his left. On the other side, he worked his way upward between two slabs and then forward into a tubular passage in solid rock. It ended straight ahead but turned left where a faint glow of light played on the walls. He moved slowly into a wide, low passage. Back to the south, it opened into the roof of the big chamber; he could look across into the upper level back to where the team waited, unseen. He had a bypass to the truncation of the upper level; they could continue on. He stayed where he was, backed into the upper level far enough that he couldn't be seen by a glance upward from below. Josh lay next to him, a grin on his face.

"Well, old man, I see why you are on this trip," Josh said appreciatively. "I would never have found that route on my own."

"We will put it down to experience and luck," David replied, minimizing the compliment. "Go back on this route and bring the team forward. It will be tight in a few spots for the bigger guys like Tim, Sam, and Pete. We are right on top of people, move slowly as silence is critical now. When you get back here, keep the team away where they can't be seen, and wait for me. No independent wandering around. I will scout ahead."

CHAPTER 17

DISCOVERY

JOSH NODDED IN AGREEMENT and went back the way they had come. David crept forward. The passage was very low, half a meter high. On elbows and toes, David continued moving ahead. The upper-level ceiling was illuminated by light coming up through several holes in the floor, which were also the holes in the ceiling of the lower-level large passages below. The sound of voices and human activity grew louder. Knowing his white face would be lit by the light coming up, he was careful to peer down one of the holes at an angle that kept his face dark.

Below was a scene that David had not expected. A number of people, almost all men, milled about in a broad chamber the size of a small ballroom. Tables with tablecloths and folding chairs were set up across the floor, enough to hold thirty or forty people. The place was arranged as a banquet, the people behaving as if it was a pre-dinner mixer although it was only mid-day. David took out his point-and-shoot waterproof camera. He made certain the shutter sound was off, and doubly sure the strobe was off. He started taking pictures. It wasn't a cell phone; that is what most people used these days, and they got great pictures. But cell phones weren't waterproof to ten meters depth. Like David, his camera was tried and true — it always worked.

The scene below was well lit; he held the camera steady but the shutter speed seemed reasonably fast. He used the 3X telephoto option to get individual images of the people he saw. There was a wide variety of dress, from traditional Middle Eastern garb, to African tribal, to typical business casual. He went on to another hole; this was broader, the top of a breached curved dome, which allowed him to see more of the walls of the chamber. In the front of the room a screen was set up, with a computer projector back among the dining tables. What is going on, a fucking time-share pitch? thought David as he proceeded to a third hole which gave him more perspective on the set up and people below. David got a sinking feeling that his team had stumbled onto something far bigger than three hostages.

He went back to the new meeting point. The team had assembled. They went to the starfish pattern. David explained what he had seen. All agreed they were observing something entirely different than what they had thought was going on. David warned them to stay well clear of the floor holes; they couldn't afford to roll a pebble or shift some sand down one. They would move past the large party chamber to see if they could find a hole into the hostage cell, which David felt would be at the north end of the cave. They continued on. There were quite a few holes connecting the two levels. David knew they were truncated bell holes, cylindrically-shaped vertical pipes produced by dissolution when the cave had been full of water in a freshwater lens. No need to explain any of that to the team, but it was a routine feature of flank margin caves, and the holes gave the impression that the floor/ceiling of the two levels had been conveniently and pervasively perforated.

All the holes they found went into chambers and passages below that had human activity but no evidence of the hostages. The upper level ended in rimouts to the north. David diligently poked into each one. He looked into yet another rimout and saw a hole in the back wall at floor level, with a smaller hole above it up near the ceiling. He stuck his head in the lower hole; the upper one was too small, only about ten centimeters across. It was a bell hole, and it went vertically down to a dimly lit chamber. David waited. He heard some mumbled voices, and shuffling. A figure crossed under the hole and leaned against the wall. Tall, blonde, in a shirt and jeans. A Westerner. He had found the hostages. He pulled his head and shoulders out of the hole, and waved Josh, who had been trailing him, to join him.

"I think we have them," David said with repressed enthusiasm. "Take a look."

Josh put his head into the hole and looked down. He brought his head out in a minute, gave a thumbs-up, and nodded in agreement.

"Now we have to communicate," David noted. He took a small 'write in the rain' notepad from his chest zipper pocket, and a pencil. He tore out a page, on it he wrote:

> No talking! Answer the following questions with a nod yes or no or spread hands to say you can't answer. Signal by number of fingers displayed which questions you are answering.
> 1. Are you under direct observation?
> 2. Are there three males present?
> 3. Is anyone sick or injured?
> 4. Are you ready to leave?

David whispered to Josh, "Break out our vertical gear, see if you can set up a haul system using the little hole at ceiling level." David wrapped the page around a pebble, securing it with a rubber band. He picked up a couple of more pebbles and stuck his head and shoulders back in the hole. The vertical cylinder was about half a meter wide. He waited until a person walked below and dropped a pebble. No response to the first one, but the second one hit the person on the shoulder, and he looked up to where David had his flashlight illuminating his face. The person waved, and two other men arrived and looked up. That action answered David's first and most critical question, but he dropped the note anyway.

The tallest man picked up the note, he looked solid, fit. Probably the PADI-trained diver, David thought. The man read it over, straining a bit in the dim light. Then he looked up and showed one finger, with a definite 'no' nod. Up went two fingers with a 'yes' nod. For three fingers, a 'no' nod, which gave David relief. An emphatic 'yes' nod for question number four. David made a shushing motion with a finger to his lips, then gave a two-handed time out signal and the OK signal, which got an identical response. David backed out.

"Who has some string or fine line?" David asked. Jesus raised his hand and dug out some shot cord. "Josh, use my pencil and notebook to explain we are coming for them, for them to stay patient and wait, and answer any questions they have. No verbal communication. Make sure they understand to leave no evidence of our messages."

Josh gathered the gear and stuck his head in the hole. David turned to the rest of the team, who had their haul line out and were arranging the rigging and pulleys. "We will run the haul line down the upper hole," David explained. "We have plenty of rigging points." David pointed to an abundance of stalagmites and other natural anchors. "The hole is tight, they won't be able to exit the lower hole by facing it, their femurs are too long with their knees locked. They will come up facing away, arch their head back and slither out of the hole on their spine with a flex of their knees. They may find it uncomfortable but there is no other option. I'll go down and get them loaded up."

A pulley was placed in the upper hole, wedged in with a chock. A 3:1 system was set up going back out of the rimout into the upper level. Sam unfolded a stainless-steel arrangement that locked into a coat hanger type structure that went on the end of the line; the hostages would stand in it, hold the thin rope, and go up.

David tapped Josh on his back, and he pulled out of the lower hole with a note in his hand. "They are more than ready," Josh said eagerly. "They are also scared and will need some TLC."

Josh moved away and David approached the hole. First David would go down. He got his feet into the coat hanger, and with tension on the line, dropped his feet and lower legs over the edge. He continued his slide into the hole on his back, his weight carried by the coat hanger, then he could reach in, grab the line, and get lowered a little more, popping his head and shoulders fully into the vertical cylinder, and standing upright. He was slowly lowered down. He had his finger to his lips; it was a full seven meters from the base of the hole to the floor of the cell. He was rushed by the hostages anyway, with tugging and slapping of his back. He again made the silent gesture and the three men calmed down. The chamber being used as a cell was oblong, eight meters wide and six meters deep; the opening to the rest of the cave was about a meter in diameter and a meter long, with a door or other blockage on the end. Light filtered in through some small holes up near the ceiling above the door. It meant no one could casually look in. There were tarps on the floor, a twenty-liter plastic paint can with a tight lid in a corner, the toilet, David assumed. No furniture, some trash was in another corner.

David had to do triage. The fittest hostage would go up first; if he couldn't make it, then the other two were in trouble. It was simple to display how they were to ascend: step into the coat hanger, hold one of their hands above their head and grasp the rope, don't let go until they were pulled into the upper level. The first man went up gracefully, like he was ascending into heaven, which for him was close to the truth. There were a few soft grunts, a pause, then the line came down again and the second man went in and up. More soft grunting. David looked at the third man, the chunkiest of the three. He looked scared.

"Is Joanie OK?" he asked.

"She is fine — safe and sound," David answered, noting that, like Willard, this man knew there were to be four originally. "You know, they were going to cut everyone's throats on video? You are very lucky we are getting you out of here." David said those words in case this man had thoughts of continuing his betrayal. The man gulped, nodded, and as the line came back down, quickly stepped in and grabbed the line as instructed. He went up. More grunts, soft but they went on for a minute or more. Finally, the line came back down, David climbed aboard, and was whisked up into the cylinder. He rotated, arched his head backward into the hole, and was pulled forcefully out of the bell hole. He made not a sound.

※　※　※

Phil had been startled, thrilled, and uneasy all in a moment. A face above him, at the top of that small hole in the cave ceiling, lit from the side like an apparition from a horror movie. He feared that now gasoline would pour down and be lit, or that a cloud of white gas would fume from that portal and choke him in agony. He steadied himself and saw that the face looked Western; it was hard to tell with the distance and poor lighting involved. Then came the dropped note, and the signaling, and finally, an average-sized man clinging to a rope, coming to join them. A new prisoner and a new delivery method. The thought was fleeting, it was a rescue, the note was proof of that. Phil realized the man was coming to assist their departure, that the man would be the last person out. Phil was impressed, to even get here took courage, but with discovery possible at any moment, this man came to help. To see them up and out of here, from below.

The man touched down, and was swarmed by Phil, Jim, and Walt. It took a minute to settle everyone down. Phil was waved over first, and shown how to stand in the metal triangle, how to hold the rope, one hand high, one hand low to stay in tight with the rope during ascent. He understood he would be first, reverse triage, get the most likely survivor out first, and work down to the worst probability. That would be Walt. Phil looked over to see if Walt was about to shout a warning to their wardens. The way their rescuer looked at Walt indicated he saw the risk as well.

The man whispered with authority, an unusual talent. He didn't name any names, he probably didn't know their names, for operational security. Phil was struck again about his situation. Even in rescue, he was still a commodity — a box, something that had fallen off the back of a Fed Ex truck — and now he was being recovered. Not rescued — you rescued people, not packages. Then Phil got a good look at their rescuer. He was old, not wizened old, not feeble old, but time-worn old. Experience hung on him like loose clothes; his instructions came with the tone of someone who had done this before, in some way, somehow. A theater play with the same lines but on a different set.

His mind plagued with questions, he rose upward, suddenly uncon-cerned. It was as if his mom was tucking him into bed after he had been woken by a nightmare. He was safe now, he was free now, he would see tomorrow in an entirely different place. He didn't know he had switched one tomb for another, a tomb that moved within the sea. But resurrection was ahead.

CHAPTER 18

BUGGING OUT WITH A BANG

FLIPPING OVER ON HIS BELLY, David said, "Secure all the gear, don't worry about footprints and scuff marks. They will know people were here, we just don't want them to know which people. Josh, let's lead people out. Who has the explosives?"

"I have everything we need," Sam said.

"OK, you are with me. The rest — head out, and pronto," David announced. "Be careful at the ladder entrance. We don't know if the dead guard has been discovered yet."

The team moved off, the hostages in their provided knee and elbow pads. In the end, it was decided the hostages would not use the flashlights. The available light from the Seals would have to be sufficient — no telling what the hostages would do with a flashlight in their hands. As the caterpillar train of Seals and hostages began their long cave trek back to the surface and on to the sub, Sam and David stopped off above the party chamber.

"Here is what I want to do," David explained, as he dug the plastic bag from their landing point out of a pocket and unwound the polypro line from his waist. "I want the explosives in the bag, set to go off one second after a small charge severs the cord holding the bag in place."

"You want an air blast explosion?" Sam asked, looking down the hole at the people gathering there.

"Exactly. Can we time it for twenty-five minutes?" David queried.

"You want twenty-five minutes, and then twenty-five minutes, one second, correct?" Sam confirmed.

"That'll do it," David agreed.

"The timer will be on the bag, so it gets blown to smithereens and leaves no record," Sam explained. "I'll use det cord to create the one second delay. It will be 'pop', 'roll', and 'boom'," he was smiling strangely, excited but wondering why David felt comfortable sending all those below into hell. Did he know they deserved what was coming? He seemed to know everything else, so Sam let it ride.

"Do it," was David's response as he took more pictures of the people below. He kept doing so until Sam tapped him on the shoulder.

"Time to go," Sam said. The cord was tied to a stalagmite at one end, tied to the bag at the other end of the slope into the hole. A piece of what looked like putty had been squeezed onto the cord, with the detonator line running to the bag and explosives where a little timer sat, no blinking light or countdown as in the movies; it could be a dead Apple watch to an outside observer. All that would be left for investigation would be a ratty piece of severed rope flotsam from the beach, tied to a stalagmite.

They made their way out as swiftly as possible. For a big man, Sam was agile and only slowed at the tight spots that bypassed the big collapse. At the ladder entrance, the body was still in the pit; apparently, no one had yet checked on the guard, or just had and were out of the cave to tell someone in command. It made no difference now; by the time anyone decided to do something, the blast would occur, and all bets were off. They crawled carefully over the trip wire, which David was glad to see was still in place. With a couple of minutes to go they were squeezing up the dug entrance, picking up David's machete and Sam's assault rifle, and were down the path a few meters.

Just then, a loud booming sound punctuated the sunny afternoon. Dust and leaves flew up into the air from the entrance they had just used. Black smoke began to pour from the lower-level cliff-side entrances. It must be death and total confusion down in the cave, thought David. Sam and David kept moving, sliding, crawling, pushing, and bushwhacking. They met Wu at the end of the bush trail and, with him, popped out onto the rocky bench. Looking back north, David noticed black smoke still pouring out of the cliff line from numerous entrances. What the explosion didn't kill, the smoke had.

"What is our status?" David asked Wu.

"All the hostages are either in the sub trunk or on their way to it," Wu answered on assumption. "No difficulties getting out of the cave. They were very professional and appreciative. The large one took some pushing and squeezing in the collapse section. We do have a problem, however. That four-person team we saw this morning is now running back here." Wu pointed south. The man in the black uniform was in the lead, walking very fast, his three escorts trailing behind. They would be up on the bench in a couple of minutes.

"Wu, you and Sam set up to take out the three escorts," David instructed. "When you hear me shoot the lead guy in the black uniform, you shoot the escorts."

The trail the four men would take wound up the cliff onto the rocky bench and worked its way between limestone pinnacles to the north side of the point. David picked a spot where the trail swung slightly east to get around a boulder and slipped behind a pinnacle. He would be only a couple of meters away from the lead man as he passed by. The location would allow the man to clearly see all the smoke from the hostage cave; he might slow or stop to take it all in. Then David would act. He heard the footfall of a man walking at a fast pace, and the sound of strong breathing through the mouth. David double checked the safety, gave the pistol a full cock, and gripped the pistol butt firmly. The man appeared. As he slowed to look ahead, David stepped out and fired once into the left side of the man's head. The man dropped immediately and did not move, blood pooling in a pocket in the rock. Behind David, he heard several bursts of gunfire, then the shout "Clear." He looked south, and saw three men in tan uniforms down, and Sam and Wu kicking their AK-47 weapons away. Wu shouted "All clear" in further confirmation down the hole to the small staging cave and those who remained below.

David's hands were shaking as he looked at the man in the black uniform lying face down. He steadied himself and rolled the corpse over onto its back and took out his camera. He laid his machete next to the body for scale and took several pictures. He then took several more shots of the man's face, turning the head to give a right profile as he had shot the left side of the head, and taking several more pictures, using his pistol for scale. He then frisked the man, who had a small handgun in a holster in the small of his back; its orientation suggested the man had been right-handed.

There was a document pouch under the man's shirt, hanging on a cord that went around his neck. There was nothing else in any of the pockets. David removed the cloth-on-plastic pouch, unzipped it, and pulled out a sheath of papers. The writing on the front was Korean. David quickly flipped through the pages. On the fourth page was a diagram of a submarine with three objects on its deck immediately behind the conning tower. The objects were drawn as circles, and they had the international symbol for radiation hazard on them. Later pages had diagrams of those circles; it was clear David was looking at renderings of atomic weapons. David tore off the cover page and set the document and the pouch down. Sam was next to him now, and David waved him to silence.

David dipped the dead man's left fingers in blood that had oozed from the head wound and rolled the man's fingerprints onto the blank back of the title page. David repeated the exercise for the right hand. Wu came up as well, having reported to the remaining people in the staging cave below.

"Search the other three bodies for papers and documents, then dump the four bodies and weapons into the sea on the north side of the point," David ordered as he waved the page in the air to dry the blood prints. He got out his pencil and labeled the prints 'left' and 'right' on the title page. Then he folded it and put it back in the pouch with the main document and zipped it up. Sam and Wu had found a few items on the other dead men and had put them all in three different ziplock baggies, each representing one man. David photographed those bodies as well, with facial close ups. The bodies were then carried to the cliff edge and dropped into the water below, the guns followed. Then they entered the staging cave by way of the cliff-top hole.

Josh was still there; everyone else was gone. David put his gear and the pouch into the cylinder Josh had prepared, and Josh sealed it. Sam and Wu did the same for the last remaining cylinder. Now, they waited for the divers and their scooters to show up.

"Sam and Wu," David called out. "Josh and I will take the next ride and lock into the trunk next. I have very disturbing information. If I don't make it, inform the Captain that he has at least one North Korean submarine in this area." At that point, a navy diver broke the surface. David put on his mask and snorkel and slid into the water and got on the octopus regulator while the diver attached the cylinder. Then, they were off to the South Dakota, with Josh's scooter immediately behind David's. They squeezed into the open trunk with their cylinder, switched to the inside hookah regulators, closed the hatch, and started the draw-down action. The light eventually went green on the bottom hatch with their feet placed on the ladder rungs on each side of the trunk. The hatch opened from below. The cylinder was passed on down, and David quickly scrambled down the short ladder to the deck. Chief Ronnals gave David a towel; David pulled off his mask and snorkel, did a quick wipe of his face, and looked at the Chief.

"Get on the horn to the Captain and give him the following message, 'Possible North Korean submarine in your immediate vicinity.' Got it? Repeat it back to me." The Chief did so and went to the phone. The Chief frowned at the apparent reply. Josh was down now as well. He helped David open their cylinder, at which time David grabbed the pouch and his camera. He stripped off his wet clothes, accepted boxer shorts, a white T-shirt, a sweatshirt, pants, and slippers from an eager and helpful petty officer. Then he walked quickly to the bridge as Chief Ronnals followed closely behind.

"The Captain was not pleased by your message. He may not see you. In fact, he may have you physically removed from the bridge if you go there," the Chief said.

"I understand, Chief," David replied. "I will have to take that risk. Please find Mr. Glenn and give him the same message I asked you to give the Captain. Tell him it is imperative he meet me on the bridge. My thanks for your efforts."

"My thanks to you, Mr. David, for getting the hostages back. Well done," the Chief responded.

"Our task has just begun, Chief. We have a big problem ahead," David answered and hurried on as the Chief went down another passage in search of Glenn.

CHAPTER 19

WARFARE INSIDE A SUBMARINE

DAVID CLIMBED UP ONTO THE BRIDGE. The Captain saw him and for a moment just stared, a harsh look on his face.

"Do you think this is all joke, Mr. David?" the Captain yelled. "Do you think you can throw crap at me and not face the consequences?"

"Captain, I can document my statement given to you by Chief Ronnals," David replied calmly.

"We have no evidence of any submersible near us," the Captain continued to shout.

"Captain, we are above the layer in tropical waters. We can't detect him, and he can't detect us," David countered.

At this point, Chief Ronnals appeared with Glenn. The Captain became nearly apoplectic. "Do you think this is a house party? All of you get off my bridge." The Captain didn't move; he was less a tsunami and more of a volcano set to erupt.

Glenn stepped forward. "Captain, you command the vessel, but I command the mission. We will hear what Mr. David has to say. Then you and I can address the issue of our presence on the bridge. David?"

"I shot and killed a man in a black uniform who was trying to get back to the cave where the hostages had been held," David began. "He had a pouch hung from his neck inside his shirt. Here is what was inside." David zipped open the pouch and took out the document. He laid out the cover page face down so that the blood fingerprints were visible. David was pleased to see they hadn't smeared.

"What the hell is that?" the Captain inquired in a quiet voice, the volcano replaced by a summer breeze.

"I used the man's blood to roll his fingerprints," David said. "We now have both his prints, and his DNA. I took mugshots of his face. We may be able to identify him." David picked up the paper so the title page could be seen. "The language seems to be Korean. I believe the man was North Korean."

Glenn leaned in. "It's Korean all right," he stated.

"When I paged through the document, I found diagrams," David continued. "Those diagrams show a submarine with three nuclear weapons stacked behind the conning tower, and instructions on how to arm those weapons. These findings may explain what we found inside Daan's cave."

A petty officer came up to the bridge, whispered into Chief Ronnals' ear, and left. "Captain, we are completely secured from all lock-out activities, all related equipment is stowed," the Chief said.

"You shot a man, Mr. David?" the Captain asked.

"And strangled another as he was about to shoot one of the Seals in the cave," Glenn added. "Then he blew up a whole bunch of terrorists."

"That was the explosion we picked up on our hydrophones?" the Captain asked.

"If there is a North Korean submarine nearby, they heard it, too, and may have gone to full alert," David supplied.

"Helmsman, move us away from the shore quietly, and take us down below the layer even more quietly. Sonar, keep me informed." The Captain looked over at David. "We will see what we have, Mr. David."

It got very quiet on the bridge. The helmsman called out depth numbers. In these waters the layer, or thermocline, could be as much as 600 feet deep, David thought, using navy measurement. When in Rome…

Lieutenant Patterson came over and looked at the submarine in the figure shown in the document. "It looks like a Golf-class Russian submarine," he said. "North Korea obtained ten of these diesel boats back in the early 1990s, supposedly for scrap but the rumor is they updated and refit them and put the boats in service. They certainly have the deck space for cargo as shown here."

"Bridge, sonar, we have a passive sonar contact bearing 072 degrees true. Running diagnostics now," came over the intercom. The Captain gave David an appraising look. The com came back on, "Bridge, sonar, the noise signature matches a Sang-O class North Korean submarine."

"Care to explain that, Mr. David?" the Captain didn't taunt, but it put David on the spot.

"It is over 4,000 km from North Korea to Pulau Ternate. North Korea only has diesel boats," David offered. "They wouldn't send a single diesel boat that far carrying external atomic weapons without an escort. The Sang-O is probably one of two escorts, the other is likely patrolling the mouth of the bay. It is the rear-guard boat. The one we hear is the point man."

"So where is the Golf?" the Captain pressed.

"Lying doggo at depth, I suspect," David answered. "If it was to deliver those weapons to the people I just blew up, the North Korean I shot was to get them from the rocky point to the south, as the submarine could tie up at the cliff because there is no shallow shelf at the point. The wooden crane there would lift the weapons. They would probably be transferred to a smaller boat to get them to Daan's cave. All the subs are diesel. They have to come up at least to periscope depth to operate their snorkel, charge their batteries, and freshen the boat. Probably tonight."

"So, we should go south and wait for the Golf boat to come up?" the Captain seemed to be playing with David.

"No, Captain. The Sang-O is probably patrolling right now, running up and down the bay, but on the western side," David ventured. "Sonar should report that the sound is increasing and decreasing in a regular pattern."

The Captain looked at Chief Ronnals, who took off for the sonar shack, David surmised. "We are quiet when we move, he is not. Why not move south?" the Captain inquired.

Chief Ronnals returned and the Captain waved him to speak. "Sonar says the Sang-O is moving up and down the west side of the bay."

The Captain looked at David, wanting an answer. David gave it. "Multi-ship tactics, Captain. The North Koreans know what they have, and what they don't have. They can't match us in quiet technology, or endurance, and not in detection equipment either. But what they can do is put a noisy boat on one side of a bay, have a dead quiet submarine on the other, and if you move between those boats, you will occult the Sang-O and the Golf will hear the sound diminution and know you are here."

"What would you do then, Mr. David?" the Captain asked.

"You could keep just to the north of the Golf," David began, "and wait until each boat comes up to use their snorkel. Then you can go deep, get under their sound channel, and come up behind them where they least expect you. But I wouldn't do that. I'd stay right where we are now."

"Because?" the Captain asked, short and sweet.

"There are three subs in a confined space right now. The rear-guard boat patrolling at the north end of the bay makes four," David replied. "I wouldn't want three hostile submersibles between me and open water, even if they are inferior boats. Numbers can matter".

"So we wait here?" asked the Captain.

"No advantage now in moving, only risk," was David's answer.

"Mr. David, you are not ordered from my bridge, but I recommend you go clean up, get debriefed, have a meal and get some rest," the Captain said. "We will talk later as I want the whole story."

"Yes sir," David replied, and he left the bridge.

CHAPTER 20

DISCUSSIONS

DAVID SAID TO GLENN AS THEY LEFT THE BRIDGE, "Hostage three, the heavy set one, asked about 'Joanie' when I was down in the cave chamber to get him out as the last one there. I assume that is the female who missed being kidnapped because of the car accident. So, like Willard, he knew four were to be taken." David then went back to sickbay and took a quick navy shower. Having worked on desert islands where he had to bring in his own drinking water, David thought navy shower water-use restrictions were fine.

Glenn had gone back to debriefing the three hostages. They had remained un-named to the extraction team. David had had to be descriptive to identify the problem hostage to Glenn. One more task on Glenn's list. So far, the stories of the three hostages matched up: each kidnapped at gunpoint by masked men at a high school, driven away with a bag over his head, hidden separately for a day, then out on a small boat as a group to a large boat, five or so days there, then on a small boat and into the cave chamber. On both the large boat and in the cave, fed and watered twice a day, given a pail to poop in, a tarp to sleep on the floor, allowed to talk to each other. No interrogations, no beatings, just left alone. Fear and boredom had warred with each other. Escape seemed impossible and, unlike for POWs, attempting to escape wasn't required by standing orders.

* * *

Phil was exhausted, not by lack of sleep or hard physical work, but by what it had taken to hold on, to keep going, to not let his mind take his soul into some dark crevice and hunker down to await the end. The man who called himself Glenn had been polite, even warm, but Phil could see he was playing a role, the good cop. At least Glenn knew his name, called him by it, treated him like a living, breathing person. The questions were predictable, even those about Walter Pinny. Phil understood the kidnappings had been assisted by inside information; it seemed perfectly reasonable that Walt could have been suckered and given them all up. No wonder he had been in some sort of mental agony in the cave. Walt's emotions had overridden his thoughts, and he had made a deal, in a fit of pique, to satisfy his greed, to elevate himself on the bodies of his colleagues, only to end up at the bottom of that pile. Phil had no proof, only supposition, but Glenn seemed satisfied. Phil had asked about Joanie; he hadn't seen her at all since the inside of the Embassy that fateful morning. He was pleased beyond measure to learn she had avoided the kidnapping — escaped was too strong a word. Joanie was still a kid in Phil's eyes; he wondered how much she had grown up in a day.

✴ ✴ ✴

After David cleaned up, he realized he was starving. He went to the enlisted men's mess and slipped in quietly but was seen immediately. The men present said nothing, but all stood up and saluted David. He stiffened, returned the salute with a nod, and went over to the chow line. "What have we got today?" David asked the first-class cook.

"Anything you want, sir," was the reply.

"Cheeseburger and fries with a chocolate milkshake OK?" David responded. "And I am not a sir."

"You are here. Lettuce, tomato, ketchup?" from the cook.

"Great, and a Coke, too, unless you have Mountain Dew," David answered with a grin.

"Sit down, I'll bring it to you," was the cook's reply.

"Treat me like an officer and I'll get a big head," David replied. "Keep me in enlisted status and I'll sleep like a baby." That got a laugh from the cook, who waved David away. He sat down, pulled out his 'write in the rain' booklet and jotted down some ideas and interpretations from what had been a very full day. His meal came, and he tore into it. As he was finishing up, Chief Ronnals came in.

"Captain wants to see you in his cabin, but at your convenience," the Chief said.

"Who else has he seen?" David asked.

The Chief paused for a moment, and guessed it was public knowledge to anyone in the passageway to know who had gone in. "Lieutenant Josh, for about thirty minutes."

It was long enough for a quick debrief of the entire day's events. "Thanks Chief, I know the way, I'll finish up here and go in five minutes."

"The Captain has had a change of mind about you. He got schooled on his own bridge in front of his crew, and he knows it. He respects how you kept it focused on the facts," Chief Ronnals volunteered. "Do you disarm ticking time bombs as well?"

David chuckled. "Thanks once again, Chief. My mouth has gotten me in trouble more than once, most often when I am telling the truth as I see it." The Chief left with a smile. David finished his Mountain Dew and returned his tray. Then it was down the passageway to the Captain's cabin. He knocked twice, got the standard "Enter" command, and walked in. Glenn was already there, sitting. The Captain pointed to the remaining chair. David sat, recognizing a different tone than the one from the first meeting here.

"I have done my own debriefing of a few people, Mr. David, I need you to explain to me what is going on," Captain Gardesol said. Now that he and David were on speaking terms, David could think of him as a person and not a command figure.

"Captain, the whole hostage kidnap plot was a sideshow to the main event," David began. "The scheme was for North Korea to transfer three nuclear weapons to one or more terrorist groups. The Golf submarine has the weapons, and the North Korean officer was to bring them to the terrorist representatives in Daan's cave. Based on how things were set up in the cave, I am willing to venture that North Korea was going to auction the weapons, probably to three separate groups. North Korea badly needs revenue, and the leadership knows it can thrive if there is chaos in the world. They would drop off the radar screen if one or more big cities were to be vaporized. I suspect that there was to be an intermediary involved at the cave. North Korea wouldn't want to be explicitly identified as the source of the weapons. They would be immediately exterminated."

Captain Gardesol looked pensive. "It is an incredible risk for North Korea to take," he commented. "If a weapon was used and they were identified as the supplier, the consequences would be catastrophic. Could they also be planning on laying a false flag?"

"What if the bomb is of their design, but they were able to obtain fissionable material from another source, like the material that went missing during the collapse of the Soviet Union?" David proposed. "After the first blast, the isotopic signature of the fallout would be different from what we already have on record for the North Koreans. Blame would be deflected, but North Korea would have the cash and the desired turmoil."

"What a plot, if true," Glenn interjected.

"Captain Gardesol, what are your rules of engagement with the North Koreans?" David asked. "We need to remove the three submarines from the board." David paused, then went on. "We need to sink the Golf in shallow water and put the two Sang-O boats into the abyssal depths."

"You want to recover the nuclear weapons on the Golf?" the Captain asked. "In terms of rules of engagement, I have great latitude in how I respond to North Korean aggression. I can sink a sub if it is a threat to me or others. Or three if need be."

"We do a controlled sinking of the Golf and make the other two submarines disappear," David responded. "Leave the North Koreans in the dark as to what happened. We left no trace of U.S. activity in the cave or on the approaches. I even policed my own brass when I shot the North Korean, and had the other men do the same at their kill site. We need to run a mission tonight."

"What mission?" Glenn said.

"We send some Seals north to steal a boat from the vicinity of Daan's cave and drive it to a nearby island," David explained. "Then we 'arrange' for it to be discovered by a friendly force, who learns from the three hostages in the boat of their miraculous escape when an explosion blew the door off their cell and they ran for it."

"How do we set this up and maintain radio silence?' Glenn asked, always thinking of operational security.

"Seals and Glenn with a radio set at a land location away from here," David suggested. "Set the meet, and we can parade the hostages around with no further explanation. It will also deflect any consideration of a U.S. action. We would have taken the men with us if it had been our operation."

"The timeline?" the Captain asked.

"Deal with the subs now, hostages on the run could well be a couple of days in transit to where they get 'found' by our friends," David answered.

"How would you attack the subs?" the Captain continued.

"The Sang-O to the north, if he is really there. We sink first as he will be in deep water already." David stated. "Then we use a modified warhead for a limited explosion to get the Golf gently on the bottom while still in the bay, so we can lock-out divers and recover the three nuclear weapons. Then we mine the Golf to really destroy it so any follow up can't determine what happened. We can make it look like an internal explosion. The third sub, we can wait on. He may try to hide for a while, but he has to come up to snorkel or suffocate where he is. When he does snorkel, he will run and we let him, to deep water, then we blast him to the abyss."

"You are talking 150 to 200 hundred men killed," Glenn noted.

"Versus ten million or more in three cities. A good trade, in my book," David countered.

CHAPTER 21

PREPARATIONS

IT WAS LESS THAN A KILOMETER from where the *South Dakota* stood guard on the two North Korean subs to where a boat might be found that could become the hostage escape vehicle. The Seals, in this case Pete, Sam and Josh, who most fit the physiques of the three former hostages, each piggybacked on a scooter with a navy diver and went north. They found a scorched five-meter-long boat adrift and climbed aboard. It had an outboard and some fuel; they had brought more, plus water and rations. It was possible that any Indonesian patrols in this area had been compromised by the hostage takers, so they went on north as stealthily as they could in the dark and on out of the bay, heading east to Halmahera, a large island with many communities and options to be 'discovered' later. The original idea of putting the actual hostages in the boat later had been discarded — so had the idea of putting a radio ashore and contacting U.S. forces. The Seals would call in by normal means to Jakarta and set up a recovery. They would be visible enough that word would get back that three bedraggled Americans had arrived on Halmahera by boat and subsequently picked up by American authorities. To the remains of the terrorist organization, and to the North Koreans, what happened on Pulau Ternate would seem to not directly involve American forces or agents.

The *South Dakota* had remained shallow after coming up to launch the Seals and later recover the navy divers and their gear. It was full dark, at just after 2300 hours, when sonar reported sounds of submarines coming to near surface position, one on the west side of the bay which was identified as the known Sang-O, and one close by, near the point with the crane on it, which was assumed to be the Golf. The *South Dakota* was between the two, a bit north; the three submarines formed a flat triangle with the U.S. sub at the apex. Running diesel engines were heard on the *South Dakota*, which meant the snorkels were up and they were charging their batteries and letting air exchange occur in the vessels. Then the *South Dakota* was able to observe, by each of its two periscopes, signals by blinker light between the two submarines. It was a short signaling sequence. Glenn interpreted it as confirmation by both subs to proceed with the plan. Things remained quiet. Captain Gardesol moved the *South Dakota* east to try and catch any light signals going to the crane area on the point, but the shelf configuration prevented a good angle. David had suggested putting an observer on shore, but the Captain wanted to be able to leave the scene in a hurry. In addition, the conditions onshore could be chaotic and a mess after the blast, no place to drop an observer. Any light transmission by the Golf would be in code and not readily identifiable by the *South Dakota*, so they just sat and waited. At 0030 hours, the submarine at the crane point surfaced; it was indeed a Golf-class boat. It waited there for two hours, then slowly submerged again, but kept its diesels running on its snorkel. It again sent a light signal to the Sang-O boat on the west side of the bay.

"OK Mr. David, what do you think is going on?" Captain Gardesol asked.

"The Golf attempted to make a land contact, but the North Korean officer wasn't there to answer," David replied. "I assume they have a contingency plan and will try again tomorrow night. If that is a negative, I expect them to assume the mission is cancelled or compromised, and they will leave the scene. North Korea as yet doesn't know what happened here, but it might be aware by tomorrow night, in which case the subs will scatter when they come up to snorkel and raise their radio mast."

"Mr. Glenn?" the Captain followed up.

"I concur," Glenn aid. "However, by tomorrow night our Seals may have made contact with Jakarta. They are only to report that the hostages are safe and that they are acting as the hostages and need to be recovered. It is important that we deal with the submarines and hand the U.S. a *fait accompli*."

"My thoughts as well, gentlemen. Good to see we are on the same page," Gardesol replied. "I think you can stand down. It is hurry up and wait for about 24 hours."

David and Glenn took their leave and headed to the mess for refreshments and conversation. This time of night, David stayed away from caffeine and had a root beer; Glenn stuck with coffee.

"I looked at all the pictures you shot in the cave, and later on the point," Glenn began. "It was quite a gathering in the cave. If your explosions caught them unawares, most of those people are dead. Five kilos of C4 as an air blast in a confined space, then a subsequent fire — that group is decimated. We should be able to identify quite a few of the attendees. Your imagery is very good. I imagine we will get an ID on the North Korean officer as well. If we recover the atomic weapons from the Golf, the intelligence coup will be complete."

"Not just the intelligence. The North Korans will be out three submarines and a number of terrorist organizations will have lost important leadership," David added. "We will also have a much better idea of the intent of those organizations, as well as the level of threat North Korea poses."

David slept much more than he had planned. No one had seen a need to wake him. He pulled himself together slowly, and went for breakfast, which was actually more like brunch. Again, he was treated with respect, and had gotten halfway through steak and eggs when Lieutenant Patterson sat down.

"Quite a show you put on yesterday," Patterson said.

"Which one? The show in the cave, the one on the rock bench, or that tap dance on the bridge?" David asked.

"The stuff on the island was not a show, it was a lesson," Patterson replied.

"So was what I did on the bridge," David countered. "It was critical that the Captain understood what was going on and the consequences of our next actions. He responded very well. He assessed new data in real time, got his emotions out of the way, and dealt with it. Good leadership, and the crew knows it."

"Still, they are in awe of how you got that bridge exchange done," Patterson continued. "What happened on the island is now a legend. Garroted a guard, then shot a North Korean officer at close range and ran his prints in his own blood. In between, saved three hostages and wiped out numerous terrorists. Then came home and had dinner. If there had been a north 40, you would have plowed it, too."

"Thanks, Patterson, but I was doing my job," David tried to explain. He had killed people, in a number of ways, and he felt the burden. Then he remembered the looks on the faces of the three hostages, the relief and excitement in their voices, and he was reconciled that he had done what he had to do. Now, a new problem lay at his feet. As always, he had a plan. He suspected the tactical details he had suggested would be changed, but the central issue was to act. In this case, Captain Gardesol's attitude was an advantage. It hadn't taken much to push him to agree to do what had to be done.

"OK, I understand, but you own this crew now," Patterson stated, breaking David's revelry. "I came here to talk about your plan for the Golf. We have a translation of the North Korean document courtesy of a scanner and a computer program. It is instructions on how to release the weapons from the Golf's deck, and how to deliver those weapons and present the arming instructions to the new owners, which are a bit complex and also triple fail-safed. So what about sinking the Golf?"

"The key will be to put her on the bottom, flooded, such that the three weapons aren't broken up or scattered around the bay," David began. "I am also concerned that the weapons may be booby-trapped or set up to self-destruct if captured. I was thinking about hitting the

Golf in the bow area, with a low-magnitude charge in the warhead, enough to penetrate and flood the boat so she settles on the bottom. Then we can go to work."

"I think we can do that, but it would go best if we didn't alert her first by sinking the Sang-O at the head of the bay," Patterson explained.

"If that Sang-O is there," David reminded. "But I agree. We target the Golf and do her, then quickly go after the mythical Sang-O to the north. That action clears our way out to the north. The last sub will be in a trailing position behind the Golf. I expect that one to go hide, maybe by lying quiet on the bottom. If it does, then we have to find it. We can't go after the atomic weapons on the Golf with that boat still active."

"That is how I see it now," Patterson agreed. "It could be that the last boat goes to rest on the bottom and dies there, committing suicide."

"I doubt it, the North Koreans are always confrontational. The sub will come up to fight. And die," David added.

The lieutenant went off to work with his Chief Torpedoman to hit a sub but not too hard. David went off to find Wu. He had been impressed with the Seal during the entire mission the day before and wanted his views as he had witnessed just about everything. After a few questions, David found him working out in a passageway.

"Wu, let me know when you take a break. I need some feedback from you if you don't mind," David requested.

"Not a problem, David. I'll be done in a couple of minutes, then do a short wipe down," Wu said. "Meet you in the crew's mess in ten?"

"Works for me," David replied. He went to the mess and sat nursing a big Mountain Dew. Wu came in, as promised, and sat down.

"So, what can I do for you?" Wu asked.

"You were in the cave, you saw how things were set up. Did I do the right thing setting the explosive charge?" David inquired.

"You have guilt feelings?" Wu responded.

"No, I want to be sure I have this gambit figured out correctly," David answered. "I am disturbed that the North Korean officer was so obvious, so exposed. How did he think he would keep the source of the nuclear weapons secret?"

"Well, first of all, his three patrol members were not Indonesian. They were Malays, at least that is what the items we took from their bodies suggests," Wu explained. "What if the North Korean officer was presenting himself as a bidder with bodyguards, and the weapons would have arrived at the cave being handled by someone else?"

"Good possibility. I had assumed he had guards supplied by the terrorists. Your interpretation makes sense. The North Korean could keep a close watch on things if he had bidder or observer status. There were some European-appearing individuals in that dining room in the cave," David noted. "What if one was presenting himself as a Russian, hawking stolen weapons from the dissolving of the Soviet Union? If the North Koreans have used fissionables from that Soviet source, and that if the terrorists present ever leak the seller's identity, the North Koreans would appear out of the loop and the Russians at fault, both by witness and by isotopes."

"Unless one of the successful bidders was Chechin, then it could be Moscow that goes up in flames," Wu countered.

"Not enough funds for them to win the bid, I'll wager," David replied. "These weapons would have gone to a group or groups with access and close ties to oil money. Leaking who had gotten the bombs, which terrorists who lost the bidding might do, would implicate Arab or Iranian deep pockets, giving the bombed countries more suspects to accuse and retaliate against. Big time global instability which the North Koreans might want."

"Maybe so," Wu conceded. "Nice work yesterday, by the way, it was interesting and a little scary to work with you. Anything else?"

"No, thanks Wu, I just needed some perspective," David admitted. Wu gave David a bit of a mock salute with a smile and left. David finished his Mountain Dew, enjoying the caffeine surge, and went to find Glenn.

CHAPTER 22

BLUE BALLS

"CAPTAIN, ARE WE PREPARED to actually sink one or more North Korean submarines without warning?" Lieutenant Patterson asked, standing in front of Gardesol in the Captain's cabin. "I am not questioning the orders, but I would like to be clear in my own head about how we explain this later."

"I understand, Lieutenant. Sit down," was the Captain's initial reply. "I have been convinced by Mr. David that we have stumbled onto a major scheme to kill millions of people and really upset the global order. Imagine what would have happened if he had not put two and two together, and had instead hidden from the North Korean and the guards, let them slip past his position so they could go on their way? The bombing of the terrorists in the cave would have stopped the current iteration of the North Korean plot, but they would simply have tried again, and we would be unaware. He took the initiative, he was thorough, and now we have an opportunity to end this line of North Korean activity. I think the situation falls under the rubric of 'clear and present danger', don't you think?"

"I agree, but aren't we getting into the weeds here by eliminating all three submarines and trying to capture the nuclear weapons?" Patterson asked.

"The thrust of Mr. David's approach," the Captain responded, "is to not only eliminate the immediate threat, but to diminish the North Korean capability to continue to pursue this approach to bandit foreign policy. Losing three submarines isn't what makes them re-think their position. It is the complete lack of knowledge that will exist in order for them to understand what happened. They will have lost three subs, a high-ranking intelligence officer, three nuclear weapons, and the trust placed in them by the terrorist groups, who will be leery of any future plot such as this one. And they won't know why or how, other than the U.S. does not seem to be involved."

"How did David figure this out?" Patterson asked.

"Great question," Gardesol stated. "I have seen this situation before, in a complex setting. Someone gets hot and sees all the pieces fall into place, not just in the moment but as an extrapolation to the future. That is one thing. The second is the will and ability to act, and act quickly. Mr. David has the hot hand, he is decisive. I am riding it."

"You have convinced me, which is a weight off my back," Patterson said. "What will be your tactical situation?"

"Sonar reports all is quiet, the Sang-O is not patrolling, that may be a default action based on the failure to engage their man on shore last night. They decided to go still," the Captain began. "I feel they will attempt once more tonight, as Mr. David suggested, and if it fails again, they will abandon the site. That is when we put the Golf on the bottom."

"Then we chase the other Sang-O to the north?" asked Patterson.

"We need to think about that action," Gardesol responded. "I don't want the Sang-O down here trying to recover the nuclear weapons from the Golf, and I also don't want him behind me while I chase down a submarine we don't even know is there. We do the Golf and the Sang-O here, in quick succession. Then we go hunting north. If there's no sub, we come back here and collect the weapons. If the sub is there, it goes to the bottom, and we come back here and collect the weapons. What do you think?"

"I concur, Captain, and my team will deliver the kills," Patterson brightened up at his Captain's comment, and seemed excited to have action at hand. He was all smiles and good cheer, preparing to kill hundreds of people he didn't know.

"Get to it, Lieutenant. I have the utmost confidence in you. Dismissed." The Captain bent his head down to paperwork on his desk as Patterson stepped quietly out of the cabin. The Captain was cheerfully whistling.

Glenn was in the wardroom having a cup of coffee; he preferred to stay away from the enlisted men's spaces. As David came in, he waved him over. David asked for and received a cup of hot chocolate.

"Where do we sit right now?" David inquired.

"I have debriefed our three former hostages as much as I think is worthwhile," Glenn said. "Hostage number three has confessed to providing written information at a drop that contained the itinerary of the four embassy workers who were to make presentations at four local high schools in Jakarta as part of a cultural exchange initiative. He was motivated by hostility toward the female potential hostage because she had rejected him, and by hostility toward one of the males — a possible love triangle situation, spurred on by some substantial cash. The oldest story in the book. We watch for things like this, but it snuck by us. I doubt the money ever appeared, they were going to eliminate him anyway," At this, Glenn made a slashing motion at his neck with the base of his hand.

"I imagine an investigation will reveal that the risk concerning hostage number three was known, and the report ended up on Willard's desk and he arranged the first contact," David suggested. "Someone had to know the necessary protocols and procedures to hook the fish."

"A mess to clean up back at Langley. I can't do anything about it here," Glenn said remorsefully. "Molly is on top of it, Josh is supposed to alert her to the problem of hostage number three. The hostages have all been briefed on the scheme of their self-rescue by boat after the explosion. They understand the need to keep the South Dakota and all of us top secret, or at least two of them do. I expect hostage number three will officially end up getting treatment for PTSD and will not be part of the official debriefing while we settle his case in the background."

"So my duties are about done?" David asked.

"We should immediately write up a narrative of all events that occurred once you locked-out yesterday. I can handle everything concerning your recruitment, the trip out to Guam, the *Harrington* gambit, and the sub ride to Pulau Ternate, but I wasn't on the island or in the cave."

"A trip report, essentially, an objective document. Keep my feelings out of it," David said in a matter-of-fact tone of voice.

"Exactly," Glenn enthused. "You should select some of your images to include as an appendix. It will be a good way to kill time before we kill subs, so to speak."

David noticed the excitement in Glenn's voice, and he had felt it all over the boat. "What we plan to do has a lot of risks," David ventured. "I still worry about booby traps."

"There was nothing in the North Korean document that indicated any such features," Glenn commented. "The arming of the bomb is not simple. Perhaps that was all they were concerned about. I worry about how sinking the Golf will affect the three weapons. I'd like them totally intact."

"I am worried about getting a torpedo up our ass," David countered. "Engaging two or maybe three submarines almost all at once is not easy, even with our technological advantage. If you hear the sonar shack call out 'high speed screws', you will know, well, that we are screwed."

David went back to sickbay, and using the unoccupied corpsman's desk, began to type up his narrative on a notebook computer given him by Glenn. Nothing was to go on his personal machine. It was a bit cathartic to lay it all down in words, to review what had happened and how the decision making had gone. He worked straight through to chow. He would have preferred using his own device, his computer went with him around the world; it had some sophisticated encryption algorithms, but he had shut it down and stuck it in his duffel anyway. He went off to eat.

He got nods again as he went through the line. When he sat down, Chief Ronnals joined him, asking if it was OK first, which David indicated it was.

"Looks like action tonight," the Chief was almost gleeful. "Never thought I'd see it before I retire. Years, hell, decades of chasing, being sneaky, testing all our weapons, and then standing down. A giant case of submarine blue balls. But we are going to ee- jack- u- late tonight!" Each syllable was pronounced as a single word. David envisioned torpedoes as sperm, the target submarines forcibly fertilized.

"I just want it to go well," David said softly. "I got enough action yesterday to last me a while."

"No regrets, though?" the Chief looked a bit concerned.

"No, none, Chief," David replied. "It was necessary, we did our job, we tied up the loose ends, we got in and out clean. No casualties, no evidence left behind, three hostages safe in the bosom of this boat."

"We won't be able to put markings on the conning tower for our kills, but we can put them here in the mess," the Chief said jovially. He then was quiet as he ate quickly. "Got to go on watch," he said apologetically, and off he went.

David realized the Chief, hell, the entire boat was all caught up in the moment, the chance to actually do something instead of talking about it and training for it. They hadn't killed anyone yet, as David had the day before. They weren't thinking about fellow submariners who were going to die; it would be quick, but it was death nonetheless. It wasn't like in the movies, with men swimming around banging on locked hatches, a hull breach at depth and it was all over in a second or two. Families would lose a father, a son, a brother, a husband, and not know how or why. It didn't matter that the crews were living a slave's life in North Korea, they were alive now and that would end tonight.

CHAPTER 23

THREE ON ONE

DAVID WAS ON THE BRIDGE WITH GLENN. As had happened the previous night, both submarines came up to periscope depth at 2300 hours and engaged their snorkels. They exchanged a short sequence of signals by blinker light. The Golf surfaced at 0030 hours and appeared to attempt to signal the crane area of the rocky point. After two hours, the Golf again signaled the Sang-O, submerged to periscope depth, and began to move slowly north to exit the bay with the snorkel up and diesels running. The Sang-O held station where it was. The *South Dakota* had what in the old days would have been called a 'firing solution' but was now called 'target acquisition'. They would wait until the Golf reached the shelf at the mouth of the bay. The bottom was only 60 meters down, a depth that the navy divers could handle with ease to remove the nuclear weapons.

David looked at Glenn and spoke. "They are running on their snorkel, so they are airing out the boat as well as charging the batteries. All the compartment hatches will be open. Lieutenant Patterson will try to put the torpedo up forward. The whole boat should flood and go down gently by the bow. That is the theory, at least. These guys have come a long way in a diesel boat, and all on board will know the mission failed. They will be psychologically down, physically exhausted and, as a result, I hope, slack in their duties. I don't want her on the bottom with men alive in the rear compartments." David stopped suddenly and went over to Chief Ronnals.

"Chief," David said, interrupting the Chief as he was going over some readings with a machinist's mate first class. "My apologies, but what capability does the Golf have to lock-out divers, and if so, where is that located?"

The Chief looked startled, then his brow furrowed. "You think they might get down on the bottom with men alive inside?"

"It could happen. We aren't hitting the Golf too hard, so as to keep the nuclear weapons in one piece," David said. "They could lock-out and look around. Or they could scuttle the sub violently. Can we prevent that by putting shaped charges on the hull after she settles?"

"Wow, I need to talk to the Captain about this," the Chief said nervously, and he went over to talk with the duty officer.

"What was that all about?" Glenn asked.

"I just had a vision of the old James Bond movie, *Thunderball* where it ends with a massive underwater scuba fight, spear guns and dive knives and all that," David explained. "The Chief is going to bring it to the Captain's attention. The real risk is that they blow the Golf up as we try to collect the nuclear weapons."

The Golf was moving toward them. Lieutenant Patterson waited until it was 1,000 yards away and closing, using navy measurements, then he launched the torpedo, which moved lazily at low speed toward the intended track of the Golf. Doing so made the torpedo quiet and undetectable. It would go active about a hundred yards from the Golf, and speed into the forward hull and detonate. It would 'see' the Golf quite clearly with its high frequency sonar and hit where it was supposed to. The Golf would have maybe three seconds to react, which was no where near enough time to do anything. The *South Dakota* was already pulling back to the southeast, to separate from the explosion concussion and to prepare to line up on the Sang-O. That submarine had just begun to move north, the separation distance from the Golf was probably pre-planned, it looked to be somewhat more than 3,000 yards, probably 3,000 meters for the North Koreans. The *South Dakota* was closing that distance and had passive target acquisition fully established on the Sang-O when sonar reported 'our fish is active' followed two seconds later by a muffled explosion that they could hear through the hull. Sonar reported noises of escaping gas, and that the Golf was descending to the bottom.

Lieutenant Patterson launched the second torpedo; it went active after 500 yards when it armed, damn close in David's opinion. The Sang-O had sped up at the sound of the Golf explosion and had closed the distance even more. Then it heard the torpedo go active, heard the high-speed screws, and tried to evade by going down and east, looking for the layer, and ejecting pillenwerfer, gas generation packets designed to confuse the torpedo acquisition and tracking system. To no avail. The torpedo struck below the conning tower with a full warhead and blew the Sang-O apart as two large pieces and hundreds of small ones. This part of the bay was deep, over 1,000 meters, not the true abyss, but the submarine parts and pieces went down into a deeper darkness than any night sky. The North Korean submarine was there, and then it wasn't; all crew dead, and quickly. Not a visual carrying any drama, the vessel was gone in a blink of an eye in a darkness where no eye can see.

The Captain turned the South Dakota around and went toward the mouth of the bay. If there was a third sub out there, another Sang-O, he would find it and kill it. By now, the third submarine had heard two explosions, the second one bigger than the first. It had also heard a land explosion the day before. What were its orders? To flee and report back in case of an accident or incident? Hard to do so when you didn't know any facts. Perhaps better to come into the bay and determine what had happened, then leave and report in.

Sonar reported a passive contact 6,000 yards ahead, still north of the bay but closing. It was identified by its sound signature as a Sang-O; it could have been another Golf but wasn't. David was still on a roll. The Captain wanted to hit this one before it reached the shelf at the mouth of the bay. It, too, needed to go deep in pieces so it wasn't ever found. It was a repeat of the first Sang-O attack, the quarry closing the distance with the South Dakota, Lieutenant Patterson launching a single torpedo that waited until 1,500 yards to go active. The torpedo sprang forward;

the Sang-O did not hear it right away over its own noise and had just begun its first attempt at evasion when it was hit. It broke up immediately and took its final trip into the depths over 2,000 meters down.

It was quiet on the bridge. There had been a few fist pumps but no cheers, no back slapping, no 'attaboys'. A couple hundred fellow submariners were now dead. The enemy, to be sure, but still brothers of the deep. And now permanently so. The men knew they had superior equipment, training, and tactics. It had been an execution, not a fair fight. They had shot fish in a barrel. It was the quiet pride of sweeping your driveway, a good job well done, everything was cleaner for your efforts, but there was no drama and no joy. The South Dakota had had a job to do, and it was done.

"Engagement time was 17 minutes 23 seconds. Well done," the Captain said quietly. "Now we find the Golf and see what we have." The South Dakota reversed course yet again. It would hold station inside the bay, south of the shelf that now held the carcass of the Golf, and wait for daylight. The divers could inspect the Golf in the clear water then without using lights that would give away their position had the Golf any survivors and had they locked-out a diver or two.

"That was a sobering experience," Glenn said softly to David. His gleeful attitude was gone; he looked far more contemplative. David had killed the day before, up close and personal. Glenn was now a passive witness to death at a distance. It left more to the imagination.

"Millions of lives saved, keep remembering that," David advised. "It was necessary and done without personal malice."

The Captain walked up. "Well, Mr. David, your three submarines are now removed from the board. Thank you for your analysis and input."

"There could be a fourth," David said evenly to indicate he wasn't kidding.

"Dawn in two hours, then we will find out if anyone is still alive on the Golf," the Captain replied, unconcerned about a fourth submarine; his crew would detect it should it appear. "If so, we end them. Either way I expect to be the proud owner of three nuclear weapons by the end of the day."

David went to sickbay and lay down, as did Glenn. Two hours later, they were up, Glenn fortified by coffee and a doughnut, David with a Mountain Dew and a bagel. Up on the bridge, they were passive observers to what unfolded. A pair of divers went in first, just swimming. They inspected the Golf, which had a big hole just aft of the bow planes. No bubble trails, no sounds. One diver entered the submarine by way of the hole, which was several meters across. He found all the hatches open, the vessel entirely flooded. Secure. Aft of the conning tower three large cases were strapped to the deck, the three purported nuclear weapons. No apparent damage.

After this initial reconnaissance report, a second team of divers went out to begin the task of removing the three weapons. They used inflation bags to lift the cases free, a tricky business as the lift force would change as the gas in the bag expanded if it went up just a little bit. Everything had to be controlled with haul lines. They then entered the Golf and performed a thorough intelligence scavenge — code books, operating manuals, photos of gear and equipment, some weapons were removed. Tim was part of this work; he had done a fair amount of ice diving and could handle an overhead dive with skill. Then the charges were set, to make it look like the Golf had had a big internal explosion, like what had killed the Kursk in the Barents Sea in August of 2000. The bodies were counted but otherwise left alone. One interesting observation was that what looked like electrical cables had been run from the aft engine room forward past the bridge. They must have had some sort of electrical problem when charging the batteries and had jury-rigged around it. When the hull breached, the hatches between the compartments couldn't be slammed shut in time. She went down quickly with all hands as a result. No Thunderball option.

With everything set, the South Dakota pulled up close. In these clear waters and shallow depths, it might be visible from the air, so this last step had to go fast. Local authorities were probably responding to reports of underwater explosions. The U.S. Navy certainly knew with their SOSUS system for underwater sound detection. The three weapon cases were 'walked' over to the South Dakota and secured behind the conning tower, really secured as the Captain wanted to be able to make a good cruising speed without shedding weapons or weapon parts across the ocean floor. It was all done by dusk. The *South Dakota* left the bay and took a northeasterly course to the open ocean. Not long afterward, sonar reported a large explosion to their rear, unnecessary as the whole boat could hear it. The Golf was now a shattered hull, blown up from the inside.

CHAPTER 24

EXTRACTION

THE CAPTAIN HAD ASKED to see Glenn and David in his cabin. He was smiling as they came in and took the offered seats. Out came a bottle of Jack Daniels and three paper cups.

"Medicinal, of course," the Captain offered.

"I feel better already," Glenn replied.

"Wonderful tactical execution, Captain. You and your crew deserve congratulations," David noted.

"As I recall the last few days, I am astounded at what we fell into, and how we fell out of it," Gardarol surmised. "I am in your debt. America is, in fact, the world is. Three nuclear weapons in the hands of terrorists — it makes flying planes into buildings seem less than the ultimate catastrophe."

"Well, we connected the dots this time," Glenn said. "Actually, David connected the dots. I still don't know how you did that," Glenn continued, looking directly at David.

"Luck, hunches, a good education, a mind unfettered by rules and regulations, and a bit of an attitude, I guess" David explained, trying not to show an attitude. He was pleased.

The Captain leaned forward. "OK David, I have your three nuclear weapons like you wanted. Now what am I to do with them?"

"We need to find a moon pool, and all will be fine," David answered. It had been a week since David had shaved; he needed to grow his goatee back in order to have the same appearance as when he boarded the *Harrington*. It made him look scraggly, and he was sure the Captain didn't like it, even though he knew why.

"What's a moon pool?" Glenn asked.

"A moon pool is an internal opening in the hull of a ship, used to allow divers and other objects, like mini subs, to enter or leave a ship without having to face the open sea directly. Or be observed doing so," David explained. "It also allows clandestine operations, which we want. We need to find a U.S. Navy vessel with a moon pool working in the west Pacific, get under her, and let her haul the weapons up and store them in a hold."

"And what about you, are you to be hauled in as well, like a champion marlin?" Captain Gardesol asked.

"No, I get sent ashore in your zodiac on Farallon da Madinilla, and the *Harrington* picks me up" David responded. "I go back to Guam, disembark publicly, and go home to my day job."

"How do I arrange this transfer?" the Captain asked.

"Same way the North Koreans did," David replied. "Approach at night, signal your intent by blinker light, and put me ashore in the dark. They pick me up in the morning as part of a normal 'search team', and all is done. Same for whatever vessel we identify as having a moon pool."

"What about me?" Glenn asked.

"Up to you, you can stay here with the submarine and the hostages, or you can join me in the zodiac," David answered. "We could put the hostages, the remaining Seals, and Glenn ashore with me. That would allow the Captain to continue his patrol and be free of us entirely."

"Now, I like that idea," the Captain was quick to say.

Glenn looked deep in thought. He was weighing the options. "So far, we have done everything in total secrecy. No one knows who we are or what we did," he began. "We can get all our people back to Langley without any, as you say Captain, fuss or muss if we use the *Harrington* option."

The *South Dakota* continued slowly northeast. The default destination was Guam to offload the atomic weapons, but it would be more public than Glenn thought appropriate. David was typing away in sickbay when Chief Ronnals ran him down.

"The Captain is pleased to report he has found the ship you are going to moon," the Chief said, laughing. He knew damn well what a moon pool was. "The USNS Maury, T-AGS-66, is operating off Fais Island in the Kingdom of Yap. We will approach it at full dark and explain our need."

"Kingdom of Yap?" David asked. "Looks like we are going to get stoned." The Chief looked at David with a quizzical expression. "Yap is the place they use stone money," David continued, then saw the Chief's expression hadn't changed. "Never mind. Good work, Chief. How far away are we?"

"The South Dakota is now 110 nautical miles east of Koror in Palau," the Chief said. "We will be off Fais late tomorrow. Then it is only another hundred nautical miles to Guam."

"Great news, Chief. My thanks," David replied. "How did you track it down?"

"We are issued the actual and expected positions of all U.S. Navy vessels in our patrol area, as well as other vessels of interest," Ronnals explained. "To avoid friendly fire problems, be able to provide assistance and support if necessary, or for that matter, request the same."

"Not good to surface suddenly under a tour boat, correct?" David asked pointedly.

"That tourist boat was in a restricted area near Hawaii," complained Ronnals.

"Yes, it was, and that sub captain was showing off," David countered. "Anything the Captain needs me to do?"

"Continue to stay out of the way, I expect," Ronnals answered, a bit miffed. "It's worked so far." And he left David to his typing.

They had quiet seas as the South Dakota approached Fais. They located the Maury on the lee side of the small island, first by sonar signature, then by periscope. They hove to and waited for full dark. It took a few minutes to get into position, and start the light blinking, and then more minutes than the Captain was happy with to get a response. Then a lot of back and forth as the *Maury* coded to Naval Command to see if they should cooperate. The response must have been compelling, as after that exchange, things moved more briskly. The *Maury* had bow and stern thrusters and could hold station precisely even in rough seas; under the current calm conditions it was simple. The *South Dakota* slipped underneath, locked-out her divers, who went up to the moon pool for direct face-to-face contact and coordination. The weapon cartons were unleashed one by one, and each was hauled up into the moon pool, and then taken to secure stowage. It was all done well before dawn. Thanks and appreciation was given to the Captain of the *Maury*, the divers locked back into the *South Dakota*, which went deeper and then headed off to the Marianas. The *Maury* was near the end of her cruise and would go back to Guam in a few days. No need for her schedule to be adjusted; the idea was to keep everything routine.

It was only a day later, or 300 nautical miles, again at dusk, that they approached the *Harrington* north of Saipan, as she continued her patrol of the waters off Farallon da Madinilla. A zodiac boat was approaching the corvette from that island as the *South Dakota* watched by periscope, undetected. The corvette's captain was at least going through the motions of looking for a right-wing terror group. It wasn't routine work; there was a lot of unexploded ordnance lying around on shore. At full dark, the *South Dakota* attempted blinker light contact, and got a swift and sure response. Which was as it should be, as the *Maury* had sent off a message to Naval Command to instruct the *Harrington* to receive the *South Dakota*. It was decided to surface the *South Dakota* to the decks awash condition and use the *Harrington's* zodiac to make the personnel transfer. People and gear were loaded, the zodiac cast off, and the *South Dakota* slipped beneath the waves. The team had received a heartfelt goodbye from Captain Gardesol and his crew, but there was also the happy air of being under their own control again, quiet surveyors of the deep.

The recovery by the *Harrington* was short and simple; no one splashed, nor did any gear. The four remaining Seals, the three hostages, Glenn and David gathered on the aft deck in front of the helicopter pad. Captain Bishchoff scanned them over.

"I don't know what you have been doing in that submarine, my orders were to patrol out here, send teams ashore, and survey the caves," he said. "We have done so without getting anyone blown up. I assume we can head back to Orote now?"

"Yes sir, those are my instructions," Glenn said.

"Instructions you were given or instructions of yours?" Bishchoff asked, and not politely.

"Captain, I am in command of this mission, you are in command of this vessel," Glenn said calmly but firmly. "Get us to Orote and you will be done with us." The unsaid 'and we will be done with you' hung in the air. "No need to billet us. We will hang out in the crew's mess until we dock in the morning."

"So first I was a spelunker, now I am a taxi driver?" the Captain spluttered.

"Essentially, yes," Glenn countered. "And we appreciate it more than you know."

That statement seemed to mollify the Captain, who left the team in the charge of an old bosun's mate, second class. His name, barely legible on his pale blue work shirt, said 'Stevens'.

"E-5 and survive Stevens?" David asked.

"Why, yes sir. You navy once?" Stevens asked.

"Enlisted, but it was a long time ago," David replied.

The boson's mate's attitude went from negative to positive. He took them through a hatch and inside, stopping before a locker. "Put your gear in here so it is out of the way, no one will touch it," Stevens said. Unburdened, the men followed Stevens to the crew's mess where they sprawled out and took coffee or other refreshment. After a while, the Seals went out on the aft deck to catch some air. The submarine time had been one of confinement and inactivity with a single day of actual action. The three hostages, still unnamed to the team, followed; their confinement since their kidnapping had been unpleasant, stretching their legs in open air was a gift. Glenn went to a corner seat and slumped back for a nap. David got out his computer and began typing up an exam for class.

CHAPTER 25

HOMEWARD BOUND

TWO MEN, YOUNG, BIG, and with unfriendly expressions, walked into the crew's mess. Their insignia were in red, they were snipes, working in the engine room. One was a seaman, or E-3, the other an E-4, or petty officer third class. David took this all in; his situational awareness was on full alert.

The E-4 said loudly, "So these are the guys who had us out here steaming in circles for a couple of weeks?"

"A couple of ugly dirtside pussies," the E-3 added. "What do you have to say for yourselves?"

Glenn was now awake and started to get up, but David waved him back down.

"D238446," David said, as if he had recited the Gettysburg Address.

"What's that supposed to mean?" the E-3 scolded.

"It means if you guys don't straighten up, you are going down three ladders," David answered simply.

"And I'll help him," came from Stevens standing behind the two enlisted men, who jumped at his sharp words. He looked at David. "That was your service number?"

"Aye," David said. "Got my gedunk ribbon, my DD-214, and my good paper."

The two enlisted men looked baffled. "What does that all mean?" the E-4 asked.

"It means you are looking at a very old veteran, as he has a real service number instead of a social security number," Stevens explained. "The gedunk ribbon is the national defense ribbon. The DD-214 is the order that releases you from active duty, and 'good paper' is an honorable discharge, which you two may not ever get." He looked across at David. "What was your rate?"

"Sonar technician," David said.

"Did you like it?" Stevens asked.

"A great rate, secret classification, no one could come into your spaces except the officers, and not one of them went down to the sonar equipment room in the bow. A great place to skate."

"Where did you do basic?"

"Great Lakes, in June, July, and August of 1971," David replied. At this point, the two enlisted men looked concerned. They had stepped in it big time. There were many unwritten rules in the Navy — one was that you didn't dick with veterans. And they had.

David waved them over. "Come on guys, let's swap war stories. I want to learn what the new navy appears to be with people like you in the ranks. Or you can get me a bucket of steam and twenty feet of chow line." That got a laugh, and things settled down.

Later, after the two men left, Stevens asked, "Sounds like you had fun in the navy. Why did you get out?"

"Had a girl I wanted to marry, and did," David answered. "The way things turned out, I should have stayed in." Stevens gave a dry chuckle, and left to go on watch, or rather, back on watch.

"What was that all about?" Glenn asked. "What does 'E-5 and survive' mean?

"It means that if you go up to E-6 or higher, you get a lot of responsibilities, lots of paperwork. If you go down to E-4 or below, you get the shit jobs, especially as a 'deck ape', the local name for bosun's mates." David replied. "E-5 is the sweet spot, little real work, no responsibilities, life is good."

"And falling down three ladders?" Glenn persisted.

"On board ship, the ladders, really steep stairs, are spaced so that one cannot trip and fall down more than one," David said. "To say someone fell down three ladders means he was pushed, dragged to the second ladder, pushed down that one, and dragged again to the third ladder and pushed down once more."

"Why not say you would beat them up?" Glenn responded.

"I felt I should tell them in 'ship speak', so they knew that I was no novice at sea," David finished.

David napped for a while, slumped in his seat. He had stowed the computer and was set to leave the Harrington; sleeping passed the time. He and Glenn had set up David's departure from the corvette. He would be the first of the group to go, dressed as he had been when he boarded. Following him would come the Seals and the three hostages, all shackled with bags over their heads; they would be in the role of white supremacists captured by the Harrington. The hostages had been a bit nervous about being bound and hooded, but understood it was a game this time, not reality.

The Harrington docked, doubled up the lines, extended the gangway, and after a few officers and crew had disembarked, David came down the gangway with his duffel and backpack, and walked over to the headquarters building. He was sent down a hallway and led into a conference room, where he found Josh, Sam, and Pete waiting for him. There were congratulations all around, then Wu, Tim, Jesus, and Rob came in. Glenn was delivering the hostages to State Department officials who had been fully briefed and took over the charge. He showed up about fifteen minutes later.

David looked at the seven Seals, a Magnificent Seven, he thought. "Thanks, guys. Thanks for sticking with me, believing in me, and executing a difficult and complex mission," David said with more emotion than he thought would occur.

Wu was the first to respond, "I am glad we have to keep this all secret. To get schooled by an old man, a pointy headed academic liberal, well, it would kill our reputation if anyone found out." His statement earned gales of laughter.

David realized he would likely never see any of these men again, ever. He went around and shook each man's hand; Josh was last.

"I thank you for believing in me," Josh said softly. "And saving my life twice."

"Just an investment in America's future," David whispered back.

"OK men, saddle up, we have new orders and they ain't for Guam," Josh announced, and he led the team out of the room.

David looked at Glenn, "So now what?"

"Now we go home. I go home to 'Beltway' Virginia, you go to Langley," Glenn said. "We will finish up your narrative on the flight back to D.C. At Langley, you will have to do a debrief for a day or two, then you will be released to the glories of ASU."

"What do I get, Motel 6?" David asked.

"Oh no," Glenn said. "You will bunk in Langley itself, rooms and facilities we keep for defectors, captured spies, all sorts of riff raff." Glenn left, still on the high of a successful mission accomplished.

David went back out to the headquarters entrance with his gear and stood under the awning. In a minute, a car with deeply tinted windows swung by and picked him up, the driver throwing his bags in the trunk. Then it was off to Anderson Air Force Base; Glenn was already in the car. They made small talk on the drive up north. This time it was a Gulfstream 6500; the flight back would be a bit more comfortable than the flight out. Glenn had sent a prepared coded initial report out when he got to the headquarters building. David assumed it would make quite a stir back in D.C.; Glenn had to agree.

The flight back was quiet. The plane had a rear compartment with four seats, a facing two and two arrangement that fully reclined, with a small table in between. It was isolated from the rest of the plane; for this compartment, it was a right turn after going up the boarding stairs. For everyone else going to the more spacious main compartment, it was a left turn. The small space had its own lavatory, a microwave, and a stocked mini fridge. Complete isolation. Glenn and David had boarded first and had settled in. It was several hours before the rest of the passengers boarded and the plane took off. Those passengers probably did not know anyone else was even aboard besides the crew, let alone who it was.

They flew east, lost a day at the dateline, fueled in Hawaii and again at Los Angles, then on into Andrews Air Force base at D.C. It took longer than the MATS flight on the way out, but was much more comfortable, and importantly for document preparation, private. David and Glenn could talk freely, look at photos, draw diagrams, and prepare for what Glenn explained would be a detailed and long debrief. They landed at dusk and disembarked a while after everyone else had deplaned; the usual robust black SUV with tinted windows picked them up and they were whisked off to CIA headquarters at Langley. David was escorted by Glenn after the usual security and document vetting, up a code-accessed elevator, to a quiet, carpeted hallway. Around a corner and Glenn coded David into a small apartment with a kitchenette. His duffle was already there.

"There is no wifi access, the room is shielded as well," Glenn explained. "You will have to stay here in isolation until the morning. The fridge and pantry are stocked. Prepare your own meals and snacks, make yourself comfortable. I have your final report, I will meld it with my own document this evening and have a summary distributed. To give everyone at the debrief time to read it, you won't be gathered until 10:00 a.m. I'll come by about 9:30 for last minute prep. So relax, rest up. The TV has the usual cable channels if you want to distract yourself."

"Thanks, Glenn. I just want this to be over," David advised. "I do have a life back in Alabama."

Glenn nodded and left. David cooked himself some eggs with an English muffin and sausage. No alcohol, so he had a root beer and settled down to watch some sports and let his mind go blank.

CHAPTER 26

WATCHER FAILURE

IN PYONGYANG, NORTH KOREA, the General sat at his desk in Building 13. His adjutant walked in; the body language wasn't good — the left hand had a twitch and the man stopped farther away than usual. He looked uneasy, perhaps a bit frightened, sweat glistened on his forehead.

"What is the outcome of the distribution of our three gifts to the Western world," the General asked. He was excited about what was to happen, impressed by his own cleverness and the puppet strings he could pull on globally.

"There is no outcome to report," the adjutant said haltingly. He had a file in his hands, and he held it out at arm's length to the General, who took it and laid it on his desk.

"Give me an oral update and relax. I don't shoot my messengers. It is too much of an effort to replace them," the General said in a relaxed manner. He needed his adjutant to perform smoothly and efficiently. "Give me all the facts."

"We have had no report from Colonel Thae Yong-ho," the adjutant began. "We have had no report from any of the three submarines that were to make the delivery."

"What have we heard?" the General asked.

"We have reports of a major explosion at the location of the cave, of smoke pouring out of cave entrances," the adjutant detailed. "We have had inquiries from the organizations who sent representatives to the auction. They want to know what happened there. They have their own information networks and know of the explosion and fire."

"We don't know if the auction went on. We don't know who obtained the weapons," the General observed. "Was there a coup? Did one of the organizations attempt to hijack the process? Was the U.S. involved?"

"The three hostages apparently escaped," the adjutant stated. "Three Westerners, who fit the description of the American hostages were seen on Halmahera Island the day after the explosion. They were described as dirty and worn. They arrived in a battered boat with scorch and burn marks on it. They contacted American officials in Jakarta and were recovered later that same day."

"That report makes it sound like they made their own escape after the explosion," the General offered. "If the Americans had been responsible for the explosion, then they would have rescued the hostages immediately."

"That is how the event has been interpreted in the Analysis Section," agreed the adjutant.

"What about our submarines?" the General countered.

"They were supposed to report once they had cleared the archipelago and reached the open ocean," the adjutant said. "It is expected at least one of them would have made a report by now. The Analysis Section feels it is highly unlikely all three submarines would have suffered an equipment failure or other unfortunate accident at the same time."

"I agree," the General said. "A hostile act is the most likely explanation."

"Or sabotage," the adjutant suggested.

"To do so and take out three submarines at the same time would require a sophisticated plot," the General postulated. "I suspect a foreign power with submarines."

"There are not many options for that explanation," the adjutant stated. "America, Russia, or China would be the most likely candidates."

"Do not forget the Israelis. They would be especially sensitive to how the three weapons were distributed," the General argued. "There is a bigger issue. Whoever took out our submarines probably set off the explosion. There would need to have been a huge intelligence failure on our part, and an intelligence coup on our adversary's part."

"There are two ways that could have happened," the adjutant explained. "One, someone was looking into the hostage taking or, more likely, the gathering of representatives of numerous terrorist organizations. Two, someone was aware of our weapon distribution program and followed the submarines. When it was learned what we intended to do, they took action."

"Or the two incidents are independent of one another," the General surmised. "It is possible that both our submarines and the terrorists were being tracked by two independent groups. If so, then the culmination of the two events in proximity is not that surprising. Action at the focal point of our Zeus mission could be explicable."

"What do we do now?" the adjutant asked.

"We find out what happened to the weapons," the General ordered. "Did they make it to the auction? Were they intercepted enroute from the submarine to the auction, or are they still with the submarine? That answer will help us figure out the intelligence problem."

"Do you suspect a mole or internal intelligence breach?" the adjutant went pale again.

"In a mission this complex, there was ample opportunity for discovery from the outside," the General stated. "We will take that approach first before we turn our own house upside down. Try and get agents to the scene. Have we had any word from our contacts in the Indonesian military?"

"None so far. Those contacts may have been present at the cave, in which case we will need to rebuild that network," the adjutant said.

"Get me facts, then we will see what we need to do," the General concluded. "Dismissed." The adjutant left briskly.

The General had kept a positive expression during this meeting, a sort of 'this happens all the time, we will solve it' demeanor. But inside, he knew it was a catastrophe of immense proportions. The best possible explanation was that it had been a series of accidents. The worst case is that someone knew all the details and had eviscerated the entire operation. A big cost in men and material and assets, but so much more. The plot was known by someone with the resources to have eliminated the mission. There would be consequences. They could lose their most important asset, embedded deep in the CIA. His reports were another reason to think the U.S. did not have any role in the disaster. The General had opposed the scheme, but only lightly and in an offhanded way. One did not argue with the Great Leader. The responsibility for the failure of the mission would fall squarely on his shoulders. There it would stay until Kim removed those shoulders entirely. The General had to consider his options. Meticulously.

CHAPTER 27

A BRIEF DEBRIEF

DAVID OPENED HIS EYES; he was flat on his back, his covers almost up to his chin. He felt as he had when a child, safe, secure, and mostly hidden. He was relaxed — no nightmares had plagued him, his dreams were simple and buoyant. He bounced out of bed, again youthful. Jet lag had never been a problem for him; he knew the tricks to get his biological clock reset. He was drinking tea and looking at his report, as he had been doing for more than an hour, when the door opened without any notice and Glenn walked in, with Molly — a surprise.

Molly gave him an appraising look. David said, "You took me as I was coming back from overseas field work. These are the best clothes I have. If you want me in a dark suit, you will need to give it to me." David was in a clean and relatively un-patched field shirt, and white slacks, with white socks and sneakers.

"You will do fine as you are," Molly said. "Your attire will help keep the debrief team off balance." Molly, as with Glenn, spoke as if wanting to join David's clan, imitating him, which David found pleasing.

"That is necessary?" David asked.

"The CIA believes in tough testing," Glenn began. "You can expect harsh questions, disbelief, attempts to put you off your game. I have confidence you will handle it well."

"I know from personal experience you can handle it, just no head-locks, OK?" Molly said. "And no taking fingerprints in someone's own blood. I read your report," she said, smiling. David relaxed a little. He knew he was being soothed, warned but then reassured. There was true warmth there, but it was for the prize puppy who hadn't wet the floor or chewed the rug for a while. It wasn't for David himself; it was for the task at hand.

"Do we have a game plan, or do I play it as it comes?" David asked. "Do I need to show respect, hostility, blandness, a sense of humor, or what?" David continued to play by their rules.

"All of the above, at the proper time and situation," Glenn responded.

"We will be in the room but won't interject or comment without someone else asking us," Molly added.

"All right. Let me hit the head and I will be set to go," David said as he went to the bathroom.

Molly turned to Glenn, and stated, "He seems to be set, same attitude he had before he arranged the death of 300 people in a variety of settings."

"I agree, but he is also a bit of a time-bomb," Glenn answered. "If he has any psychological problems with what he did, they haven't manifested yet. He could go off if pressed too hard, especially if he doesn't respect the people grilling him."

"I have confidence in him. Remember, we were intimate for a moment," Molly said with a chuckle.

David came out of the bathroom. "Do I need to bring anything?"

"Not necessary, but you can have a notebook if you like," Glenn replied.

David grabbed his 'write in the rain' notebook and followed Glenn and Molly out the door.

The meeting room was grey, both in color and in character. It was an interior space, no windows, square in shape. Two doors were present, one at each end of the wall separating the room from the corridor. Subdued lighting, a computer projector hung from the ceiling center. The screen was on the wall across from the doors, but David was to the right of the doors, at his own little table and single chair. Facing him were two rows of chairs behind two long tables. Molly and David escorted him in, sat him down, and took seats at the second row on the left end as David looked at them. They waited several minutes, then a series of people entered; men, women, all dressed coldly in black and grey, not quite like undertakers, severe as IRS agents before an audit. There were no introductions.

"Mr. Langownaire, are you prepared to answer questions?" This from the man front and center on the first row. David was surprised, he hadn't heard his last name spoken since the initial contact at Immigration in Atlanta. He also noted the incorrect pronunciation. Some things never changed — the speed of light, the mispronunciation of his last name.

"Yes, I am," David replied simply.

"Do you know why you are here for this debriefing?" the man in the center asked.

"Yes, I do," David was again short and direct.

"What do you think this meeting is all about?" Center Man, as David had dubbed him, inquired. David's response had not been to his liking.

"I am here for three reasons," David began. "First, it is procedure, routine, so you are following the rules. Second, many of you do not quite believe what I did and wish to know how I did it — you suspect outside influence. Third, Mr. Willard wants to impeach me and accuse me of spying, when the actual truth will reveal he is a deeply embedded mole who has worked for the North Koreans and was central to this plot. He has not seen the report, does not know what is in it, but used his position to force his way in here. What we discuss here will soon be in Pyongyang unless you act." David said this looking directly at Center Man. Willard was sitting on the back far right. He had come in silently through the far door after everyone else had entered. Numerous heads turned to look at him.

"Hank, you don't have clearance to be in here," the Center Man said.

"Bill, I can be where I want to be if I suspect internal malfeasance," Willard retorted.

"There you have it," David said loudly. "Do you remember me, Mr. Willard? I introduced myself as Karl Mallin when you broke into the office Glenn and Molly were using in Atlanta. You were very surprised to see me, and you left expeditiously, but not without saying 'Good to know you are helping get our four people back.' Do you remember telling me that? I was surprised, as only three had been kidnapped, that there was a fourth intended victim who wasn't figured out until later. But you already knew. How is that, Mr. Willard?"

"You lied to me!" shouted Willard.

"Damn good idea I did, or the whole operation would have been blown," David said with agitation. "Essentially, you would have set me up to die. So this is personal."

Glenn had gotten up during this exchange and left out the door behind Willard. He returned shortly with two security guards, who posted inside the door and watched. Molly moved to stand beside David.

"Mr. Langwonaire informed us of this exchange immediately after it happened, with the opinion that Willard was a mole," Molly said, getting David's name correct. "We began an investigation, and I am sorry to inform all of you that David was accurate. We have significant evidence of Willard's activities on behalf of North Korea."

"You said you were a mining engineer, and I believed you!" Willard shouted again, too focused on his self-destructive past error, apparently oblivious to the events crashing down on him now. Then he looked around, turned to leave by the door he had come in, saw the security guards, and stopped. His shoulders sagged. He put his face in his hands and sobbed noisily. The security personnel brought his hands down, cuffed them behind his back, and led him out of the room.

David shook his head in disbelief. He had had it with all these people. His thoughts wanted to drift, to think about getting home and away from all those clowns with hands made all of thumbs, and everyone wanted him under one. He inhaled deeply, and re-focused. "Bill," he said, looking at the Center Man who was still standing, and whose name he now knew, "That takes care of item three. Item one is self-evident. Can we address item two? I'll now take questions."

Bill said nothing and sat down. A woman at the far-right side of the front row looked inquisitive. David pointed to her and asked, "Yes?"

"You are correct, you made a series of assessments, first of your situation, and then of the adversary's situation," she began. "You were accurate on all major points. It does seem like you had outside information. Can you help me understand?"

"I understand your difficulty grasping my behavior," David began. "It is in part because you are caught up in an organization with rules, procedures, protocols, and personal agendas. I am not. I think out of the box, so to speak, because I am not in the box. The initial contention of your question is completely ridiculous. If I had outside information, who else had that information to give it to me? How did I get it? What was their motive? Your question reflects your, and this organization's, self-important position. You didn't figure it out, hence no one could. First lesson in life — there is always someone out there better than you."

"You seem pretty high on yourself," Bill interrupted.

"For good reason. I am very good at taking incomplete data, assessing it, looking at options for explanation, and then testing those options," David replied. "I imagine when you debrief Willard, you will find out whether Pyongyang asked him to determine if there was any interest in me at the CIA. My mining engineer story may have saved the entire mission."

Hard faces looked back at him; David had to get past the wall of privilege CIA agents often had. "You people work hard, in a political environment that is demanding and unsettling. We all make mistakes. You don't shoot the messenger. Look at the errors made at the very start. You initiated a contact in a public place full of internationals you couldn't vet. You made assumptions about how to do the mission and didn't recognize the LZ as a trap. You failed to understand the diplomatic implications of the planned extraction. One of your own was spying on the mission behind your back. Some guy off the street shouldn't have to point this all out to you. And when he does, your first thought is 'he must be a spy'. OK, enough of my rant. Next question?"

There was silence. Bill turned to the back left of the room. "Molly, Glenn, anything you want to add?"

"The summary report you have been given is complete, factual, and without bias," Glenn explained. "Mr. Langwonaire has been truthful in all our interactions as best we can tell. He was able to lead CIA agents, Navy Seals, a submarine Captain, gain the confidence of the hostages, recognize the North Korean aspect, save a lieutenant's life twice, and give us the intelligence coup of a lifetime. What more do you want?"

"What does he want?" Bill asked.

"I want my life back," David answered. "I did my job, did it well, without complaint. Now pay me and send me home."

The lady David had scolded earlier raised her hand. "Mr. Langwonaire, what would you do next if you were in charge here? I'd like to get one more shot at your talent."

"What to do about North Korea's attempt is a matter for the President and the State Department, with input from our intelligence agencies and the Defense Department," David replied. "We are talking about complicity in the attempted murder of perhaps ten million or more people, some who assuredly would have been Americans on American soil. If we just keep quiet, North Korea won't know who did what. It won't be long before they turn on themselves, looking for the mole that they will believe must exist. They will suspect that one or more of the major powers are aware, too. They will expect massive retribution. The chance of significant paranoia and instability in North Korea, beyond anything we have seen before, is manifest."

More silence followed David's response. Bill looked around. "We are adjourned," he said. "Before lunch. Can you imagine that." It was a statement, not a question. He turned to David. "Mr. Langwonaire," pronouncing it perfectly now, "I apologize for the attitude you had to deal with. It is the nature of the business. I think we can all agree that you deserve the thanks of all of us in the CIA, and all Americans owe you as well."

"Thank you, sir, thank you all," David replied. "At the end of the day, when it all looks bad, just remember to do your job and do it well, and everything will work out. Thank you." David sat down, staring at the back wall. He had made his point; his claws were sheathed. The assembled group filed out of the room. Molly and Glenn stayed behind.

CHAPTER 28

SEVEN MINUTES AFTER MIDNIGHT

JOANIE DELLOWS WALKED DOWN A HALLWAY that reeked of concealed power and projected history. The walls were lined with paintings and prints, all from the American Revolution. Washington on the Delaware, Washington at Yorktown. A reminder to any Indonesian official who trod this dark hardwood floor that America, too, had thrown off colonial masters, and tasted the fruits of freedom. No Civil War images; Indonesia had gone through one a century after the United States, and there had been no Gettysburg Address moment, no Emancipation Proclamation document. Just gritty fighting and death. Then, as the doors to the Ambassador's office were approached, on the left-hand wall, large portraits of Muhammad Ali and Bernard Hopkins, and on the right-hand wall, Kareem Abdul-Jabbar and Hakeem Olajuwon. All action photos of famous American sports heroes who were also Muslim; boxers on the left, basketball players on the right. These had gone up, Joanie had been told, after Ambassador Linton had arrived. He was darker than any of these four. The photographs showed sports warriors in battle; Linton was always calm and cool in his business suits. He was of them, but clearly above them — he had ascended.

Two marine guards, in dress uniform, stood to either side of the large double doors. The right-hand one was opened by a guard as she came forward. She gave a nod and a polite smile as a greeting, met by an expressionless face with warm eyes. Joanie was a slice of hero herself, the one who got away, with the plastic cast on her right arm as her purple heart.

Inside, she was met immediately by Fik, who appeared as a vetted local who ran the office but was actually an American citizen. She was tiny in stature but like a border collie, clearly in charge of her sheep. She gave a quick bow, which embarrassed Joanie, and turned to lead the way to the inner sanctum. Like any good sheep, Joanie followed, trying not to hurry, careful about appearing laggard. Fik opened a door and waved Joanie in, pulling the door shut and going about her other shepherd's duties.

Seated behind the large teak desk was Ambassador Linton, a man she had seen often but spoken with not at all. In a soft chair to Joanie's left sat Matt Coglin, smiling affably, an expression designed to assure and calm. The Ambassador was inscrutable, all business, assessing that which he had read and talked about, but never consciously seen. He spoke first.

"Please sit, Ms. Dellows," he said in the deep, melodious voice that could capture audiences. He indicated a chair to her right that was the companion to the one Matt was now ensconced in. "How is the arm?"

"It is healing well. I am told I will recover full use with no future pain," Joanie answered, saying nothing about her concussion, which had cleared, but she worried about how many cells had died inside her head, and what information and skills they might have possessed. She kept her right arm in her lap, covered by her left; her injury was an embarrassment, a reminder that she had escaped and her colleagues had not. Her relief at having escaped the kidnapping warred with her concern that others had suffered, not in her place, but in a place she should have been.

The Ambassador looked over to Matt; the briefing was to begin, and Ambassador Linton was to be a witness.

"Joanie, we have information we are going to share with you, but it is critical that it is kept secret. The why will be obvious but know in advance we do this as a courtesy," Matt's voice was serious, no pretense, no acting. His eyes were calm, he wanted Joanie stable yet aware of the significance.

Joanie stiffened. There was news, and it was about Phil, Jim, and Walt. "All right, I understand." Her voice was resigned, apprehensive.

"A few days ago, the United States conducted an operation that successfully rescued three American diplomatic officials from a hostage situation," Matt's voice was more than relieved, it was triumphant. Joanie could see he was working to restrain his enthusiasm, understanding that good news such as this was the rare kernel in a field of chaff. She also realized he had used no names, no ranks, no identifiers. That alone told Joanie how secret it was, they didn't tell her what she already knew, that they knew she knew.

"I very much appreciate learning of the success of the recovery effort," she replied in her best professional tone, her insides churning with relief, guilt dripping away like ice melting from an eve, where it had hung, a sword of Damocles that threatened to pierce her soul. "However, I could have been notified in a very private way to the same effect. Why have me stroll like a champion athlete to this office? It will be the talk of the Embassy. If I stay more than fifteen minutes, people will assume other things."

Linton laughed, no longer the Ambassador but a simple spectator. "You were correct, as usual Matt. Yes, I agree and approve. Now, get her out of here to save her reputation and follow through." A very oblique answer to her question. They had plans for her.

Linton stood up; he did a graceful half bow and reached his right hand across the desk. Joanie reached out awkwardly with her left hand, and he quickly shifted arms to do a left-to-left handshake, a firm squeeze, held for more than a second, his eyes alight with humor. "It has been a pleasure, and I mean that, just a few words with you and my day is already better."

Mine too, thought Joanie, feeling the man's power, his confidence, his sexuality. Was her reputation worth it? She hadn't felt a tingle like this in months. She wanted to say 'I bet you tell all the girls that' but it would be false because what he said was true. The fellow was genuine, in a job built upon dissembling. He hungered for reality, and Joanie, with her cast, spoke of that consequence. Matt had stood and walked over, offering his hand to help her up, which she accepted. It was more than protocol; she was being handled, in a variety of ways.

"Thank you, Ambassador Linton," she said with honest sincerity. She really had wanted to say, 'you can be a dust ball under my bed anytime' and blushed at the thought. Linton saw it and chuckled.

"The feeling is mutual," he said in a whisper, and Joanie wondered if he read minds. A useful tool in diplomacy, if true.

Matt guided her out the office door and into the main administrative area, waving Fik off who had appeared as if a magical elf. Then the walk down the hall, the guards had said "Sir!" to Matt as they exited. Matt must like Fik, Joanie thought. She is one of the few people here smaller than him. The paintings, prints, and photographs were passed unseen by Joanie, as she laughed at herself. She had been entranced by the great man like a simple schoolgirl. Yet it had seemed real. Probably the glow from learning her compatriots were rescued. In what condition, she didn't know. Had they been tortured? Starved? Neutered? Those thoughts brought her to even keel, and she followed Matt in silence, a shroud he didn't break, knowing she needed to sort it all out before he made his approach.

Matt's office wasn't dingy, it was clean, and mostly ordered. It looked like a place where things got done. The open books, the stack of loose papers, the pile of manila folders gave the feel they had appeared that day to be done that day and were not the accumulation of many jobs not yet finished. She sat across from him; he relaxed behind his desk, his chair creaking as he leaned back.

"So what do you think?" Matt asked.

"In general or something specific?" Joanie inquired.

"About the rescue news."

"My first thought was relief, then I wondered what condition they were in."

"They are fine, they were mushroomed," Matt laughed. He thought it was funny, compared to what could have been.

"Kept in the dark and fed bullshit?" Joanie asked, trying to see the reason for Matt's light mood.

"Pretty much. Not beaten or tortured, not interrogated. Just kept, like cereal boxes on a pantry shelf. The ultimate plan was grim, of course, but they are happy now to have soft beds and good food — and light whenever either of them wants it."

"Either of them? Only two? I assume then that Walter Pinny is not enjoying the same, that you have fingered him as the set-up guy here in Jakarta," Joanie's comment was revelatory to her, yet it felt right.

"Yes, he has confessed and will be treated for what he is — a traitor." Matt's words came out hard, sharp, a weapon unto themselves. He realized his tone and shifted. "He will never be able to bother you again."

"If he had bothered me again, he would be dead," Joanie said, astonished at her words because they were true.

"That is what I wanted to hear," Matt said as if he had expected her venom. "What about Ambassador Linton?"

"Impressive, yet at the same time, vulnerable. He can be approached. He does seem to see things clearly."

"He clearly saw you. That reaction was unusual. What is it, your perfume?" Matt was smiling, his words again close to laughter.

"The cast. He was lucky it was plastic and not plaster. No man, nor some women, can refuse me in that case," Joanie was also laughing now, the juxtaposition of a man's heat with news of rescue, and the culling of that three-person herd filled her with contentment. "So what now?"

"I was authorized, and you saw it, to offer you a job," Matt was half smiling, half frowning. He didn't want to be turned down.

"You are only doing that to keep an eye on me," Joanie said, suddenly serious.

"Keeping an eye on you is what Linton wants to do. Me, I want you to work for us, and by us, I mean the big us, the U.S."

"To keep me out of trouble?" Joanie didn't want to end up in a back water, kept away so as to reveal little of anything.

"Ha!" Matt exclaimed. "We want you to *get* in trouble and show us how to get out of it. Ready to be a secret agent?

"Do I have to change my last name to Bond?"

CHAPTER 29

BACK TO THE CIA WORLD

"WELL, I SHOULD SAY I AM SURPRISED AT HOW THAT WENT," Glenn said. "But I am not surprised, as I feel I know you pretty well now.'

"How you handled Willard, that was quite a show," Molly said, shaking her head in disbelief.

"Captain Gardesol was tougher, and more was at stake," David replied. "I could see what Willard was going to do. I decided to head him off at the pass.

"Put his head on the chopping block is more like it," Glenn responded. "I thought he would be a tough nut to crack. You broke him in a minute. The man was in tears!"

"He is a bully, and I hate bullies. But I know how to deal with them," David answered. "It gets me in trouble from time to time, but if someone doesn't stand up, it never gets fixed. Do I get to go home now?"

"Not quite," Molly stepped in. "We need to do a final check on the report. As he left, I got permission from Bill for you to review the entire report for continuity, consistency, and accuracy. We will have to do it in our secure documents room."

"When do we start?" asked David.

"After lunch. As for lunch, we will bring something up to your room and join you if that is OK," Molly said. "What do you want?"

"Pizza," David was quick to say. "Sausage and mushroom, with a cold root beer."

They both escorted David back to his room, promising to return with the goodies. David lay down on the bed, suddenly tired. He had gone on a rant, several rants actually, and he was lucky it hadn't turned out badly. He hadn't processed it all, the entire mission, hadn't yet seen the truth of what had happened, his role in it, the consequences. His mind felt tired, out of sync. He had been playing a high-level game too long. His brain was cramped the way his fingers got if he did too much on the game console. He fell asleep.

As soon as the door opened and he could smell pizza, David woke up. They sat at the little table and ate, swapping war stories, which mostly consisted of David starting, with Glenn jumping in to say, "Then he told the Captain this" and "the Chief couldn't believe what David said," and "I thought he was going to fight those two sailors." It was fun to hear how Glenn interpreted what went on, with Molly looking over at him; she believed it all. A few minutes alone with him in the Atlanta airport had convinced her David could do anything. He gave her a wink. She returned one in kind.

The Secure Documents Room was exactly what its title said. It was shielded and sound-proofed and access was by way of an airlock set up that had security personnel on both sides. It was an interior room with no windows. Cell phones, laptops, and other devices, like thumb drives, were not allowed in. Each computer in the room, and the copier, logged every action, every keystroke. A vault with a bank safe door held all hard copies of sensitive documents. Those hard copies could not leave the room without a security escort keeping eyes on the document at all times.

At the outer entrance, David was frisked, searched, eyeballed, and questioned. He had to take his shoes off and wear paper slippers. Off went the belt, the pockets were emptied. He was allowed to keep a class ring on after it was examined. Then through to the second entrance door. More checking. His retina was scanned, he was fingerprinted (but not in his own blood), DNA swabbed and photographed. If he had been an alien, he would have gotten an anal probe. He did avoid a cavity check, however.

Finally inside, he sat down at a desk and Glenn placed the hard copy of the manuscript in front of him. The only hard copy in existence. This wasn't the summary the review committee had gotten the previous night. This was the full deal. Glenn told him that after he did his own submission, the file had been stripped from his loaner computer. David's own file had been stripped as well. It didn't matter, David had it all in his organic memory; he scrubbed that only occasionally, with ethanol.

Glenn left. David started reading. He was to make any notes on an adjacent pad of paper, in pencil, although there were a few pens lying around, some in blue for official signatures, others in black. The writing was concise, efficient, and accurate. The story told was compelling because it was so bare — no flourishes, no exaggeration, no anecdotes. As Joe Friday said, 'Just the facts, ma'am'. Words that might be new to the reader were underlined, and a glossary was attached as an appendix. There wasn't to be any running around looking for a dictionary or a textbook by anyone who had access to the document. There were a few people walking around who ignored him. David had a task, they knew it, and they left him alone.

It was interesting to David to read how Glenn and Molly described him from that very first day, how he had 'disagreed' with their assessment and had offered an 'alternative opinion' that later proved to be correct. At least his facts weren't alternative, just his opinion. The section he had written was cut down only a small amount from what he had done, indicating that he, too, was sparse, concise, and without flourishes. Page 53 had the words stalactites and stalagmites written on it. He noticed those two words were not underlined. A taste of the 'spelunker bunker' rose in him, the typical disregard of cave science. He looked at the words, looked at a fine-tipped black pen lying on the desk. Using his pencil as a ruler, he drew an underline for each word, slowly and carefully. No one in the room apparently noticed. He kept reading. He chuckled later when he saw how Glenn had described his confrontation with Captain Gardesol; it read like David had been the soul of discretion. The facts were accurate, but the flavor was gone. He finished his read, and stood up, stretching his back, and loosening his legs.

Suddenly, there was some disturbance at the inner door; two men were flashing a sheet of paper at the inner security guards. The supervisor came over. He read the letter, frowning. One of the two men had a black briefcase, right out of the spy novels. It appeared heavy, probably indestructible by casual methods. It was clipped to the man's wrist with a handcuff, the chain going back to the briefcase handle. The supervisor walked the two men over to the desk where the only hard copy of the report lay. It was put into a large envelope, which was then sealed, the seal written over by the supervisor and both men. The envelope was then put into the briefcase, which was locked with a small lock; the key was held by the supervisor. David assumed the duplicate key to open it was at the briefcase's destination; it certainly wouldn't travel with the two men. The two men signed some documents. A security official came through the inner door. He talked to the two men, also signed a document, and the three of them went out the inner door. When the door was closed, the supervisor cursed mightily.

David went over to the man. He asked, "What was that all about?"

The supervisor looked at him, and said, "You weren't supposed to see any of that. Goddamned White House, always throwing their weight around." Then he realized he should be quiet.

Maybe the supervisor thought so, but David didn't. "You just sent the full hostage report to the White House?" asked David, the incredulity obvious in his voice. "Are you crazy? That report will be leaked within days."

"Don't I know it," the man confessed. "Come on, your work here is over, so let's get you out of here. You cannot tell anyone what you saw here tonight."

"I understand," David replied, "Boy, do I understand." He cycled through both doors and found Glenn waiting for him outside.

"I can't talk to you about it," was the first thing David said.

"Sure you can, I am your CIA handler, the rules are different for me," Glenn responded. "I know what happened anyway. Think the report's subject will be leaked?"

"I don't know. It is more than explosive. I hope someone in the West Wing keeps it under wraps," David said, a morose statement reflecting reality. "Get me to my room and get me home tomorrow."

"Aye, Aye, Sir," Glenn said with a smile. "Other than the activity at the end, how was the read?"

"Excellent," David said. "Factual, descriptive, effective," David replied. "We should write corporate reports together."

When David got to his room, he was agitated. He packed up his things as much as he could, had a snack of ice cream, and went to bed. He lay awake a short while, running through the day's events, which had been powerful and had ended in calamity. Not only for the United States, but for David himself. Then he crashed.

*　*　*

In North Korea, the General sat in his fighter. He flew twice a month to maintain his pilot rating. His flights usually took him near the DMZ, so he could directly observe the configuration of the South Korean defensive posture. He always had a two-fighter escort, as much to keep him in line as to ward off any adventuresome pilots from the South. He did his typical pass, west to east, and at the end of the line he began his pull to the north. His escort, anticipating his turn, shot out ahead. The General suddenly reversed course and sped southeast, out over the Sea of Japan, then quickly southwest into South Korean airspace. He put down his landing gear and slowed enough that his plane got a little shaky. South Korean fighters, who always paralleled his patrols from their side to the DMZ, immediately flew up. It took the other two North Korean pilots more than 20 seconds to realize what had happened, then it was too late. The General had successfully defected, his plane heading south with an escort to touch down at an American-controlled air base. He was sorry for what would happen to his adjutant, but someone had to take the blame if the real culprit could not be punished. The two North Korean pilots would also get harsh treatment. Such was life in the North. He, at least, had escaped the Great Leader's clutches. Now he would sell his trove of intelligence for a good, if anonymous, life in the United States. Pyongyang would realize that now the U.S. would know everything about the North Korean plan to distribute nuclear weapons to terrorist groups. Things would get ugly. Maybe he should have defected to a less confrontational place, like New Zealand.

CHAPTER 30

FALSE ENDING

THE MORNING WAS UNEVENTFUL. David made himself a small breakfast of toast and jam with tea and afterwards, a banana. Glenn appeared.

"You are booked from Reagan to Atlanta to Montgomery," Glenn said. "We have direct deposited your pay in your savings account. It has a small bonus to cover your car parking, meals enroute, etc."

"So it is over?" David asked.

"Yes it is, and a fabulous time it was," Glenn chortled. "I mean it. I have never had a field experience like I had with you! Nor one of such consequence." He gave David a card. "The numbers on the front, and the email address, are for routine problems. For emergencies, use the material on the back." David looked at some handwritten numbers and pocketed the card.

Glenn walked David down to the main entrance, and into a taxi. At least it wasn't an Uber. He was taken to Reagan, dropped off, worked his way through check-in and security, and sat in the departure lounge. His flight was called an hour later, he boarded, economy, of course, but an aisle seat at least. Clear sky, no delays, into ATL at gate A-4. His Montgomery flight was at D-42, about as far away as possible at Hartsfield, but he had 75 minutes, so he took the train and settled in at the end of D Concourse. Off on the puddle-jumper to Montgomery, with only a 20-minute delay, and finally on home ground. It was mid-day; he parked his car on campus and went to his office by way of the Department Head's office. His Department Head had received a call from the Navy saying he would be in that afternoon, so he was met with expectation and questions about his 'rescue mission'. He got similar questions from his colleagues and his students. He and Glenn had worked up a simple narrative, to which David added a few anecdotes, and after a few days, interest waned. He was back in the saddle and trotting along. The teaching went well, it always did. He finally caught up on backed-up email, found out a paper had been accepted for publication, which felt good in a way that teaching didn't, sort of how eating a great meal and sex both felt good but were different (excepting Tom Jones).

So it went for several weeks. Then one Tuesday morning, after his Geomorphology class, he found an email with no subject. It read, 'call me, use the back of the card.' Uh-Oh, thought David. It was Glenn. David had a sinking feeling. Life is going to get different, again, he thought. Maybe permanently this time. He closed his office door and made the call.

"Hello, David, good of you to call," said Glenn's voice.

"Well, I was pretty much ordered to," David replied. "I know something bad has happened, so let me have it."

There was a pause, then from Glenn, "We have just learned that today, at 3:00 PM eastern time, the complete CIA report on your mission will be distributed to major news outlets across the country."

"I am not surprised, once it went to the White House, it was only a matter of time," David replied, his tone steady. "I am surprised, however, that the full report was leaked, not just a summary. A lot of people and craft just got compromised." David paused; Glenn was silent. "OK, I am going to get hounded by the news media, what am I allowed to say, and what should I not say?"

"The full report will be public, you can say anything you want about the contents of the report as long as you do not reveal anything not explicitly stated in the report," Glenn advised.

"I see," David said, then it was his turn to pause. "I will arrange a news conference for tomorrow afternoon, to get all the news out, answer all the questions, and keep the news trucks from lining up on my street. Hopefully I will lance the boil, so to speak, and media pressure on me personally will drop dramatically. Is this approach OK with you, Glenn?"

"Yes, it's a good idea," Glenn responded. "I will watch it, to see who asks what. I am also interested in how you handle the media. They are much more slippery than Captain Gardesol." Another pause. "David, I am very sorry about this, but let me assure you, the damage is not as bad as you think. I cannot tell you more, but some of the problems we had discussed from the mission would have occurred anyway. I will send you the URL all the media outlets will get in five hours, so you can have your very own hard copy early. Goodbye."

David said "Goodbye," as well, but it was to a dead line. The URL appeared within moments. He downloaded the pdf and printed it out, it took a while. Then he called Patty Onsett in University Relations.

He got Patty's secretary, a gay male named Robert, not Bob, part of the ASU's diversity goal. He was very competent and easy to work with. "Robert, I need to talk with Patty, it is very, very important."

"So important you can't share it with me?" Robert did a good false petulance act.

"It is a time issue, Robert. Patty will have to act and get out in front of this problem before two o'clock today," David replied, recognizing he was in the CTZ. "So, I really need you to get her on the line."

"Got it," was all Robert said, and soon David was speaking to Patty.

"Well, David, you have Robert in a tizzy, what's going on?" Patty was always cool and professional.

"Today, at 3:00 p.m. Eastern time a confidential CIA document dealing with a recent exceptional clandestine mission will be illegally leaked to the news media," David explained. "I, and ASU, are mentioned prominently in that document, so we will all be in the news. I'd like to work with you to get out in front of this situation."

"So you weren't rescuing Chamorro fishermen, David?" Patty asked, her smile came through the phone line like it was fiber optic cable.

"I have the pdf of the document, I think you should see it," David offered.

"Then what, David?" Patty asked.

"Then you and I schedule a press conference for tomorrow afternoon," David responded, "so we don't have press vans tearing up the Quad and shoving microphones into people's faces."

"I see, well send it to me," Patty suggested.

"No, I'll bring a thumb drive, no email," David said.

"Still playing spy, I see. Well good, bring it over," Patty stated. "I'll call the President and get his permission. He won't refuse me."

David went over to Patty's office in Howard Hall, 'HH' the students called it. He breezed by Robert, ignoring his protest and went into Patty's office.

"The President is onboard, but he doesn't know if he is going to like the results," Patty opened. "He agrees we have to get out in front, good or bad. Let me see it," she said as she held out her hand. David gave her the drive, she plugged it in, the report was the only file on the drive. After a few tense seconds, it came up.

"Read the Executive Summary to get an idea where this is all going," David recommended. Then he went out to hang with Robert so she could read without him hovering. It took more time than David thought necessary before she stepped out, waved him in, closed the door behind him, and told him to sit down, which he did.

"Holy shit, David! You rolled a dead man's prints in his own blood? A man you shot?" Patty was aghast.

"Got his DNA that way. I was in a hurry, I had no ink," David explained.

"OK, I see why you came to me with this," Patty continued. "You are correct. A press conference is about as controlled an environment as we can get in order to address the multitude of questions that we will receive. I will instruct Robert to answer all inquiries with a statement that there will be a press conference tomorrow afternoon at 1:30 in Alumni House, in the small auditorium."

"Make it the large auditorium," David suggested. "Things will go better if the press is spread out, not bunched together like cattle at a feed lot. Better camera angles, too."

"Now you will be the star?" Patty joked.

"More like we make ASU the star," David rejoined. "The better ASU looks and behaves, the better press we get for all the follow-up stories. Make sure the President reads the Executive Summary. Robert, too. He is your front line. He needs to know the facts."

"What do you do next?" Patty asked.

"I go hide out," David said. "After 2 p.m. CST, it is open season on me. There will be a lag time, for sure, but by nightfall I expect people at my door. Can you call the mayor and get my house some police protection?"

"Where will you be?" Patty again asked.

"I don't know, someplace the press won't expect me to be," David replied.

"Good, stay at my place," Patty suggested. "You aren't allergic to cats, are you?"

"No, cats are fine, I appreciate the offer, Patty," David said with emotion. "You offer not only a place to hide, but protection as well. I'll go back to my office, get some things, go by my place as I haven't been there in weeks, then I'll come over."

"No, I'll pick you up. In fact, when you leave your office, I'll pick you up with your luggage. Leave your car in faculty parking, do your business at your place, and then we go to my place."

"No fuss, no muss," David said laughing. Then he got up and left. David was different with people he knew, especially those he'd known for years. It meant they knew him, and if they did not accept him as he was, they tolerated him with good cheer. It was a comfort level he could live with. He was home as he ever was, even if it would be someplace else tonight.

CHAPTER 31

FORECAST: STORMY

PATTY HAD GOTTEN ALL CAUGHT UP in the 'spy thing', looking around from the front seat of her car to see who was watching, which only served to make people notice her. David got in, told her to calm down and just act normally. They arrived at her house and both read a copy of the full report, with CNN on in the background with the sound off. About 2:30 p.m., the 'Breaking News' banner floated across the screen. Patty noticed it and turned on the volume as a runner at the bottom of the screen announced, 'North Korea's Plan to Help Terrorists Kill Millions Defeated'. The narrative was breathless, but the topic warranted it. David had been close to it all, hip deep as it were; for Patty it was still discovery. She listened with keen interest, even though she had better facts in the manuscript on her lap. She was also a press secretary, so the drama was right up her alley.

"They haven't really distilled anything yet, just raw facts and sensational words right now," David said.

"Damn right it is sensational, David," Patty shouted over the narrator's voice. "It was the crime of the century, and you stopped it!"

"Hitler did worse," David commented.

"That was last century," Patty countered. "Boy, you did the right thing coming to me. You are the hero. You saved millions of lives, and not by pushing a button, but by thinking it through. And also by killing quite a few people, all who deserved to die. The press will be all over you. You will need an agent. Can't be me, but I know who you should use."

"I just want to teach and do my research," David was almost whiney.

"Those days are over, forever," Patty advised. "Just ask Sully Sullenberger."

"Great," was David's short reply, not a cheer but a complaint.

They spent the afternoon listening to CNN, MSNBC, Fox, and reading up on the manuscript. Patty made spaghetti for dinner with rolls, salad, and red wine. They ate on snack tables so they could keep up with the news. The later network news reports were more organized, some showing scenes from ASU and David's house, where a city patrol car was parked. The officer told any who arrived that David wasn't in the house, he was in seclusion, but that there would be a press conference the next afternoon at 1:30. By mid-evening word had gotten around, and no more press showed up. The officer finally left at 10 p.m. David knew he owed the mayor a major 'thank you'.

The later news shows were informative, with talking heads discussing how the U.S. should respond to the North Korean action; others focused on how the leak occurred and the subsequent consequences. The President tweeted solely on how the U.S. had kicked North Korea's ass and how hellfire and fury would now fall on the Hermit Kingdom. That response only confirmed David's view of the source of the leak. Patty showed David her guest room, and after convincing two cats that there were other habitats in the house besides this bed, David pulled back the covers and crashed. He had a big, long day ahead of him.

David slept in a little. Patty had gone off early to set up the press conference. Robert would come by before noon and pick up David and bring him to a private lunch with the ASU President and a few other campus dignitaries. David had a bowl of cereal as he watched the cable news channels. There was speculation about the ASU news conference coming up later. David half expected to be told not to participate, but nothing had come through his cell or email to suggest such an action. Comments from the administration in D.C. were vague and noncommittal. 'We are assessing the situation' and 'We are evaluating developments' and 'The proper officials are meeting to consider the options'. Meaning that they too were caught flat-footed and had not considered a complete and public exposure of what was now called in the media the 'Three Bomb Case' or 'TBC'. David understood he would be the first individual to deliver an in-person Q & A regarding the entire episode. Yah, no pressure. He remembered Glenn's advice going into his CIA debriefing. He would be himself. He knew that approach could have consequences, given his direct mouth and foot connection, but he really had nothing to lose. Over thirty years in the Alabama public employee's retirement system meant he could quit and do what he liked, hopefully on a remote and obscure island with plenty of caves.

Robert came by, and David, dressed in a sports coat and tie picked out by Patty for good contrast on digital TV, climbed into Robert's car. They went to the loading dock at HH and David scrambled in a door and up a set of metal stairs for two flights into a hallway that went eventually to the President's grand office. David was skulking again as he had on Guam. He knew he had better get good at it; his private life was over forever.

No Fortune 500 company would be ashamed of the President's elaborate digs. Along with the ASU President were the provost, David's Dean, Patty, and the ASU staff lawyer. After introductions all around, they went into the private dining room where the President usually hosted rich alumni and influential state politicians. A light lunch of soup, cutlets, biscuits, and salad was served. David availed himself of sweet tea, Mountain Dew not being available.

The President began the conversation, "Well, Dr. Langownaire, con-gratulations on successfully executing a real James Bond mission. I am impressed that a man of your age could accomplish all that gritty work. It gives us younger fellows a lot of hope!" That comment brought out chuckles, even from David. The President was portly and flabby; he would be gasping going down three navy ladders on his own, let alone go up them, despite being ten years younger than David. David hadn't even noticed the mispronunciation of his name. "There is a problem, however," the President continued. "I received a phone call from the White House a few minutes ago asking me to not have the press conference."

David was taken aback, although he was not truly surprised. The White House didn't want any glory grabbing; that reward was reserved for the occupant of the West Wing. He said, "Of course you told them that the press conference would proceed."

"Well, I told them that I would consider their request," the President said slowly, which meant he had said no such thing, and had told the White House he would cancel the press conference.

David went into full 'David mode'. "You have two options, sir. One is to proceed with the press conference as planned. The other is to watch me go across the street to the Hilton Garden Inn and give it in their lobby."

"You wouldn't dare," the President bristled.

The ASU lawyer broke in, "You could be fired for cause!" She looked a little unsure.

"I have my thirty years in. I can retire now," David countered. "Look at the optics. How about a headline reading 'American Hero Silenced by Pompous University Administrator'? How about me standing on the HH steps shouting, 'Freedom of speech today, freedom of speech tomorrow, freedom of speech forever!' ASU, and you personally, can catch a wave of public approval by not only allowing, but supporting, this press conference. The local headline is 'Alabama Tells the D.C. Swamp to Stick It'. They will love it from Mobile to Huntsville."

The President looked around the table at people nodding. The lawyer gave a shrug. "I don't like to be threatened," he said.

"Me neither, Mr. President," David replied. "Can I tell you what it felt like to roll a dead man's fingerprints in his own blood?" His comment had the desired effect.

The President looked at Patty. "Put on a good show. I never liked that city slicker jerk anyway." He rose and left the room, his lunch unfinished. After some hesitation, the Provost and Dean did, too, but the lawyer, Anne Brosseck, stayed.

"Nice job. Now that the President has given the OK to all of this, what can I do to help?" she asked, abruptly changing her tone.

"Run interference if the feds try to disrupt the press conference," David replied. "I think it is unlikely as they currently believe there will be no press conference. Still, campus security would be good."

"Perhaps request a few State Police?" Patty suggested.

"I can handle that," Anne responded.

They all finished their lunch — the key lime pie for dessert was especially good. David and Patty went over his opening statement. It was close to time.

CHAPTER 32

FULL PRESS

THE AUDITORIUM WAS PACKED, as David had predicted.

"Full house! You sure are popular," Patty teased.

"I am the only game in town, and nationally, for that matter, I am not surprised," David responded. "It's not about me. It's about what I have to say. Let's do it."

Patty walked out on the stage to the podium. David followed her out and stood behind her and to her left. Strobes fired. Patty had put the spotlight overhead and slightly out towards the audience, so David would be able to see the questioners but not be in shadow. The whole room was well lit.

"Ladies and gentlemen," Patty began. "This press conference is to allow the media to ask questions of Dr. David Langwonaire, Professor of Geology in the Department of Natural Sciences here at Alabama Southeast University, as regards the CIA report that was released yesterday to you all." She managed not to say 'y'all'. "Here is how we will conduct business. Dr. Langwonaire will initially read a prepared statement, then we will handle questions. I will recognize each questioner. If I don't recognize you, don't shout out. You will be ignored. Please state your name and your media organization, then ask the question. If you wish to follow up, look to me for approval. Dr. Langwonaire will stay at the podium and answer questions for as long as it takes, so be patient, you will get your turn."

There was silence in the auditorium that was quite unexpected, an air that this gathering was a no-nonsense situation and decorum mattered. Patty turned to David and waved him forward. He strode confidently to the podium. He had notes in his pocket which he placed on the podium, but knew he wouldn't look at them. He understood what he was going to say. He felt like he was going to teach evolution to creationists; he was in a battle.

"The release of the CIA document to the media yesterday has altered my life forever," he began. "Through no intent of my own, I have now become a public figure, an event I had hoped would never come. This press conference is an attempt to try and control some aspects of that public personage. I will answer all questions I can. I have been instructed that I can answer any questions about material explicitly mentioned in the CIA report. If I decline to answer a question, it will be because I either do not know the answer, or I know the answer but am not allowed to reveal that answer. Do not attempt to approach me on the street or come to my house. I will not talk to you. I may do an extended interview later, but only after I assess your behavior. We are at a time in America where the media is under assault. A free press is enshrined in the Constitution. You do your professional duty, and I will do mine. Let the American people see the press conduct themselves with dignity and character. We break no norms here today." He turned to Patty and waved her forward beside the podium. Hands went up in the audience. Patty pointed to one.

"Karl Kingsley, NBC News. Sir, can you explain the consequences of the leak, and how the leak occurred?"

"Thank you, Karl," David began. "Up until yesterday afternoon, the North Korean government was in a quandary. They had set in motion a plan to distribute three nuclear weapons to terrorist groups. It may have been, in part, for simple financial gain, but their major intent was to create disorder and chaos in the world as a whole, so that they could continue to operate as a feudal kingdom without interference from the outside. That scheme literally blew up in their faces. We now enter a very uncertain time. The North Korean crime is known worldwide, and there will be consequences, as yet unstated. It may be that the terrorist organizations who participated will be identified, and there will be further consequences. For both situations, we need to work with global partners because we are all at risk. Our recent attempts to negotiate with the North Korean government can now be seen as the colossal blunder that it was." David paused for a moment to let it all sink in.

"As for the leak itself, there are a number of explanations. One is that it was an accident, someone pushed the wrong key. Possible, given the clumsiness with security of this administration, but extremely unlikely. Another explanation was a consideration that North Korea would eventually figure out what had happened. By purposely releasing the data now, we have told the North Koreans, and the rest of the world, that we know what they are doing, and that we will act decisively and with prejudice to terminate such schemes. We now have a free hand to do what we please with North Korea, and we will have global backing to do it. Finally, the document may have been leaked so that the President could have something to brag about. The release of the full, detailed document suggests a very amateur approach, a desire to act quickly, take the stage, bask in the glory of others' work, with no thought of the consequences."

Karl looked to Patty for a follow up, David nodded. "Are you saying that the President of the United States leaked a top-secret document for personal validation?"

"I mention it as a possibility because the nature of the leak is so ham-handed, so unnecessarily revealing of methods and practices. If there are better explanations than what I have given, I would like to hear them."

The hands were up again. Patty pointed to her right.

"Leslie Wasson, Washington Examiner. Could the CIA have leaked the document to embarrass the President, given their secret war with him?"

"Leslie, I just spent several weeks working with CIA personnel in pursuit of the mission revealed in the CIA report," David explained. "I found them to be professional, dedicated to the U.S. Constitution, effective, and extremely careful with their security procedures and information protocols. In my opinion, they would never have leaked the report."

Wasson followed up without waiting for Patty to approve. "That is just your opinion, correct?"

"Correct," David answered. "My assessments are usually accurate, as a read of the CIA report demonstrates. Factual proof of what really happened waits to be developed. Then we can revisit this question." David, the previous evening, had discovered that proof, but he chose to keep it silent for now.

Patty made another selection.

"Joe Stakowski, CNN. Following up in a way to your last answer, reading the report shows many places where you took incomplete information and arrived at a quick, and as it turns out, correct conclusion that others had missed. How did you do that?"

"I have been a practicing scientist for more than four decades," David stated. "My job requires me to assess and evaluate data, what we call 'observations', in order to develop an explanation, what we call an 'interpretation'. I am good at what I do. I was prepared for a situation where partial and incomplete data required an immediate response. As an analogy, baseball batters on a hitting streak talk about how they are 'seeing the ball well', which means they are picking up the ball rotation visually and can decide if the pitch is a curve ball, a slider, or a fast ball. An NFL quarterback will talk about how he takes the snap and the game 'slows down'. He sees the coverage, moves the safety with his eyes, and makes the completion. A basketball player will talk about being 'in the zone' as shots keep falling from the three-point line. I was on a hot streak. I was making decisions and they were just dropping correctly."

Joe looked over to Patty, who nodded.

"Are you right all of the time?" Joe asked.

"Heavens no! We all make mistakes," David laughed. "My problem is I am right more than 90% of the time. So the 10% of the time I am wrong, I don't think I am wrong, and I can go way off into the weeds doing the wrong thing before I realize my mistake. If you are right 60% of the time, then you know you are wrong the other 40%. It makes you cautious, hesitant. In my case, I tend to be decisive because I am confident. I act, and I act quickly. When I am wrong, then it is really wrong. I acknowledge my mistakes, to myself, and to others. Once I see I was wrong, I quickly act to correct the situation, I don't alibi, make excuses, or pretend it didn't happen."

Patty pointed to a lady in the second row.

"Emily Ouizo, ABC News. Dr. Langwonaire, you are mentioned in the report as having brought all sorts of knowledge to bear on the mission, such as your understanding of how a soccer field should be laid out, how the Indonesians viewed their colonial history, how caves are configured. How did you acquire those smarts?"

"When my mother was still alive, and I would visit her in upstate New York, she would sit with my young second cousins and watch Jeopardy every afternoon," David began. "She would go through an entire show and miss one, maybe two questions. My cousins would say, 'Granny, you are so smart!' And she would say, 'no boys, I'm educated'. It is both a hardware and a software problem. To do what I do as a faculty member here at ASU, I have to be smart, I have to have a brain that works well. I also need to have good software. Not just memory, but determination, motivation, perhaps a bit of a cavalier attitude, a sense of daring. In the old days, I would be described as 'well read'. I have always felt that knowledge was its own reward. We live in a society where college students can tell you all the characters in the latest streaming TV series but can't tell you who their U.S. Senator is. Ignorance has consequences."

There was no follow up, Patty pointed to her left, second row.

"Connie Destain, Fox News. How did it feel to commit cold-blooded murder on Pulau Ternate?" There were a few gasps from the audience,

Destain was smiling, preening. She knew her name would be on commentators' lips tonight and tomorrow.

"It would be hard to explain to you, Connie, as I doubt you have ever killed anything larger than a mosquito," David said flatly. "Let us examine your initial premise. Was it murder? The first individual I killed was about to shoot a U.S. Navy Seal, I think a case could be made for justifiable homicide, don't you? As for the terrorists gathered in the cave, they were participants in a hostage scheme, and we had prior documentation that those terrorists were going to execute three kidnapped diplomatic personnel by cutting off their heads. If that is not justified, perhaps pre-emptive strike would be a better term? The North Korean officer I shot was also a participant in the hostage kidnapping scheme. Kidnapping is still punishable by a death sentence in many jurisdictions. He was also proximal to the site where we were trying to get the recovered hostages to safety. He was a clear and present danger. So, I think the term 'murder' is not applicable. Was it 'cold-blooded killing'? Most certainly, yes. I was cool, calm, focused. I knew what I was doing, I was not in the throes of passion. I had no hate or anger. I had a job to do, and I did it. Everyone who died at my hand was an enemy combatant."

Patty did not even give Destain an option to follow up. She pointed to the third row.

"Collin Wasterman, *Wall Street Journal*. Dr. Langwonaire, you have been proximal to the events regarding North Korea's so-called Three Bomb Case. Do you have any opinions on what the United States should do in response?"

"A very difficult question, Collin, and a good one," David said, looking pointedly at Destain as he said 'and a good one.' "North Korea, by attempting to distribute three nuclear weapons to terrorist groups, essentially committed an act of war. Not only against us, but the entire world. If we are to retaliate, then it should be with full congressional approval. The constitution is an exceptional document. We should use it properly and use it more often. Congress has the sole authority to declare war. We should not act alone. We should build a global coalition and decide how we address the North Korea problem. War? Sanctions? Blockade? Rogue states need to know that there will be consequences for bad behavior. At the same time, I would not commit American lives for the wrong reason or without purpose or an end game, as was done in Iraq two decades ago. This is a time for true leadership, not posturing. The final decision is way above my pay grade."

Patty pointed back to the fourth row.

"Gerald Lappman, *Louisville Courier Journal*. Do you consider yourself an American Hero?"

"Well, I am definitely 'Merican," David said, using southern slang. Mild laughter drifted across the room. "I do not consider myself a hero. I was hired to do a job, and I did it. The job turned out to be somewhat more complex than originally advertised. I did what I knew I had to do. A hero is the woman who runs into a burning building to save a child she has never seen before, or the man who jumps in the river to rescue a drowning person he doesn't know. Heroism is putting yourself at risk when you don't have to, when you are not expected to. Sully Sullenberger objected to being called a hero, as he pointed out, 'I was on the plane, too'. The real heroes don't know in advance they are going to be a hero. I knew in advance what I was doing. I had hoped it would go unnoticed by the public, and certainly unnoticed by the press. But it did not. Don't make my situation worse by calling me a hero. Just say 'job well done' and let's all get on with life."

"Lisa Reynolds, *Entertainment Weekly*. Who would you like to play your role in the movie about this CIA mission, Matt Damon or Brad Pitt?"

"Neither," David replied. "I have no intention of authorizing any movie or book that deals with my participation."

"You would turn down all that fame and money?" Lisa followed up.

"I didn't do it for either. I just did my job," David answered — simple, factual, and true. He admitted to himself it would be Tom Hanks, anyway.

The press conference went on and on. David patiently answered all questions, declining some that asked about specific procedures, or about his feelings. The steam gradually went out of the room. Eventually, a little before five o'clock, Patty asked if there were more questions. There were none. She declared the press conference over.

As she did, Karl Kingsley stood up and said loudly, "Thank you, Dr. Langwonaire, for answering all of our questions today, and thank you for saving millions of lives." Someone started clapping and soon loud applause filled the auditorium. David gave a small nod of the head and left the stage. He understood the appreciation, but he would have preferred it never happened.

CHAPTER 33

THE OTHERS

MANDY WALKED SLOWLY ACROSS THE FLAT, clipped lawn of the city park as dusk approached. Phil was walking to her, and it wasn't as Mandy had imagined it would be. No mad dash into his arms, as would have happened in a romantic movie. Each kept their steady, casual walk. An outside observer would have found it difficult to determine if the pace was languid in order to savor the moment, or hesitant to avoid it.

Phil commonly confused Mandy; he was handsome, athletic and smart, but seemed insecure. He became a scuba diver, he said, to test himself, to see if he was good enough. Then he took a diplomatic posting half-way across the world, again, he said, to test himself. To test for what? Courage? Or commitment? She loved him, but at times she felt she was outside looking in, not quite able to open the door into his life. Now he had been tested, not in a physical way, but mentally, confronted with an awful end. She had read the leaked CIA report and was certain Phil had, too. He probably anticipated what was coming as he languished in that dark cave so distant from home. She imagined the only darkness greater was that in his own mind as the days went on and all he had were his thoughts, which spiraled down and down. Freed by a miracle, by one man who seemed some sort of cold construct, a robot who assessed and acted. She had watched the press conference this afternoon, and wondered what sort of man who achieved what he had would tell the world 'thanks, but leave me alone'?

Phil had called her immediately afterwards, said he was in town, could they meet at the park? The first she had heard from him; she assumed he was in some kind of CIA or State Department debriefing quarantine. David Langwonaire's press conference seemed to have been a trigger. The man had basically told everyone to get over it, let's move on. So, Phil had moved, perhaps not onward, but to a different place, and here they were.

"Hi," Mandy said softly when they were only feet apart. It felt like a prison visit; some glass wall still separated them.

"Hi," Phil repeated, his words a whisper, almost inaudible. His eyes were scanning Mandy, her face, her form, where she stood.

"I'm here, and I am so glad to see you," Mandy tried an opening. No touch, no hug, no kiss, just happy to see him alive. But whole? She was unsure of what lingered in his head, in his heart.

Suddenly he was closer, face to face, his eyes locked on hers. "I thought I would die in that dank hole, and what troubled me most was that I hadn't said it, I hadn't tried it, I didn't know if I would succeed or fail." Phil's voice was still a whisper, as if it were all a dream and any loud noise would end it all.

"Say what, try what?" Mandy's eyes remained locked, her voice had dropped to a whisper as well; they were conspirators now. He had a secret — would he share it?

"I love you Mandy," Phil said, a shock as it was a near shout; the sound and substance staggered her. Phil grasped her the way a man does a life ring in the storm-tossed sea. Mandy hugged him back, feeling her need open to encapsulate him. He held her strongly, not in a painful crush, but as one does on a windswept deck — to secure, to save, to see life's continuation. There they stood, Mandy's hug as fierce as his. The door was open, and the animals were loose.

"My thoughts were everywhere, but they always circled back to you. You were my place of calm in the silence that seemed dead but raged in my mind. You were the antidote for the sameness of where I was." His voice was pleading, the penitent in confessional, his lips close to her ear, his words instantly in her head.

"Now we are here, we are in the same place. Will you be my partner, so we can face it all together?" Mandy's words were an offer, a suggestion, a key in heart's door.

"Yes," came his reply, his commitment, their future. All in one word.

* * *

Josh studied the plan. It was called a stabilization mission, which meant they were going to stabilize a local area in sub-Saharan Africa by assassinating a warlord. A polite word, fraught with political implications, but it was killing. Justified? Certainly, Josh thought. The man assaulted schools, killed adults as if they were bugs, took young women into bondage, raped, and abused them. So, yes, a deserved ending. Still, it took something from him every time, a cost, a price, it left a wound that would scar. He had many scars now. When would scars be all that was left?

He had read the CIA report, seen the press conference, and wondered about the man who had led them into the darkness and brought prisoners to light. And twice saved his life. To see his own mission errors written down was bad enough, but to know the world saw his mistakes, too, caused its own special pain. That pain was healing, that scar would join the others. There was command, and there was leadership. Dr. David Langwonaire led the best way possible, by focusing on the task and enticing those with him to focus as well. The man was a teacher, by his own admission. He placed a suite of choices in front of you, asked you to look at the data, and to make a decision. One he had already reached, with a speed which illuminated as it blinded. How did one reach that steady place, that bubble that seemed separate from the world? Was David alone, or exalted? Did he care? Was being alone his reward or his punishment? His words said it was his preferred state. Was that self-flagellation for past deeds, or just a simple environment that soothed the passage of the ragged edges of life?

Experiences change people; that is what life and learning do. The Indonesian mission was more than an experience, it was a cusp. Josh would not re-up when his enlistment ended. He worked his body, as a Seal, harder than he worked his mind. It was time to switch. David talked of his love for his teaching; Josh wanted to experience that joy. Teaching was a type of leading, where you encouraged students to lead themselves. As a teacher, you could both be within yourself and without. And you didn't have to kill anybody.

CHAPTER 34

ACCOSTED AGAIN

"THAT WENT WELL," was Patty's first comment.

"I guess so, the appetite of the media is endless," David replied.

Two men approached David, campus security stepped up, but the men flashed badges and came on through.

"Dr. David Langownair?" the lead man asked. The running joke that was his name never failed to amuse David.

David said nothing. He looked away, then stepped over to Patty. One of the men grabbed David's left arm, David wheeled and decked him with a right cross. The other man pulled out a gun and demanded, "get down, get down." Two campus security officers and a State Trooper ran up. The State Trooper took charge.

"Holster your weapon, sir, or I will arrest you," the trooper said. The man looked confused. His colleague was sitting up, rubbing his jaw.

"He hit my partner," the man with the gun complained.

"Those men never identified themselves. That one," David said, pointing to the man on the floor, "grabbed me. I felt an assault was happening, so I defended myself. I would like to press charges of assault on that one," he again pointed to the man on the floor, who was slowly getting up. "The other one pulled a weapon on me, that is a felony as well."

"Uh, officer," one of the campus security men said, "they flashed badges at me."

"But not to him?" the trooper asked, indicating David.

"No, they just walked up and grabbed him," the security guard said.

"I saw it all and will gladly testify," Patty added.

The trooper turned to the two men. "You will show me your identification."

The two men looked at each other. One said, "We aren't supposed to casually show our ID."

"You will show it to me, or you will be immediately cuffed and incarcerated, am I clear?" was the trooper's response.

The men grudgingly held out their ID cases.

"FBI, I see," the trooper stated. "What do you want with Dr. Langwonaire?" David was pleased to see his name properly pronounced. "Do you have a warrant?"

"Uh, no, no we don't, we, we just want to talk with him," the punched-out one said.

"He apparently did not want to talk with you, correct?" the trooper persisted. The trooper turned to David and said, "Sir, what do you wish to do?"

"I'll talk with them, but you confiscate their weapons first," David replied.

"Oh shit," the one with the gun said, "let me do something." He took a page out of a notebook, wrote something on it, and gingerly held the note out to David, who took it.

The note said, 'Glenn said to say this was about the back of the card.' David looked up, turned to the trooper, "It is OK, they have validated their interest in me, no further action is necessary. I thank you for your quick and professional action. You guys as well, many thanks," he said to the two campus security men. Those three men walked away.

"Your names, gentlemen," David said.

Punched-out responded first. "Sal Munoz, FBI."

Gun guy followed. "Peter Comstock, also FBI."

"All right, what is this all about?" David queried.

"We are supposed to see you alone," Sal said, looking at Patty.

"Patty stays, or I walk. I need a witness given your stupid display here today," David was harsh.

"Glenn said to be careful around you," Peter said. "I thought it was all hype."

"So now you know," David said. "Now, let's see if we can be productive. Patty your office is close, let's go there." David let Patty precede him, and followed, the two FBI agents coming along like ducklings.

"What do you want to know?" David asked, as they all sat in Patty's inner office, with flowers in places that didn't obscure lines of vision, chairs that were artful but comfortable.

"Who leaked the CIA report on the TBC?" Peter questioned.

"How am I supposed to assist in this process?" David inquired in return.

"You were the last person to see the complete report before it left CIA headquarters," Peter pressed. "What did you observe?"

David related the events that had occurred as the White House courier had appeared and the hard copy of the report, the only one in existence, had been carried away under guard. They questioned David for quite some time, going back and forth into the early evening. Finally, it appeared they were done. But David wasn't done.

"You have access to a CIA-approved copy?" David asked.

"Yes, we do, and we have been over it with a fine-toothed comb," Sal responded.

"Tell Glenn to study Pluto and do a blink comparator test, and then get back to me," David stated.

"What does that mean?" Peter asked.

"Relay my message and we will see," was all that David would say.

The FBI agents left. Patty and David drove to her place after picking up Chinese take-out.

They watched the news that night; it was full of more punditry regarding the ASU news conference. Fox was critical as expected, since David had questioned the President's character and competence, whereas MSNBC thought those comments were outstanding. There was much debate regarding how the U.S. should respond, with Fox arguing for unilateral massive U.S. response to level the country and MSNBC making the case for a global, coordinated response with increasing sanctions escalating to a full blockade. Both extremes would punish the North Korean people, who were essentially slaves already. David doubted that the Great Leader and his minions would suffer much.

The second major topic was the hunt for the leaker. As to be expected, Fox was certain it was the evil CIA, MSNBC had no doubts it was the narcissistic President. The punditry was as usual, inflammatory and fact-challenged by Fox, factual and I-told-you-so by MSNBC with the other news outlets somewhere in the middle ground. MSNBC's Candace Collins, or 'CC' as she called herself, spent her introductory remarks answering the question of who was Dr. David Langwonaire? That was interesting and a bit frightening to David, the most private of people. CC's team had dug up a lot of David's past, which fortunately was dry and uninteresting. His teaching awards, his research papers, navy time, divorce, all got mentioned. He wondered what his ex thought about it all. It had been over for decades; they were both very different people now. With a lack of dirt to revel in, most of the subsequent discussion was about David's analysis and decision making, and how he was able to do it all so successfully. Fortunately, there was no video of a younger David cavorting in bars on islands across the world. By the time cell phones had become universal with their see-everything cameras, David had calmed down quite a bit. Nothing to see here. It was still an ego-rush to be talked about, even more so as that talk was positive, even laudatory. He had done what he had done; it was officially documented by the U.S. government. He could neither run, nor hide from it. So, as he had done at the CIA meeting and at the press conference, and would continue to do, he would be himself, react in the moment, and let the chips fall where they may.

"David Langledangle," Patty teased, "All-American hero. You are on ego-steroids! Your hat size will change just like Barry Bond's."

"All true, I'm afraid," David answered. "I am getting praise, and I like it. I also know some of it is unwarranted, and that the media can turn on an individual in a moment. My life is going to be forever different.

If I could keep my mouth shut, things might eventually wind down. But I know me — I'll say or do something that will keep the fires roaring. Do you think it is pathological on my part?"

"A male with an oversized ego?" Patty responded. "If you are pathological, that pathology is universal. It has been a busy day. Are you going to teach your classes tomorrow?"

"I'll try. I don't want my students caught up in this," David replied. "Perhaps a call to Anne in the morning to have campus security nearby."

"Time to crash, we will see what the morning brings," Patty said, yawning. They both took to their respective beds, but Patty's eyes followed him down the hall.

Patty dropped David off, he would continue to stay at her residence until the press caught on, at which time he would go back to his place. No sense in getting Patty caught up in news reports of mythical hidden trysts at her house. He went to his office; there was a member of campus security in the hall, one of the men from the day before.

"Thanks again for your support yesterday," David said.

"I'm just glad I didn't piss you off, your right cross is lethal," the man replied with a smile. "Bob Simmons," he stuck out his hand, which David took with a firm handshake. He went on, "Carla is downstairs, to handle the press."

Carla had discouraged several members of the press already. "We have a job to do," several had complained.

"The professor has one, too," Carla explained, "and students who have paid to listen to him do his job."

"The First Amendment guarantees freedom of the press," the press members offered.

Carla worked full time as campus security because it allowed her to take six credit hours a semester tuition-free. She had a major in Journalism and a minor in Ethics, an interesting combination. "The rights of the press come with obligations and responsibilities," she noted. "Did you ask your questions yesterday at the press conference?"

"We didn't attend," was the response.

"Oh, so you essentially cut class yesterday and now want special treatment?" Carla countered. "Not going to happen. You gentlemen just move along."

David went to his office and prepped for his nine o'clock Oceanography class. The class went well; he had opened with a brief statement that he was finished with his work for the U.S. government and it was time for him, and them, to get back on track. His 11:00 am Geophysics class went pretty much the same, although those students were a cut above his 9:00 class. Geophysics was an elective, not a requirement for the Geosciences major the way Oceanography was. The Geophysics students were clever; they were learning the section on gravity and asking how gravity could be used to detect submarines or caves. David explained that for the former, not good, but for the latter, excellent. They couldn't get him to tell any 'war stories' about the CIA mission, but he approved of their creative attempts to do so.

CHAPTER 35

ANOTHER COMPANY

DAVID HAD PACKED A LUNCH, as he usually did, and worked at his desk catching up on email and writing an exam for next week's Geomorphology course, his Tuesday-Thursday class. He wrote up a thank-you card for the mayor and one for the State Trooper. In an environment where people rarely did RSVP to an invitation, even when one was asked for, David's attention to old-fashioned courtesy had paid off for him many times over the years. A few students came by for office hours, about half with serious questions and about half trying to talk about the CIA mission.

As 4:00 approached, there was a knock on his open door. It was Sal and Peter, the FBI twins, with Bob as escort.

"Thanks Bob, I'll see these gentlemen," David said. Sal was sporting a faint bruise on his jaw.

"Can we close the door?" Peter asked politely. "What we have to talk about is a direct result of what you said to us yesterday about Pluto."

"Yes, agreed," David replied. "Have a seat." Neither man did.

"We have determined," Sal began, "that the CIA copy and the leaked copy are different."

"How so?" David asked. He knew, but he wanted to see where all this was going.

"Page 53 of the leaked copy has the words 'stalactite' and 'stalagmite' underlined," Sal continued. "The CIA copies, both the single newly generated hard copy and the pre-existing digital file, do not have those words underlined. Do you know anything about this situation?"

"Why tell you guys anything?" David complained. "You will only run to the Attorney General and he will make it all disappear."

"That is not how it is going to work," Peter interjected. "We have been assured by the Director of the FBI that we have total independence and there will be no interference from the Attorney General."

"We are sharing everything, and I mean everything, with both the House and Senate Intelligence Committees," Sal added.

"You have made an initial assessment, haven't you?" David suggested.

"Given which two words were underlined, and our understanding of who was around the document just before it was collected by the White House courier, we of course suspect you," Sal stated.

"So how was it done, if it had been me?" David asked.

"The FBI documents lab says the underlining was drawn in by pen," Peter explained. "Which is why all the CIA digital records don't show it, and the subsequently printed CIA hard copy does not show it."

"The key is to know whether the document left the CIA with the alteration, or if it was subsequently added after receipt by the White House," David proposed.

"If you did the underlining and watched the entire procedure of collection of the document by the White House courier, then the chain of custody issue is demonstrated," Peter stated. "It completely implicates the White House in the leaking of the document."

"Which you already suspected, given what I said at the press conference yesterday," David contended.

"In our business, suspicion is useful, but proof is the gold standard," Sal commented.

"Well, gentlemen, you have it all figured out, so now the question is what happens next?" David observed. "Or do you want me to recommend a course of action?"

"You have known about this all along but did not say anything about it at the press conference yesterday," Sal said.

"And you, at that time, didn't know. You had to be led there," David rejoined.

"Alright, no need to pick on each other," Peter intervened. "David, tell us how you see it and what you would do."

"This was classic bragging by the President," David began. "He knows it was wrong, so he chooses a pathway that will keep the adults in the room from blocking him. I'd look at the Vice President. He will do whatever the President tells him to do. If it all blows up, the President will blame the VP and cut him loose, as he has done to others in his administration so often before. Check the sign in/sign out logs at the White House. Look for the VP to have been in and out twice the same evening. The President had to have the hard copy scanned to make the pdf. There was no original digital copy available. The VP may have been smart enough to not scan it at the Naval Observatory, but have an underling run it out to a commercial operation. I bet whoever did it charged it to a VP account, or paid cash but then turned in the receipt. The copy machine that made the digital copy will have it in memory. You can run this all down easily."

"The White House and the VP won't take kindly to the FBI probing around," Sal said.

"You tell them it is routine exclusion of all possible subjects. Once you are finished, you can focus on the real crooks," David suggested. "Look bored, with a 'I just want to get things done' demeanor, and it should fly. Getting into the various copy establishments can be done as part of an investigation into fake drivers' licenses, or social security cards, etc."

"What is the trigger?" Peter asked.

"I go on the Candace Collins Show and reveal that I did the underlining," David offered. "That will create panic in certain quarters and flush some participants out into the open."

Peter and Sal looked at each other. "All right, we will get back to you," Sal said. "Until then, just sit on this, OK?"

"Fine with me," David said. "Good hunting."

David let Patty drive him to her place again. They watched the evening news while sharing a pizza with a few Miller Lites. While the TBC was still news, David himself had become a minor factor. That pleased him, no end. The later cable news outlets had a surprise. On MSNBC, Candace Collins had dug up one of David's former students, Trent Collupts, who now ran an alternate source energy company, *Solar Wind and Tidal*, or SWAT, which was doing quite well. He had been David's student over 15 years ago — smart guy, had an attitude.

CC started off by saying, "After last night's show, and my segment on Professor David Langwonaire, we were contacted by a bevy of the professor's former students, who were uniform in their praise of him as a person and as a teacher. One of them volunteered to come in tonight and give me and our audience a broader feel for the man who pretty much single handedly stopped the biggest terror event ever."

CC turned to the guest chair as the camera panned back to show them both. "Mr. Collupts," she began.

"Please, call me Trent," he said.

"Trent, we have heard here at MSNBC from many of Professor Langwonaire's former students about the excellence of his personal attributes and his teaching. Can you explain why he generates such feelings?"

"Dr. DL, as we used to call him, was what you want in a teacher," Trent began. "It wasn't obvious at first. For some people, it wasn't obvious until years later. He came to class prepared, he was enthusiastic, he clearly wanted us to succeed, he wanted mental discipline, and our best effort. He was creative, and forced you to participate, and we had a lot of fun. In the end, that was the key, he made learning fun, even if he did mentally beat us up from time to time."

"What did he do, exactly?" CC asked.

"We had weekly assignments, usually quantitative, which means there was a numerically correct answer," Trent began. "You did the work, solved the problem properly, got the paper back, and you got an 85 grade. You would complain, and he would answer, 'You got the correct answer, that is good. Good is 85, a solid B. You want an A, that is for excellence. You want an A from me, you have to show me something.' The irony is that he curved at the end of the semester; he told us all he would do so, and an 85 average became an A. But the stigma of an 85 still hung with you. I got a 94 once, I still have that paper pasted on my fridge."

"He did the same with exams?" CC pursued.

"No, that was different," Trent explained. "He gave twenty questions, multiple choice, or as he liked to say, 'multiple guess'. Five choices, the usual A, B, C, D, then a choice E, or 'Some combination of the above, you choose.' Ouch, that was tough. But the catch was you could write next to the question, or on the back of the page, or another sheet of paper, why you had picked the answers you chose. And also why you didn't select the other choices. He told us, 'Every time you take one of these multiple choice exams, you go down the list. You accept A, or decline A; why? Same for all the choices.' He would say it wasn't about knowing the facts, it was about understanding them and using them and seeing alternatives. It certainly applies in life, as I have found out."

"Did it do any good, what you wrote?" CC followed up.

"It was a big deal. At the top he wrote on the exam sheet, 'If you don't write, don't complain later.' If you didn't select his default answer, he would read what you wrote, and give partial or even full credit for a good argument. If you selected the default answer, he wouldn't read what you wrote as he said there was no telling what dumb thing you might have said. So it was risk-free. The biggest prize was to have a minus zero, which meant you had missed the default, but your argument was more than worthy, and you got full credit anyway."

"That worked for you?" CC asked.

"Big time. It made you not only know the material, it motivated you to think about it, to understand how you yourself got the answer you chose. You had to defend your choice. In class the next meeting, we would go over the exam in detail. Sometimes there were near fights, but he made us think, a skill I have never lost and use every day. A couple times a semester, a student would have an argument that was really good, that Dr. DL would say he had never heard before, that it taught him."

"You said he got the exam back the next class?" CC asked. "Isn't that unusual?"

"Not for Dr. DL," Trent commented. "Every exam, every assignment, was back in our hands, graded, the next time we met with him. He wanted us to remember where our head had been when we gave our answers, so we could learn from it. With him, it was always about learning. He saw exams and homework as a learning tool first, and an assessment tool second. He was tough, he could be snide, belittle you, but at the end, all he wanted was your success."

"So, you are not surprised at what he did in Indonesia?" CC asked.

"Not at all. It shows how he taught us — look at the information, make an interpretation, then see how that works, then what are the alternatives?" Trent continued, "I owe my success to learning how to think from Dr. DL."

"My thanks to Trent Collupts, President of Solar, Wind and Tides, or SWAT," CC concluded. "Back after this commercial break."

Patty looked at David with a different expression than she had ever used before. "I had you down as a loner, standoffish, focused on self," she said. "That interview was a pleasant surprise."

"For me as well," David sighed. "What I do with my students is my way of improving the world."

"Saving millions of lives isn't?" Patty countered.

"That was a one-off. Teaching builds and lasts lifetimes," David responded.

※　※　※

Things got quieter and quieter. David was back at his house; he had had few unwelcome guests. He had hopes that maybe his life would settle down, get back to what was normal to him. He was planning his next research trip, this time to the Aegean. His caver team was eager and ready. It was evening, he was watching Premier League reruns, when he got a knock on the door. It was Sal Munoz. No avoiding what was to come.

He opened the door. "Hello, Sal. How are you doing? How is the jaw?" David inquired.

Sal made a reflexive touch to his jaw, then said, "Just fine, how is your hand?"

"Still a bit sore, I should have used my kick," David said, smiling. "I assume things are going to happen, and I am in the middle."

"It was your idea, and we like it," Sal responded. "I can't give you many details, but if we are asking you to go on CC's show and reveal the underlining, then you have a good idea what we found. But I can't confirm anything more."

"How do you want me to play it?" David asked.

"Just as you said," Sal began. "We have a person you should contact at MSNBC who will start the booking process." He handed over a slip of paper. "You are highly desired as an interviewee, so you can assume events will move quickly. Just go on TV, explain what you did and what you saw. Feel free to say that the leak had to be from the White House. Then we will see what happens. We have solid evidence of what you expected, and your interview may make one or more people do something rash."

"Once more into the breech, dear friends, is that it?" David asked.

"Pretty much, David. You are the gift that keeps on giving," Sal replied. "I'll catch you later." He got up off the couch and went out the door.

CHAPTER 36

QUAKE TV

DAVID SAW NO REASON TO PUT IT OFF. The next day, he called the number and talked to Ms. Rose Franks, which had to be a stage name. He would fly up tomorrow on an early flight from MGM, Montgomery to ATL, Atlanta to LGA, Laguardia. Limo pick-up and on to the studio. One night in a hotel, then his return the next day. What a hassle — but at least it wasn't a MATS flight, or sickbay in a sub.

The flights were smooth, on time, the limo wasn't plush, but the driver was excellent. A lot of hurry up and wait at the studio. He had told Rose that CC had to have a printed copy of the CIA report and a magnifying glass, and if so, she would get a scoop. He knew it was unlikely to be on for even ten minutes, but the bomb he was to drop could be done in 60 seconds. Anyway, CC was primed; she would get the printout and the magnifying glass.

"We welcome tonight a true American icon, Dr. David Langwonaire," CC announced in her smooth style. "Dr. Langwonaire, to start us off, explain how you were able to determine where the hostages were being held?"

"I was only able to narrow it down to a region of eastern Indonesia, based on a lot of assumptions that could have just as easily been incorrect," David explained. "As the leaked report shows, the CIA already knew which island the hostages were being held on, a great piece of work on their part. My input only demonstrated that it was necessary to provide me with a cover story if they wanted me to participate."

"So, hunting for neo-Nazis in the Mariana Islands became your cover story?" CC asked.

"As events played out, the North Koreans were either totally uninterested in me, or they were interested and they bought the cover story," David commented. "Either way, the mission went to a successful conclusion."

"The CIA decided they needed their own cave specialist to execute the rescue — why you?" CC inquired.

"Studying caves is clearly a specialty with few scientific experts," David began. "Studying caves on islands is a very small segment of that specialty. I am about the only person in the world doing that sort of work. The caves we find on the coasts of many islands, and along continental coasts such as the Yucatan in Mexico, form in a different way than the caves most people are familiar with. To rescue the hostages, the extraction team needed to know how the cave would be laid out, what routes would work, and how to avoid detection. I showed them how. That is why the cover story was necessary. If the CIA showed interest in me, and the North Koreans were paying attention, they would know that some or all of their plot had been discovered."

"Interesting," CC commented. "You told me to have a copy of the leaked CIA report and a magnifying glass here tonight, and I do." CC pushed a stack of papers to a position between her and David. Then she whipped out a large magnifying glass. "I am ready to Sherlock Holmes," she said with a grin.

"Excellent," David replied. "It is time to demonstrate who leaked the CIA report. Go to page 50." CC did so and looked at David questioningly. "You see that there are several words that have been underlined."

"Yes, I see them," she said. "I see 'claymore' and 'garrote', among others."

"The CIA report policy is to underline words that may not be known to a potential reader, such as an administrator or bureaucrat," David explained. "There is a glossary in the back."

"How does this underlining tell us anything about the leaker?" CC was still polite, but David could see she was wondering if she was being played.

"Go to page 53," David instructed. "What words are underlined?"

"Only 'stalactite' and 'stalagmite', no others," CC responded.

"Are those words in the glossary?" David asked.

CC did a quick flipping of pages at the back of the report. "No," was all she said.

"Now look at those two words with the magnifying glass, and then look at the underlined words on page 50," David ordered.

There was silence for a minute while CC looked first at page 53, then at page 50, and back and forth several times. "The underlines are different," she said with surprise. CC then flipped to several other pages and looked at underlined words there. "There is something different about the underlining of the words on page 53." She gave David a hard look. "How do you know about this? Did you discover it on your own?"

"I know about it because I put those underlines there myself," David announced. "With a fine-point black pen, by hand. Just moments before the White House courier showed up with a Presidential order demanding release of the hard copy immediately to the White House with no delay. I watched as the document was sealed in an envelope, placed in the special with-handcuffs briefcase, and the courier and his escort left."

"You did it?" CC was a bit incredulous. She turned to face the camera. "This action means that the White House leaked the CIA report, not the CIA"

"I did not intend to AF the White House," David said. "I was just a little pissed that cave science always gets laughed at. People treat cave scientists like they are crazy, so I brought attention to two words people commonly get mixed up."

"We have to take a commercial break," CC said. "But before we go, what do you mean by 'AF'?"

"Your on-site historian will know," David said smiling, as the program cut away.

After a couple of minutes, CC was again on the air with David. "Tonight, I am interviewing Dr. David Langwonaire, a central player in the leaked CIA report. He has just explained to me that he made two subtle alterations to the hard copy of the CIA report, alterations done by hand, so there is no digital record. Do I have that correct, David?"

"Yes, CC, you are spot on," David replied.

"You said you did not intend to AF the White House," CC commented. "I asked a few people what that meant, and they said it was about the Battle of Midway in World War II. Can you explain?"

"It is one of the most famous counter-intelligence stories ever," David said. "In May of 1942, the U.S. Navy knew that the Japanese were planning a big attack, but we didn't know where. Was it Hawaii again, or the west coast of the United States, or some other location? The chief intelligence officer in Honolulu felt it had to be Midway Island, but our code breaking was very spotty, and all he knew for certain was that the Japanese code name for the target was 'AF', so he set a trap. He had Midway broadcast in the clear, meaning not in code, that their desalinization still had broken down. Within a day, they intercepted a coded Japanese message that said 'AF has water problems'. The target was Midway, we set our own trap, and won a stunning victory, sinking four of their carriers to only one of our own."

"So when you said you did not intend to 'AF' the White House, you meant you did not set a deliberate trap?" CC speculated.

"Exactly, I made the edit in a fit of pique," David answered. "I did not expect the White House courier to show up, take the draft I had just edited by hand, and go off with it. To later see that the leaked report had my two hand-drawn underlines told me right away that it had been leaked by the White House, and not the CIA."

"You knew this fact at your press conference and said nothing about it," CC said accusingly.

"Correct," David replied. "I wanted to see if the investigation was good enough to detect the edits. The fact that we haven't heard anything from any official body such as the CIA or FBI could mean that perhaps they didn't know until now."

"What do you think will happen now?" CC asked.

"The White House will need to change their story and quit attacking the CIA," David said calmly. "As they used to say on I Love Lucy, the White House has some 'splaining' to do."

"Do you expect any personal repercussions from this revelation?" CC asked.

"What are they going to do, shave my head and send me to Vietnam? It didn't work in 1971 and it won't work now," David responded.

"Why did you come on the show and reveal the underlining?" CC inquired.

"I thought that it would become quickly obvious that the two words I underlined were an addition, and I kept waiting for the other shoe to drop. It didn't, so I came here to make it drop. Stay tuned, things will get interesting now."

"I am sure they will," CC said with a smile. "Thank you, Dr. Langwonaire, hope to have you on again sometime."

"Thank you as well, CC," David said as the show again went to a commercial break.

"That son of a bitch," Glenn said to Molly. "Even when he fucks up, it pays off."

They had just watched David's appearance with Candace Collins in Molly's Spartan office.

"I never saw the underlining, and I have read that document several times," Molly consoled Glenn. "He wouldn't have done the CC show without clearing it with Sal and Peter, would he?"

"Hell no, he didn't clear it with them. He planned all of it," Glenn said with frustration. "It has his fingerprints all over it, this time in the President's blood. I bet even now people in the White House are running around trying to cover everything up."

"Will that work?" Molly asked.

"I doubt it. The FBI is probably watching like a hawk," Glenn observed.

"David did this to make them panic, to make them screw up," Molly exclaimed. "He is helping us out."

"He would say he was helping America out," Glenn countered. "He hates bullies. This isn't so much about protecting us as it is to put the bully-in-chief under the gun. And it may work."

By the time David completed his interview, Sal and Peter had already located the copier used in the leak plot in an office supply store in a strip mall only a few miles from the Naval Observatory residence of the Vice President. Its internal memory held the CIA report as a digital file, produced from scanning the hard copy as a pdf. The data was time-stamped, as was the security camera video that had captured the individual who brought the document to the store and had done the scanning. It was Roger Templatine, the Vice President's personal security man, errand boy, and fixer. The Secret Service had logged him out of and back into the Naval Observatory that night. He had been secretly taken into custody and, for immunity, he had agreed to wear a wire. The FBI also had the White House visitor's log showing that the night of the scanning, the VP had come to the White House, stayed about thirty minutes, then left with a briefcase he hadn't had coming in. He was back two hours later with the briefcase and left ten minutes later without the briefcase. That time window encapsulated Templatine's time window when the scanning had been done at the strip mall. When Roger Templatine confronted the Vice President after David's appearance on CC's show, he was wearing a wire. He demanded that the Vice President get the President to pardon him should Templatine be implicated in the leak scheme. Templatine had been assured that the President would pardon him, and not to worry, some White House underling would take the hit. All of this was recorded with high fidelity.

The next day, the FBI was summoned to the Senate Intelligence Committee, who wanted to know all about the underlining. The FBI consul was sent down, as some fireworks might occur. Sal and Peter were the gumshoes doing the actual investigation; they would be insulated from the politics as best as could be done. There was still a lot of 'Deep State' talk in Congress, especially on the Republican side, but polls showed that after the coronavirus debacle, the public was sick and tired of the relentless attack on U.S. institutions, and things were quieter these days. The FBI consul gave a summary report which stated the facts as they had happened. Dr. David Langwonaire had made two minor edits to the CIA report, the only hard copy in existence at the time. Within in a few minutes of having done that, the White House courier had arrived. All witnesses to the scene had the exact same story. There were no chain-of-custody issues. The three individuals who were part of the courier team had testified that the report never left their possession until it was delivered to the White House. All the documentation and receipts were in order. There was no alternative but to state that the report had been leaked some time after leaving the CIA and *after* arriving at the White House. This reporting was all done in closed session. That afternoon, the same was done for the House Intelligence Committee.

The Senate Intelligence Committee decided that it needed to talk with Dr. David Langwonaire. They had a committee staffer call the Professor.

CHAPTER 37

THE POLITICS OF POLITENESS

DAVID ANSWERED HIS PHONE while in his office in the late afternoon. "Hello, David Langwonaire speaking."

"Dr. Langwonaire, this is Alice Conzeski from the Senate Intelligence Committee," the lady on the line said. "The Committee would like you to come to Washington, D.C., and testify before the Committee regarding the situation surrounding the leaked CIA report from your mission."

"No, I will not testify," David replied. "Goodbye." And he hung up. He then called Anne Brosseck, who answered, as she had given him her direct line. "Anne, I just received a phone call from an Alice Conzeski, a staffer for the Senate Intelligence Committee in D.C. They want me to testify. I told her no. Does ASU have any opinion on the matter?"

"Uh, David," Anne began. "That was probably not a good idea. They can subpoena you and compel you to testify. ASU will take no stand either way, you are on your own."

"Anne, as I understand a recent court ruling, they can compel me to appear, but they cannot compel me to testify," David replied.

"Well, that is true, but your only option is to plead the fifth amendment," Anne responded. "Then they offer you transactional immunity and can then compel you to testify, or you can be locked up."

"Then I would need a lawyer?" David asked.

"Then you would need a lawyer," Anne agreed. "I can provide you with contact information of a few choices who have experience with this sort of thing."

"No, that won't be necessary. I think I can handle this myself," David stated. "Thanks for the input." He then rang off.

He noticed that a voicemail had been left on his phone; he was certain it was from Ms. Conzeski, so he called back.

"Dr. Langwonaire, thank you for calling back," Alice said. "If you need a subpoena to encourage you to testify, the Committee can arrange that." No fuss, no muss, she cut directly to the chase, thought David. He gave her points for that approach.

"Ms. Conzeski, is this testimony to be in an open or closed hearing?" David asked.

"Open hearing is my understanding," she answered.

"Inform the Committee I will only appear for a closed hearing. I will not testify in an open hearing," David replied.

"Why is that, Dr. Langwonaire?" Alice inquired.

"Three reasons, Ms. Conzeski," David answered.

"Please call me Alice," she interrupted.

"Not while we are in an adversarial situation," David responded. "The three reasons are: one, the topic involves national security. Two, I will not allow myself to be further publicized. Three, I am no one's political tool. Is that clear enough?"

"A subpoena will require you to appear," Alice countered.

"I understand you need to do your job, so no hard feelings," David replied. "The Committee will have to vote to approve a subpoena. I will wait and see what happens. Please be candid and complete when briefing the Committee on my response. Also, I will deal only with you, and no one else. Good day." He hung up and went about his daily business. An email popped up, from Anne; she had sent him some lawyer names and contact information anyway. She, too, knew her job.

Things were quiet for several days. David dared to hope that the Senate Intelligence Committee had decided he wasn't worth the effort. Then his phone rang.

"Hello, David Langwonaire speaking."

"Hello Dr. Langwonaire, this is Alice Conzeski with an update," she began.

"And the update is?" David asked.

"A subpoena was voted on today. You are compelled to appear," Alice continued.

"I had heard nothing on the news. I assume the Committee voted in closed session," David replied.

"That is correct," Alice responded.

"The Committee voted in secret closed session to require me to appear before them in open session? You see the irony," David asked.

"Uh, it does look unusual," Alice agreed. "Anyway, you now have been notified."

"Not until I am served in person," David replied. "You could be anybody. I have no proof you are who you say you are."

"All Committee conversations are recorded, so my verbal notification is sufficient," Alice contended.

"All my calls are recorded as well, including your inability to prove you are who you say you are," David argued.

"You recorded me without permission?" Alice asked.

"Alabama is a single approval state, so I do not need your permission. You called me, remember? You still cannot prove who you are and who you represent," David contended. "This could all be a scam."

"You are required to appear next Wednesday morning at 10:00 a.m. in the Senate hearing room," Alice said, clearly exasperated by David's antics.

"Not until I am formally served, which means you will have to find me. Good luck with that," David responded.

"Your lawyer will be required to produce you, or face discipline," Alice explained.

"I don't have a lawyer. And you will have to find me," David said.

"You don't have a lawyer?" Alice sounded very surprised.

"Where in the Constitution does it say a U.S. citizen must have a lawyer in order to speak with their government?" David asked. "Goodbye." David hung up.

David was pretty sure what would happen next. He would be served an official subpoena from the Senate Intelligence Committee, probably before or after class, as that is where they knew they could find him. Maybe served by a federal marshal, even. He sent Sal an email relating the developments, although David was certain Sal knew already. Sal would probably inform Glenn. A day later, he got a call.

"Hello?" David said.

"David, this is Glenn. I understand you will be appearing before the Senate Intelligence Committee in open session," Glenn began. "Do you plan to appear?"

"Glenn, nice to hear from you," David initiated. "Yes, I plan to appear. Any advice or instructions?"

"Same as for the press conference," Glenn said. "Although this time, the underlining you did will be the central issue, and that part is all up to you. They won't believe that you didn't do it deliberately in order to trap the White House."

"That line of thinking will blow up quickly, as it implies, I knew they would leak it," David countered. "A lose-lose situation for them."

"Whatever your motive, and I believe you did it as you explained on CC's show, well done," Glenn said with some admiration. "This event will blow up into something big."

"Thanks, Glenn. Now, why did you really call?" David asked.

"I forgot for a moment what it is like to work with you," Glenn responded. "Yes, there is another item. We need to put you on contract for a few days. We have some interviews to do with a third party."

"You have a North Korean defector, I assume," David suggested.

"Make no assumptions, even good ones," Glenn retorted. "Look to your schedule sometime after your Senate hearing."

"I haven't agreed yet to do the interview," David replied.

"Now it is my turn to make a good assumption," Glenn stated. "You wouldn't want to miss this opportunity."

"You are assuming I am not in custody after refusing to testify to the Senate Intelligence Committee," David countered. "But you are correct. I'll come. Can it be over a weekend?"

"You said you would appear," Glenn said with confusion.

"I didn't say I would testify while I am there," David answered. "Talk with you later." Glenn hung up, then David did the same; his office land line could actually be hung up. Why Glenn was surprised David suspected they had a North Korean defector amazed David. What other reason would they have to want him to participate in an interview? People who worked and lived in secrets often failed to see how obvious some outcomes were.

David was correct; he was served by a federal marshal as he exited his Oceanography class on Monday. The document contained instructions on where and when he was supposed to be, who his contact was, which was Alice, he was pleased to see. It also contained his travel arrangements and all manner of detail, like the penalties for refusing to appear. He called Patty and asked if they could do lunch, to which she agreed.

After meeting up at the off-campus coffee shop popular with faculty, the 'Grinds for the Grind', they sat at a small table and David showed her the subpoena.

"Well, the famous Dr. David Langwonaire now claims yet another national spotlight," Patty enthused.

"This is all a pain in the neck," David responded. "The Republicans control the Senate, so this will be a party line affair."

"You are a hero, David. They won't get far with you," Patty stipulated.

"This is all about discrediting me," David replied. "That is why it is a public session instead of a closed one. They want to make it look like I set the White House up."

"You didn't make the White House leak the document," Patty exclaimed.

"Doesn't matter. The words 'hoax' and 'witch hunt' and 'deep state' will fly around the Committee," David said. "I'd like to borrow your car. You can have mine in the interim."

"You are driving to Washington?" Patty asked.

"Of course," David answered. "I am going to show up at the time and place requested, but they won't know until I appear in the door."

"They are bullying you, so you are snarking them," Patty announced. "Sure, take my car. I'll even type a note and sign it saying you have my full permission to use the vehicle."

After lunch, David dropped by Anne Brosseck's office and showed her the subpoena. "Just wanted to keep you in the loop," David said. "So you can keep the Prez and everyone else informed. Bosses don't like surprises."

"Well, I know you will make things interesting in the hearing chamber," Anne replied. "Think you'll have another press conference here after you return?"

"Maybe so," David agreed. "I'll try and give you lead time if I do. It would be better here, on my home turf, than in D.C."

David went by his Department Head's office to give him the news so that his classes could get covered. He expected to be back for his Thursday Geomorphology class, but he couldn't guarantee it.

CHAPTER 38

INTO THE VALLEY OF DEATH

DAVID WAS HEADING NORTH out of Montgomery on I-85 at six o'clock on Tuesday evening, at the tail end of rush hour so the driving was smooth. He would pass Atlanta in the quiet late evening hours and go on up north to pick up I-95 at Petersburg, Virginia, and ease into D.C. before morning rush hour there. David liked driving at night; there was less traffic, and plenty of time to let thoughts wander. He parked at a Walmart inside the beltway at 6:00 in the morning, called up an Uber, and went to a doughnut shop within walking distance of the Capitol Building. There, he hung out with hot chocolate and a Boston crème doughnut, thinking about the upcoming day. People came and went, getting their super deluxe coffees. At 9:00, David bought a Mountain Dew from the soda case and strolled over to his destination as he enjoyed his favorite caffeine delivery system. He didn't understand coffee; how could something that smelled so good taste so bad?

David entered the Capitol Building and, by showing his subpoena, was eventually led to the hearing chamber. At 9:59 a.m., he entered, showing the guard at the door of the chamber his subpoena. The Senate Intelligence Committee chair, a Mr. Condlon of Wyoming, called his name and a page took David forward and seated him at a long table in front of the assembled members of the Committee. Senator Condlon was known for running a loose ship as regarded Committee rules and procedures.

"Dr. Longwonaire, do you have an opening statement?" Senator Condlon asked.

"No," David answered.

"Do you wish to wait for your legal counsel?" Senator Condlon followed up.

"I do not have legal counsel," David answered. That answer brought out some mumblings and whispers in the chamber. David continued, "Where in the Constitution does it say a citizen needs a lawyer to talk with elected public officials?"

"Are you prepared to take your oath and answer questions?" Senator Condlon continued.

"No," David answered.

"You have been subpoenaed by this Committee. You are obligated to do so," The Senator suddenly seemed to wake up.

"I have been subpoenaed to appear, and I have, "David replied. "I will not answer any questions in open session."

At this point, Senator Moorland of South Carolina asked to deal with the recalcitrant Dr. Langwonaire, and Senator Condlon gave assent. Moorland was a true firebrand, a conspiracy lover, far right-wing devotee, and a bully. Here we go, thought David.

"Dr. Langwonaire," Moorland began, drawing out David's name as if it were a joke. "What is it like in your precious ivory tower?"

"The view is excellent, Senator, but the pay could be better," David replied. There were some giggles and chuckles from the audience.

The Senator was no longer smiling. "There are severe penalties for failing to answer questions. I can assure you I can make them harsh indeed."

"You cannot do anything by yourself, Senator," David began. "Only a majority vote of the Committee can ask for and enforce any penalties." So was the battle was joined.

"You will treat me, a United States Senator, with respect," Moorland bellowed.

"I am a tax-paying United States Citizen, and a veteran, which you are not," David countered. "Respect is a two-way street. Show some, and you might get respect in return." That response drew audible gasps from the audience. Few people took on the bellicose South Carolina senator.

"I can crush you like a bug, boy," Moorland again was loud.

"Not by yourself, Senator, unless you would like to go outside and settle it mano a mano," David responded, equally forceful.

"I can have you arrested for threatening a Senator!" Moorland was now upset as only a confronted bully can be.

"I merely invited you to a test of strength. You threatened to 'crush me like a bug', the only threat was from you," David countered. "I must assume that you fear me and can only resort to threats."

Moorland turned to the Committee chair. "I want to go into closed session and vote to punish this jerk."

"Too scared to ask for a vote in open session, where the public can see who is a coward and who is not?" David challenged. "You are just a bully, Senator, and that won't work with me."

At this point, the ranking Democratic Senator, Klinwitz of New Jersey, asked the chair to initiate a dialogue with Dr. Langwonaire. The chair gratefully gave permission and recognized the Senator.

"Dr. Langwonaire, why do you object to testifying here today?" Klinwitz asked.

"What I have to say needs to be done in closed session," David replied.

"Can't you just invoke national security for certain questions?" Klinwitz continued, soft spoken and reasonable.

"Merely asking the question, and having me decline to answer it, reveals more than we wish our adversaries to know," David stated. "The best way for me to avoid that situation is to refuse to answer any question. I will invoke the fifth amendment if asked anything."

"But you are interacting with us now," Klinwitz pointed out, "it could be argued you have already waived your fifth amendment rights".

"I am not yet under oath, so your argument has no force," David responded.

"We can give you full transactional immunity and then compel you to answer," Klinwitz continued.

"You can try, but doing so will not make me answer," David began. "It doesn't matter. Giving me immunity does not immunize the United States from the damage your questions will do."

"It will be an order, a command," Klinwitz persisted.

"I will not follow an illegal order or command," David rejoined. "To say 'just following orders' did not work at Nuremburg and it won't work here."

"I can move to go into closed session, and we can vote on your fate," Klinwitz said

"Go into closed session and I will answer all your questions," David replied. He noticed a startled look on some Senator's faces, and he realized what had happened. "That is what I told Alice Conzeski. Was that information not passed along to you? Did someone on this Committee suppress that information?"

Klinwitz looked puzzled. "I did not know that. We were told that you might refuse to testify and had prepared a waiver of immunity to that end. Can you prove what you told Ms. Conzeski?" He looked around. "Where is Ms Conzeski, she is supposed to be here."

"Ms. Conzeski told me she had recorded our conversation, so you can listen to it yourself and hear my instructions that the Committee was to be informed that I would testify only in closed session." David interjected.

Senator Moorland interrupted, "I have that recording, and I can assure you that it says no such thing. Ms. Conzeski is not here, as she said things to Dr. Langwonaire that were unprofessional, so I instructed her to stay away because of her perceived bias."

"Senator Klinwitz, I also recorded that phone call, and the Senator from South Carolina is lying, pure and simple," David stated forcefully. "A recording of that call is currently in the hands of the media. While I am not under oath, as a member of this Committee Senator Moorland is, and he has just committed perjury."

The room erupted in a cacophony of voices. Condlon banged his gavel for some time before order was restored. He stared at David. "Sir, you have made a grave challenge and the consequences for you could be extreme."

"You chair this Committee, Senator, and how it behaves reflects on you," David countered. "My advice is to do your job, as you swore an oath to do when accepting the post for Senator of the United States. To accuse me of misconduct when it sits to your left is willful blindness. Goodbye." David rose and walked out of the chamber, to spontaneous applause from the spectators. At the door, the guard stepped in front of him.

"Sir, you haven't been dismissed," he said.

"Nor have I been ordered to stay," David replied. "Go home to your family tonight, understanding that they are alive today because of what I did in Indonesia."

The guard moved aside.

Senator Moorland was on his phone, talking loudly so all could hear. "Contact Homeland Security, put Dr. David Langwonaire on the no-fly list and detain him when he goes through security." He looked over to Senators Condlon and Klinwitz and said, "He will be in custody soon. I will have him and do what I please." Unfortunately for the Senator, all he said was captured on his open microphone. The scandal only deepened. David walked back to the doughnut shop, had another Boston crème and a Mountain Dew, and called an Uber to go back to his car. It was mid-day; he cleared the beltway with few problems and was on his way home, listening to NPR discuss his Senate appearance. He would teach his class on Thursday.

Glenn and Molly had watched the whole thing on TV. "Typical David," was Molly's response.

"It is amazing how he causes adversaries to make self-inflicted mistakes," was Glenn's reply.

"Will they get him at the airport?" Molly asked.

"Unlikely, as I expect he drove and used someone else's car," Glenn postulated.

"Now you are thinking like him," Molly joked.

"Never too old to learn," Glenn smiled.

CHAPTER 39

WATCHING THE WATCHER

GLENN CALLED AS DAVID WAS DRIVING, but David had turned his phone off and wrapped it in aluminum foil so that he could not be tracked. He made it home without incident near midnight and caught some sleep before rising, intending to teach his 9:30 Geomorphology class. His phone was back on, and it rang at 7:00 in the morning.

"David, that was well played," came Glenn's voice. "I tried to call you yesterday as you were driving back, but I bet you had your phone off."

"Good to see you figured out my visitation plan," David said. "I expect to be subpoenaed again, but this time for a closed session testimony. In the meantime, are you willing to pay me again for my interview skills?"

"Can you fly to Reagan Friday afternoon?" Glenn asked. "Pay will be the same as last time."

"I don't know, Senator Moorland was screaming about putting me on a no-fly list," David responded.

"Not a problem. We will fly you up here on a company jet," Glenn replied. "Molly will brief you on the way up. Will 1 p.m. from MGM work for you?"

"That will be just fine. Can I get back Sunday afternoon?" David queried.

"Certainly," Glenn answered. "You can stay in your old digs here if the Senate wants you back on Monday."

"You know they are going to subpoena me again?" David asked.

"Yes, it will be Alice by phone this afternoon. Do what she says. It will be closed session and Senator Moorland will not be available," Glenn stated.

"Heart attack?" David asked hopefully.

"No, he has been told to recuse himself until their internal investigation into his behavior has been completed," Glenn responded. "You did a number on him, and he is in serious difficulty. In addition, Alice Conzeski is much beloved by the Committee, his falsehoods about her are actually more impactful for his fate."

"See you Friday afternoon," David replied and hung up.

David's day went fine; about mid-afternoon he got another call, it was Alice Conzeski. "Ms Conzeski, my apologies for any difficulty I may have caused you in regard to my Senate hearing," David began.

"Oh, no problem, no problem at all," Alice answered. "I should be thanking you. Senator Moorland has been extremely unprofessional with me for some time, and your bit of non-testimony testimony has freed me from him forever."

"So the Senate Intelligence Committee wants me back for another shot?" David asked.

"Yes, and it will be closed session with no Senator Moorland present," Alice responded. "You can also expect Senator Condlon to be much more agreeable. Can you be there at 10:00 Monday morning?"

"I will be there," David answered.

"Good, I will meet you personally in the Rotunda at 9:30, and thank you again," Alice said and hung up.

David sent email to Anne and to his Department Head saying he was missing class again for Senate testimony. He had swapped Patty's car for his own on the way in that morning. He was set to do the rare CIA-Senate double play.

This time he was in a Gulfstream G150, a much smaller plane than what he had flown back from Guam, but it was just him and Molly. It was greetings and small talk until they were in the air, then David initiated his questions.

"So, who do you have?" David asked. "I wouldn't be surprised if it was the man in charge of the whole operation."

"Why do you say that?" Molly countered.

"Had to be someone who was in great danger before the CIA report leaked, but who also had means to escape," David answered. "Did he fly out?"

"Does it seem that obvious to you?" Molly asked. "Oh, never mind. The man is Choe Tu-bong, who is known as 'the General', which is how he prefers to be addressed. He is understood to have been head of one of their most secret intelligence arms, 'Building 13', but little is known about him personally. He deflects most inquiries into his past. The man you killed on Pulau Ternate, Colonel Thae Yong-ho, was his most gifted and important asset. The General speaks very good English."

"When did this defection occur?" David was intrigued but also worried.

"Three days after you sunk the submarines," Molly replied.

"The North Koreans were aware that their plot was a failure long before the White House leaked the document," David surmised. That was why Glenn had been unconcerned by the White House leak. "Did they do anything to indicate that they were responding to the General's defection?"

"They went very quiet," Molly replied. "No weapon tests, no bellicose press releases, no maneuvers."

"Afraid we would go totally ballistic, perhaps literally, once they realized who the General had defected to," David stated. "So all they learned from the leaked report was how the events played out, some details of our craft, and that we have a vain man as President."

"The latter statement may be incorrect," Molly interjected. "The President's behavior confuses the North Koreans. They cannot believe that what the President says and does is the real thing. They think it might be an elaborate game to cover his true intentions."

"Has the General seen the full CIA report?" David asked. "He has been in your custody for more than a month."

"We have done a thorough debriefing of the General," Molly replied. "We think he is doling out his responses carefully. He always wants to bargain. He wants a car, a house, a flat screen TV. He wants to ski at Vail and dive on John Pennycamp. No, he hasn't seen the report."

"Why not?" David asked.

"Glenn thinks we should hold something back," Molly replied. "The General is very curious about how we discovered the plot."

"You want me to interview him in person?" David inquired. "I expect he will recognize me. Has my name come up?"

"He hasn't mentioned you, although he has been quite forthcoming about the plot," Molly began. "Since we did discover it, he assumes we know all about it."

"Does he ask how we found out?" David continued. "Has he offered any explanations for our intelligence coup?"

"All we have said is that such a complicated plot with so many players could be expected to get noticed and examined." Molly stated. "He seems to agree. He complained that he advised against the mission, but cautiously as the Great Leader demanded that it move forward. They called it 'Project Zeus'. When he heard about the explosion in the cave, then no report from Colonel Thae Yong-ho, and then the three missing submarines, he realized he would soon be purged, so he defected before anyone higher up knew of the failure of the mission."

"So why bring me in?" David asked. "You are stuck, aren't you? He won't give and neither will you. I am supposed to break the logjam."

"As usual, perceptive," Molly responded. "What we want you to do is simple. Go in and talk with him, reveal whatever you like, see what you can get. Be yourself, it seems to work."

David and Molly spent some time going over transcripts of numerous interviews, but only sketchily. They were soon on approach at Andrews Air Force Base, picked up at the plane by the standard black SUV, and whisked away to Langley.

"When do I meet his honor, the General?" David asked as they skipped around traffic. The SUV had blue and whites, and the driver flashed them when it was useful.

"Tonight," Molly replied. "You are in the same suite you had last time. It will be pizza and root beer as Glenn and I do one more briefing, then you see him."

"Alone, or with one or both of you?" David asked.

"Just you. He is shackled during interviews, about which he complains often and loudly," Molly said with a wry smile. "He was going to murder ten million people and he wants us to treat him like royalty? We will be, of course, watching and recording."

"I won't have to pee in the corner?" David inquired, chuckling.

"Only if you want to, but I doubt it will have any effect on him," Molly replied.

"It would if I peed in his face," David argued. "Imagine, waterboarding with urine, a new technique." At this Molly rolled her eyes, then looked at David sharply.

"You wouldn't, would you?" she asked suddenly.

"Of course I would, if I thought it would work," David responded.

They were at Langley, and he was soon stamped, photo'd, verified, and sent to his room like a bad boy. He showered, shaved, and cleaned up. They had been keeping the General isolated from true time. David would act like it was early morning. The main advantage from David's point of view was that the General might think that the grilling would go on for a full day.

The door opened and it was Molly and Glenn with pizza. As usual, they didn't knock. The briefing offered nothing new, and Glenn's frustration was readily apparent. They were really hoping David would get the General to say something novel, convinced the well had not yet gone dry. Amid pizza crusts and empty cups, David pressed one more time.

"What is it exactly that you are looking for?" David said with some exasperation. Then he had an inspiration. "Did you run his DNA?"

"Why would we do that?" Molly responded.

"He is hiding something about his past," David said slowly. "Perhaps he has family here in the U.S., or perhaps he was the war child of an American soldier, maybe even a POW. You have run his prints?"

"Yes, nothing there," answered Glenn. "We did it in ink for better resolution." That came out with a smirk.

"OK, let's go see him," David said finally. "Pay close attention to his reaction when I walk in. I will introduce myself as 'Karl Mallin'. I'll try to start out subtle."

CHAPTER 40

WHAT IS HE?

DAVID GOT A LOOK AT THE GENERAL from the observation room. He was reasonably fit, balding a little, and he tended to move the fingers of his left hand in a repetitive manner, one that David suddenly understood.

"He plays poker," David immediately stated.

"What?" Glenn asked, startled.

"That finger motion with his left hand, that is how poker players move their chips around across the back of their hand when they are thinking hard before making a bet or a call," David said. "I recognize it. He played poker once, maybe professionally. Could he be a mole of his very own?"

Glenn looked at Molly, who said, "We gave him a full medical screening, he is borderline diabetic. We can easily map his DNA." She left the room, probably to initiate the testing process.

"Well, David," Glenn said appreciatively, "that is why you are here."

Molly came back and gave a thumbs-up sign. Glenn said, "OK, go down the hall. The guard will open the door. You stroll in and do your thing. I expect the General to be cool, calm, and pretty much non-reactive. The change of scenery you present will not get an immediate response from him."

David did as instructed; the guard opened the door and David strolled in like he was about to conduct his Geophysics class, a cup of hot tea in his left hand. The General's eyes flicked briefly up at his face, then he whipped his head up and stared at David.

"I knew it, damn it I knew it," he shouted, lunging forward against his manacles then sitting back down.

David didn't flinch. "So I am no surprise? Pretty much as I thought."

"I knew you would be trouble," the General was close to yelling. "I had you researched top to bottom. You weren't looking for neo-Nazis in the Marianas. You were on Pulau Ternate, messing with Project Zeus."

"It wasn't me alone, I had some help," David replied calmly.

"If I had known you were working with the CIA, I would have aborted the whole thing," the General sputtered. "You know what you are, don't you?"

"I am me, and that has always been sufficient," David replied, wondering what the hell was going on.

"Of course it has. The ones like you always know," the General said. "Thae had a little of it, but he had ambitions. He didn't have the moral fiber needed to make full use of his gift. This changes everything." The General slumped back in his chair, his manacles clanking. Then he sat up straight. "You identified Willard as our mole, didn't you? With your type, it only takes seconds."

For once, David didn't know what to say or what to do. "You have been most accessible. I need little more for now. You must begin to play the hand dealt to you. I will be observing." David turned, knocked on the door, and went out into the hall as the guard opened it. Behind him, the General buried his face in the palms of his hands and did not move. David went back into the observation room.

"What the hell was that all about?" Glenn was almost shouting himself. "The General completely lost it. He recognized you right away, and more importantly, recognized that you were the single most important factor in the failure of Project Zeus. Care to explain that?"

"He seems to think I have some special ability to solve problems, and to assess people," David replied. "I have always known this. I didn't realize that I was such a rare beast. You will want to pursue the topic with him, but obliquely. He knew I was dangerous because he had me researched. What research? It was more than what is on my Department webpage. He had people who knew me interviewed, possibly as part of a fictional background check. He had a suspicion from the start. Why?"

"Our mission would have entirely collapsed if you hadn't suggested the neo-Nazi ruse," Molly said. "He had eyes on you the whole time. It wasn't all wasted effort."

"Be sure the Captain of the *Harrington* learns that his mission was much more important than he knew at the time and a major success," David stated.

"David, we need to find out what you are," Glenn said softly.

"I doubt you will. This is a quantum state problem," David explained. "The mere act of observing what I am will make me not be what I am. So stay clear." David was as sure of that statement as any he had ever made in his life. He was what he was because no one cared. However, the General knew. "The focus needs to be on the General and what he knows about the situation. I literally cannot be around him when that is going on."

Another Glenn-to-Molly mutual stare. "Alright for now," Glenn said.

Molly walked him out to the hall, and they went back up to his suite. She coded him in. "What do we do with you?" she asked.

"Nothing, that is the whole point," David replied. "I do what I do because I am free, unbound, able to let my mind run as it will. I am not a tool for anyone's use. I don't accept bad moral behavior, bullies, con men, or anything that is functionally dishonest in the intellectual sense. The General was right, I knew Willard was a bad egg immediately, in one gestalt moment. The same for Senator Moorland. In the morning, tell me how it went tonight with the General. I expect him to be very cooperative."

Molly looked bewildered. "You have this great gift, and you work at a small, second tier college, making contributions in a subfield of a subfield. Why?"

"Because it makes me happy, Molly," David said with real passion. "I can do what I like to do, I can make a difference, and in the academic realm, I do not stand out. I do not deliberately hide myself. I found a wonderful niche and it works for me, Oh God it works for me."

"You don't have ambitions?" Molly was still confused.

"Molly, I know myself, and know what works for me, and that is the life I lead," David spoke softly but with earnestness. "Success is defined by how I feel about me. My work benefits others, both my students and my field of study. I injure no one who does not deserve it."

"That sounds a bit arrogant, that you can choose what and who is deserving of injury," Molly said with caution.

"That is exactly true," David responded. "The General knows it as well. I make the correct decisions, Molly. That is who or what I am. The truly scary part is how quick that decision comes."

"But you could do so much more," Molly protested.

"It is what I call the Superman Problem," David answered. "That comic book character cannot save everyone, fix every situation, he must choose. The needs of the world outnumber the time I have, I must select those moments that I feel are critical. I cannot save them all, I can save very few, in fact. And if I did a lot of saving, then I distort the world by my actions. I make my greatest impact by my students, not in changing them, but by showing them a path that allows them to choose how much of themselves to maximize. It is all about free will and choice. And consequences, of course."

Molly looked at David, her eyes brimming with tears. "You are unlike any human being I have ever met. I see that you are correct, for one such as you the trail you make in life must be the one you carve, not others." She then hurried out the door.

The little fridge had some cold beer this time. David pulled one out, sat in the stuffed chair, and took a long pull. One of the happiest persons in the world was also one of the most selfish. He knew it, it worked for him, and it hurt no one who was good.

END

ACKNOWLEDGMENTS

Much appreciation for all my friends who read early drafts of this work, and provided commentary and insight, especially Jim Carew, who is responsible for the title. Special thanks to Lisa Shrewsberry and to Michelle M. White for their patient editing skills. Most of all, my joy at having Joan as my colleague, friend, partner and critic, who made it all possible. *No Night As Dark* deals with caves and submarines; caves and the ocean depths are truly dark, and as the book describes, that darkness can seep into the soul. I deeply respect all those who go to such places, and how they assisted me through the years.

ABOUT THE AUTHOR

John Mylroie is Professor Emeritus of Geology at Mississippi State University. After childhood in rural upstate New York, he attended Syracuse University, graduating in 1971 with a Zoology degree Summa Cum Laude and Phi Beta Kappa, and also lettering on the soccer team. He met Joan Saxon, a fellow Zoology major and Phi Beta Kappa, in Chemistry lecture his freshman year; they were married in 1970. Draft number 69 in the first draft lottery sent John to the Navy for a year as a sonar technician. While subsequently working in the electronics laboratory of the Biology Department at SUNY Albany, John decided to turn his sporting interest in caves into a career. He entered the Geology PhD program at Rensselaer Polytechnic Institute in 1974, graduating in 1977 and taking a faculty position at Murray State University where Joan earned a MSc in microbiology and taught as an instructor.

John and Joan decided to start a family in 1981, and by November 1983 had three sons, the latter two appearing as undiagnosed identical twins (surprise!). With five mouths to feed, John took the Department

Head position in the Geology and Geography Department (now Geosciences) at Mississippi State University in 1985. Joan later became a Geography instructor. He continued his island cave research program, often taking the entire family into the field. The National Speleological Society awarded John their Science Award for his work on island caves in 2000, and the Honorary Member award, the society's highest award, for lifetime contributions to cave science in 2008. Joan and John have completed field work in 25 countries, and they have published hundreds of professional papers, reports, field guides, and articles. Their work on islands across the Atlantic, Pacific, and Indian Oceans, as well as the Caribbean and Mediterranean Seas, has given them insight into how peoples and cultures interact with the environment in remote settings.

After a career of writing factual material in scientific literature, John decided it was time to make things up and write fiction. He has written books in the science fiction, fantasy, mystery, and spy thriller genres. No Night As Dark is his second step into publication, the first book in his ten-book "David Langwonaire Thriller Series." The fifth book, The 12th Girl, is already available. The rest are in production, so stay tuned!

The author can be reached at cikmpub@gmail.com.

Made in the USA
Middletown, DE
21 November 2023

43149016R00137